Last Car to Annwn Station
Michael Merriam
Copyright © 2022 by Michael Merriam
ISBN 978-1-7343603-8-7
Library of Congress Control Number: 2022939586

Queen of Swords Press LLC
Minneapolis, MN
www.queenofswordpress.com
Published in the United States

Cover Design by Kanaxa Designs.
Interior Design by Terry Roy of Teryvisions.

LAST CAR TO ANNWN STATION

MICHAEL MERRIAM

Contents

Acknowledgments vii

Introduction xi

Monday, 23rd of October 1

Tuesday, 24th of October 17

Wednesday, 25th of October 46

Thursday, 26th of October 71

Friday, 27th of October 95

Saturday, 28th of October 122

Sunday, 29th of October 168

Monday, 30th of October 189

Tuesday, 31st of October 212

Wednesday, 1st of November 253

Sunday, 17th of December 268

About the Author 275

About Queen of Swords Press 276

Acknowledgments

I'D LIKE TO THANK my wife, Sherry L.M. Merriam, who was the first reader and helped me edit the manuscript into something I could submit to publishers.

Thanks to Adam Stemple, Alison Ching, Jaye Lawrence, Joanne Anderton, Kevin McIntyre and Hilary Moon Murphy, all of whom read the novel in various drafts and offered thoughts, ideas, occasional smacks to the back of the head and all the encouragement I needed to finish it.

A special thanks to the editors and staff at Queen of Swords Press for choosing to bring this novel to you, the reader. They are a joy to work with.

To everyone on LiveJournal who cheered me on as I wrote the novel and who, when I described it as "a dark urban fantasy, revenge and redemption paranormal romance and supernatural horror novel with mythological and fairy tale overtones and lesbian protagonists, featuring the ghost of the defunct Twin Cities streetcar system," had a good laugh about me finding my little niche.

Dedicated to Mr. Thomas Lowry (February 27, 1843–February 4, 1909). For the streetcars.

Introduction

THIS BOOK IS A love letter.

When my wife and I moved to the Twin Cities of Minneapolis and St. Paul at the turn of the last century, we didn't know how hard we would fall in love with these two cities. And when you love something, you want to learn everything about it. Which is how I discovered the Twin Cities once boasted one of the world's most extensive streetcar systems.

There are still a few of these cars running today, part of the Minnesota Streetcar Museum. Remember this: it is the important bit.

You need to understand that I hold a firm belief in—and fascination with—the concept of spirit of place. I believe that buildings, lakes, and cities have their own spirits. The initial concept for the book in your hands was built around this idea of spirit of place.

I was looking out at the sparkling waters of one of the many magnificent lakes in Minneapolis when behind me I heard a bell ring. I turned to find a big yellow beauty of a streetcar rolling up to a museum station. That's when it hit me. *As long as one streetcar still runs its route in the Twin Cities, the ghost of all the streetcars still existed just under reality.* That evening when I got home, I started writing what I then called "The Phantom Streetcar Novel."

Other concepts crept in, of course. I was sitting in a coffeeshop and had a stray thought about the late singer Roy Orbison. That thought became the opening line to the novel. I worked with Welsh mythology because, well, my ancestors are mostly Welsh.

And so, this book is a love letter. It is a love letter to my adopted home, the Twin Cities of Minneapolis and St. Paul. It is a love letter to those lovely old streetcars. It is a love letter to the mythology of my ancestors. At the core, this is a story about the power of love, be it romantic, platonic, or something else entirely.

I give this love letter to you, reader.

Last Car to Annwn Station

Michael Merriam

Monday, 23rd of October

*S*omewhere in the world, at any given moment, Roy Orbison is *singing.*

Mae Malveaux blinked at her reflection in the washroom mirror as she slapped a bit of water on her face.

And I really need a vacation.

She sighed and returned to her desk, trying to tune out the tinny music coming from the office to her left. She had left her door open in a vain attempt to get some fresh air in the windless space her desk and file cabinet were wedged into. Instead, her neighbor's radio was filling the airspace. For the sixth time today, she had heard Roy Orbison singing. It was starting to get under her skin. She did not understand why the fates seemed determined to haunt her with the voice of a dead man in large sunglasses.

An opened folder sat waiting for her return, right where she had left it. This particular case was another thing Mae did not understand. Despite persistent abuse and neglect, on four occasions, judges had returned Chrysandra Arneson to the custody of her mother, Marie Arneson.

Child Protective Services, after contact from school officials and doctors, had removed the girl from the home within six months after each judicial order. Now Marie, having completed a drug rehabilitation program and found gainful employment, was again seeking custody of her twelve-year-old daughter.

In each of the previous rulings, the judges had cited the need to "keep the family unit intact" as one of the driving reasons for returning the little girl to her mother's care.

Mae suspected it had more to do with the woman's family being white, wealthy and suburban. The Arneson family, already established among the elites of the Twin Cities after decades of doing business in the brewing and milling industries, had made a fortune in the 1950s when the public transportation system in the Twin Cities switched from streetcars to buses.

Mae had spoken to the child's grandparents, but while they were happy to be her temporary guardians, they did not want to be responsible for Chrysandra long-term. Instead, the elder Arnesons were single-minded in their belief that Marie was a good mother and that for some reason the State of Minnesota had singled out their precious daughter for harassment. Mae felt the Arnesons were willfully ignoring evidence that Marie was abusing their granddaughter, pretending the constant parade of bruises, burns and broken bones over the last three years were all accidental. The identity of the child's father was unknown, and Marie Arneson and her family refused to share any information about him, closing off that avenue of aid from Mae.

Mae groaned with relief when the song ended and she heard the solid click of the radio being switched off. She had the beginning of a migraine. When she had walked into her morning meeting with Juvenile Court Judge Slotky on a matter unrelated to this case, she had found herself in an impromptu negotiation conference with the attorney representing Marie Arneson. Judge Slotky seemed sure they could work out a deal without the need for a court session.

This morning's ambush was bad enough, but lawyer William Jefferson Hodgins's refusal to take her seriously had infuriated Mae. At one point Hodgins and Judge Slotky began talking to each other as if Mae were not even in the room. The "old boys" in local law circles saw her childlike frame, pale complexion and thin, slightly stringy blond hair, and brushed her off. Mae had refused to agree to anything and stormed out of the judge's chambers.

"Hey, I thought you left hours ago."

Mae looked up, startled by the voice. Jill frowned down at her and Mae gave her a lopsided smile. They had been office pals since Jill began working for the county a year ago, meeting socially outside of the office for drinks and lunches on a regular basis. Jill was younger than Mae, barely past thirty, and worked in the law library upstairs. She dressed conservatively and kept her hair up at work, exuding a "sexy librarian" aura, with her black hair, pale blue eyes and long legs. The men who worked in the Government Center were stupid for her. If Mae was being honest, she was a little stupid for Jill as well. Jill seemed mostly oblivious to the attention of her male coworkers. Mae hadn't acted on her attraction to Jill, content to build a close friendship. For now…

"I'm nearly done."

"Mae, sweetie, when was the last time you did something fun?"

Mae blinked in confusion. "I have fun. All the time."

"Um-hmm."

"Really!"

"Well, Miss Fun, I'm meeting Teresa, Stacy and some of the other girls in the building down at the Fine Line tonight for dancing, booze and hot, hot boys. And hot, hot girls. You're welcome to come with."

"On a Monday night?"

"That's when the hot boys troll for football widows."

"Maybe some other night. I'm really worn out." Mae rubbed her head for emphasis. She appreciated the offer, but the noise and crowds of the Minneapolis club scene were the last thing she wanted to face tonight. "I think I'm going to wrap up and head home."

"Suit yourself," Jill said. "The offer stands if you change your mind."

Turning back to her file after Jill walked away, Mae flipped through its contents. One of the serious concerns with this case was the lack of photographic evidence. Without pictures to document and corroborate the medical and police reports, Mae had trouble convincing the judge of the severity of the situation. When she had asked *why* there were no photos, her boss had shrugged and told her that by odd coincidence, every time photos of Chrysandra Arneson were taken, the camera failed or the memory card went bad.

Deciding she needed to go home before the migraine took full effect, she closed the folder and stuffed the entire manila-covered mess into her bag. She was not allowed to take files out of the office, but she knew the other lawyers did it. And maybe she'd spot something she hadn't seen before if she looked at it later.

Mae rode the elevator to the lobby. Stopping at the security checkpoint long enough to claim her can of pepper spray, she stepped into the gathering dusk and made her way toward the light rail station.

Climbing aboard the sleek, modern machine, she closed her eyes and dozed for the short trip to Hennepin Avenue. At her stop, Mae checked her surroundings. There had been a rash of robberies along Hennepin in the last two weeks. A small, professionally dressed woman would present a tempting target. She stood with a group of people awaiting buses and checked to make sure the can of pepper spray she carried was within easy reach.

The ringing of a bell startled her. Mae took a step backward at the sight of a big yellow streetcar. She *had* heard there was a plan to bring back the old streetcars. "Heritage Lines," Metro Transit called the resurgent machines. They would intersect the modern and highly popular light rail in downtown Minneapolis. She had not realized the streetcars were running, had not even noticed the tracks when she crossed the street.

Mae looked around. The open doors of the yellow streetcar beckoned. She glanced at her fellow travelers. No one seemed to notice the old streetcar. Mae read the route sign on the side of the car: "Hennepin Avenue Express." She lived in Uptown, so the streetcar would work as well as a bus.

"The fare is ten cents, miss."

She hesitated for an instant, starting to protest that she had a pass, but let her curiosity win out. Mae fumbled in her bag. Finding five tarnished pennies and a nickel, she dropped them into the fare box. The sturdy-looking man in an old-fashioned conductor's suit offered her a slip of paper.

"Your transfer, miss. You'll be needing that."

She took the slip and turned toward the interior of the streetcar. Mae froze for an instant, then the car's bell rang twice before it lurched, making Mae lose her balance. As the car rolled forward with a sharp clack-clack, she gazed in bewilderment at the other occupants.

It was as if Halloween had arrived early, and all the riders of the streetcar except her were on their way to a costume party. Mae grabbed the long overhead rail, more to steady herself from the shock than against the swaying of the streetcar. She locked eyes with a man in a business suit who had the head of a bison. He snorted and nodded solemnly to her. A small woman with fragile-looking wings and electric-blue hair stood near her. Too short to reach the rail, she clung to the support pole. The woman smiled up at Mae and leaned toward her.

"These seats aren't exactly friendly to someone with wings. Hi, I'm Elliefandi. You can call me Ellie, if you want."

Mae barely followed the high-pitched and rapid speech. "I'm Mae," she mumbled, looking out the window.

Hennepin Avenue passed by outside the window, but it was not exactly *her* Hennepin Avenue. The shops were dark and squat. There was none of the usual hustle and activity as they turned left at the Basilica of St. Mary and started toward Uptown. The Walker Arts Center and Sculpture Garden looked gray and cold and washed out.

"Don't worry," the winged woman said as they crossed Franklin Avenue and began to click along, gathering speed. "It'll all be there once you go back."

"Go back?" Mae asked. She could hear the note of panic in her own voice.

Ellie smiled. "Of course!" Her smile faded. "You've got your transfer, right?

Mae held up the slip of paper.

"And a return fare?"

"I—I'm pretty sure I've got enough loose change."

"Good, good. Old man Lowry's cars, they'll take you where you need to go. Getting back, now that can be a bit of trouble."

The car's bell rang twice and the machine jerked to a stop in front of the Uptown Bar. Mae was surprised, since only a moment before they had crossed Franklin Avenue, now ten blocks behind them. The bison-headed man stood and exited the car from the rear. Mae moved to follow the bison-man, having missed her usual stop, the Uptown Transit Station, completely. The back doors slammed shut and would not budge for her, no matter how hard she pushed on them.

"This must not be your stop," the winged woman said.

Mae turned to call out to the conductor and motorman that she wanted to exit. Her voice caught in her throat as two riders boarded at the front.

The first seemed blessedly normal to Mae's eyes. He wore black slacks and shoes, with a white dress shirt and black tie, loose at the

Ellie placed herself between the new voice and Mae, thwarting the creature in the hat from his apparent desire to sit next to Mae. "And what, exactly, do you think you're doing?"

"But—but I've been working sendings to her all day using this voice! I need to—"

Mae's head snapped up and she glared at the…well, she was not entirely sure what he was. "Wait a minute. Are you the reason I've been hearing Roy Orbison all day?"

The creature smiled at her and doffed his hat, giving her a small bow. "Yes. I wanted to make sure you would recognize me when *I* came to you. I am Kravis ap Thimp, your ladyship. I am at your service. In fact, I'm commanded to your service."

Mae blinked. "Commanded?"

"Aye, Miss Mae, I've been sent by—"

The streetcar jolted to a sudden stop, causing Mae to pitch sideways and fall between the bench in front of her and the one she had been sitting on.

Howling, high and hollow, filled her ears.

"Well, this is unexpected," she heard Death say.

Ellie flapped her wings, rising toward the roof. Mae heard Kravis's voice, tight and frantic, speaking in a language she did not understand.

"What's happening?" Mae asked, trying to stand. Around her, she heard screams and the sounds of the other passengers fleeing the car. A strong, clawed hand grabbed her elbow and lifted her from the floor. She found herself looking into the eyes of the ugly, gray-faced creature.

"The Cŵn Annwn have broken the magic of the streetcars. Things will move quickly now."

Mae frowned. "Wait! The what?"

Kravis grabbed her by the elbow and started to drag her toward the exit at the rear. "No time to explain. We have a connection to make."

Death allowed them to squeeze past as he stood in the middle of the aisle. "Run, Maeve Malveaux. The hounds are kin to me, and I wield some small power over them. I shall hold them here, for a time."

Clutching her bag, Mae followed Kravis and Ellie out the back door as several white-coated, red-eared hounds charged down the streetcar's narrow aisle toward the unflinching figure of Death.

Mae and Kravis dashed around the streetcar while Ellie zipped ahead of them, flying quickly despite her fragile-looking wings. Around them, creatures and spirits scattered, running away from the streetcar in every direction.

"Come on, woman, run faster!" Kravis urged Mae.

Mae ran as hard as her short legs allowed, her messenger bag flopping against her side, the strap pulling on her neck. She looked up at where Kravis seemed to be leading her. Lakeview Cemetery loomed, dark and brooding, its wrought iron gates closed, chained and padlocked.

Ellie turned in the air and faced them. "Kravis, I'm not sure going in there is the best idea! The restless dead—"

"It's the fast and straight path. Come on!" he called to Mae, who was starting to lag behind.

The howls at her back gave her a fresh burst of panic-powered speed.

"The gate!" Mae gasped. She knew there was no way she would be able to jump it, not at her height, and she would never be able to climb it before the hounds caught up to them.

She need not have worried. Without slowing down, Kravis lowered his shoulder and—with a defiant yell—smashed into the wrought iron, shattering the lock and flinging the gate wide open.

Mae leaped over Kravis as he tumbled and rolled down the path. Kravis, his shoulder smoking and torn where it had struck the gate, sprang to his feet as the first of the hounds reached them. He grabbed the hound and slung it into the nearest piece of statuary. There was a hollow snapping, and the snow-white hound lay still.

"Run!" Kravis yelled at Mae and Ellie. "Get to the platform across from the lake! Ellie, you have to lead her."

"This way," Ellie said, taking Mae by the hand. Mae stumbled on tree limbs and debris littering the ground. Small stones and markers that were barely above the earth and hidden by the snow threatened to trip her as she ran. Around her, the howls and barks of the pale hounds filled the night air.

A wail of pain and despair rose high and terrible behind Mae, and was abruptly cut off. The hairs on the back of her neck stood on end. She imagined she could feel the hot breath of the hounds behind her, their wicked, yellowed teeth inches from the back of her throat, ready to rip both flesh and life from her body.

Mae looked over her shoulder, trying to find where her attackers would be coming from. Something on the ground, she could not tell if it was a white branch or a skeletal hand, snagged her leg and she flipped. Mae curled into a ball and rolled down the steep hill toward the fence below. She thought she heard Ellie scream her name. Mae closed her eyes as she tumbled. She expected her life to end any second, whether at the teeth of the ghost-white hounds or by the snapping of her own neck, and she did not want to see what finally killed her.

Mae came up against the fence, bouncing off the steel enclosure and lying on her stomach, gasping.

"Get up!" Ellie's frantic, shrill voice broke through Mae's stunned brain.

Mae rose to her hands and knees. She looked up toward the sounds of howling and barking, but could not see any of the hounds.

"Mae! Mae, we have to go!"

"My bag," Mae said. Her messenger bag lay a few feet away, its contents scattered on the ground.

"We don't have time!"

Mae scrambled back to her bag. She gathered up the file she had taken from work and checked to make sure no pages lay on the ground. She picked up her keys and pepper spray.

"Mae!"

"I've almost got it all!"

A low growl sent a shiver down Mae's back. She looked up to find one of the hounds had reached her, ahead of its pack, and was staring at her, its teeth bared and hackles on end. The hound's ears lay back on its head, eyes wide as it prepared to spring at her.

She aimed the can of pepper spray, pulled the pin and fired directly into the hound's face. The creature howled and dropped to the ground, rolling in a frantic attempt to clear its eyes of the stinging chemicals. Mae stood and ran to the fence, leaving the injured hound behind.

"We have to get to the next platform," Ellie said, nodding at the small raised wooden structure next to a set of rails. "Can you climb?"

Mae nodded. She tossed her bag over her shoulder and climbed over as the remaining hounds reached the fence. Her slacks caught and ripped on the top row of barbed wire and she fell flat onto her back once on the other side of the fence, pants ripped at the right calf. Mae rolled over, grabbed her bag and half-walked, half-crawled to the platform and the waiting streetcar.

"Miss?" she heard a voice say.

Mae looked up at the big yellow streetcar. "Harriet-Como Line" read the sign. She looked around for her companion, but Ellie was nowhere to be found. She reached into her slacks and pulled out a piece of paper.

"I have a transfer."

The man took the piece of paper and examined it carefully. His jaw worked in agitation. "Um…okay then. Do you mind if I hang on to this? I'd like to put it on display at the museum."

It was Mae's turn to be confused. She looked at the car's other occupants.

The insides of the streetcar were decorated in paper ghosts and bats. Jack-o'-lanterns lay on the floor, secured by mounds of straw. A dozen children and their parents sat inside, most of the children in Halloween costumes. Mae glanced at the driver. She was dressed as a pirate. The conductor was obviously supposed to be Frankenstein's monster.

Mae smiled shyly and moved toward the back of the streetcar, all too aware how she must appear to these people, with her blouse untucked, her hair full of twigs and leaves, covered head to toe in dirt and makeup running down her face. She took a seat and tried to become as small and invisible as possible.

Several of the children looked from her back to their parents, obviously curious. A couple pointed and whispered only to be hushed by parents too embarrassed to acknowledge her presence.

She watched out the window as the streetcar slowly made its way to the small station near Lake Harriet. Mae knew where she was. All she needed to do was make the short walk up to the Linden Hills neighborhood shopping district and she could catch a Number Six bus back to Uptown Station and home.

She wondered what had happened to Ellie and Kravis. She—she had no idea what had happened, except that it seemed like something out of a nightmare. Or one of the stories her father had told her as a child, stories filled with fairy folk and other impossible things.

She exited out the back of the streetcar as soon as it came to a stop, determined to reach the bus station before some well-meaning person called the police. The last thing she wanted to do was field questions with no sensible answers.

She reached the stop as the bus pulled up to the curb. Passing her card over the reader, she gave the other riders a quick look. They all appeared blessedly normal, even the young woman with the spiky pink hair and nose ring. Mae settled on the back bench and stared out the window, watching the night pass by.

When she reached the sanctuary of her apartment, she dashed straight into her bathroom, turned on the shower, stripped off her dirty clothes, and stepped under the driving stream of warm liquid. Feeling safe at last, she cried until the hot water ran out.

Dear Wall,

Today I stole this pencil from one of the minders. He did not notice when I reached out and plucked it from his shirt pocket, the stupid oaf. I managed to hide it through breakfast, and slipped back to my room with it. Mother would be proud to know that I'm still fighting to escape. When Chrysandra came to visit me, she looked right at the pencil, right where I had forgotten and left it on my dresser, and didn't give any clue that she saw it. I can still hide a few things with magic. Of course hiding things from Chrysandra is not terribly hard.

I'll have to be careful and write as tiny as possible, since I've only so much wall. I hope they don't find out what I've done. I can hide you words too, but it's harder. Words want to slide out of their places and be read. It's what you words do. Still, it would be very helpful if you would keep yourselves hidden when Chrysandra, Elise, "Mother" and especially Mr. Hodgins come into the room. You can be my secret.

They don't actually make pencil lead from real lead, do they?

"Mother" came to visit me last night. Of course, she's not really my mother. My real mother is far more beautiful and terrible than this shell of a woman. She won't tell me her real name. She insists on me calling her "mother" and since that's the only name I have for her I do. It keeps her calm.

"Mother" made me sit on her lap. She brushed out my hair and yammered on about nothing. I'm worried about my hair left on the brush. Mother—my real mother—told me that humans are big on sympathetic magic. They could use my own hair to bind me tighter.

I tried to trick "Mother" into telling me her name, but Elise is ever watchful. "Mother" always brings me a gift when she visits. Usually it's clothing, or something pretty but utterly useless, like ribbons and other bits for my hair.

Tonight, she had a small gift bag. She pulled out a picture book about the local streetcars and handed it to me. She said "Grandmother" and "Grandfather" had taken her for a ride on one at the lake and she thought I'd like it.

I thought I was going to scream. I thought for sure they were taunting me or at least trying to trick me somehow. I took the book from her thin fingers, watching Elise the whole time.

I realized that they don't know.

I thanked "Mother" and hugged her, which did make Elise look at me carefully. She must have been satisfied, because she didn't take the book. "Mother" cried and hugged me back, too hard, too bony. Elise practically had to pry her off me.

I could almost feel sorry for her, poor broken thing.

Humans are not the only ones who can perform sympathetic magic.

I had to bite through my own lip to get the three drops of blood. I placed them on the picture I tore from the book, laid my charm—my call for rescue—on it, and tossed it into the fireplace as we walked to dinner. I could tell Elise suspected something, and later I saw the blond man and Mr. Hodgins studying the fireplace, trying to decide what I'd done.

I wonder what my summoning will bring?

That's enough for now. We'll see if Elise notices you words when she comes to take me to lunch. If she doesn't, I will write more tomorrow.

Tuesday, 24ᵗʰ of October

MAE ARRIVED AT HER office the next morning, the previous evening's events still sharp in her memory. She had hoped after a night's sleep they might fade, but instead she had tossed and turned all night, her mind filled with the terrifying image of the white hounds chasing her. Rationally, she knew last night could not have happened. Except it had. Instead of sleeping, she had lain awake all night and tried to remember every tale her father had told her and everything she had picked up from her comparative mythology class in college. The important thing that struck her was how poorly it typically went for humans who dealt with mythological creatures.

She had uneasily ridden the bus into downtown, alert for the appearance of streetcars and nightmare creatures. No ghostly conductors asked for fares, no monsters jumped out of the shadows at her and she didn't even hear the voice of Roy Orbison.

Mae was not reassured by any of this and, all the way to her desk, nervously jingled the loose change she had placed in her pocket as a just-in-case measure.

The one consolation was that the morning was quiet at work. It gave her a chance to spend some time on the Internet refreshing her knowledge about the Cŵn Annwn. Her father had taught her more about Welsh mythology than she had ever thought necessary, but now she was desperate to brush up on those lessons. She was not reassured. The Cŵn Annwn were the hounds of the Wild Hunt, responsible for helping to bring souls from the mortal realm to Annwn, the ancient Welsh afterlife. If the white hounds *were* real, and they *were* after her, she was in deep trouble.

Mae closed her browser and turned to her work, desperate for a little normalcy. She had several files open on her desk and, like everyone else in the office, carried a caseload that was, according to policy and statute, too large. Budget cuts at all levels made this a simple fact of life for everyone in the county attorney's office. Mae knew that cases—cases that represented real children who needed protection and aid—were falling through the cracks. It frustrated her. She knew she couldn't save them all, but she meant to save as many as she could, despite what felt like utter indifference on the part of policy makers. Those policy makers weren't the ones looking these children in the eyes

"Hey, Mae."

She looked up from her paperwork to find Jill settled on the corner of her desk.

"Hey you."

"I just wanted to let you know I might miss class next week."

Three months ago, they had signed up for a self-defense and martial arts class that met every other Tuesday night, though after watching Jill in action, Mae wondered why the younger woman needed it. Jill habitually mauled and manhandled their instructors.

"I'll let Richard know. Is everything all right?"

Jill nodded and stood up. "Family obligations. Look, I'd better get back upstairs before Millard wakes up and finds me gone." Jill took a deep breath. "You want to come to lunch with me this afternoon? We could walk down to Kieran's."

"Okay. That sounds like fun."

Jill favored her with a smile filled with perfect white teeth. "Great! I'll swing by your desk and collect you in a couple of hours."

Mae held her own smile in place until Jill vanished out her door. She let out a deep sigh, all of her social anxieties kicking in. They had been friends for a year, and had gone out for drinks and food several times, though nothing anyone would call a date. Mae had to admit she enjoyed Jill's irrepressible personality, and she was tired of living like a hermit. Jill had given signals. Well, she hoped they were signals. It wasn't as if she and Jill had talked much about relationships since neither of them had dated anyone in the entire time they had known each other, and Mae tended to be private about her personal life. She just assumed that Jill knew that she liked girls. The question was whether or not Jill realized that she hoped that her friend did too.

She resisted the urge to run to the washroom and check her clothes, hair and makeup. Instead, she took a shaky breath and tried to sit still. She resisted a *renewed* urge to run to the washroom, this time to throw up. Mae turned her attention back to the mound of paperwork on her desk, hoping to distract herself. *It's just lunch.* She tried to steady her shaking hands. *Nothing to worry about.*

Two hours and a short walk filled with awkward silence later, Mae found herself fidgeting in a chair, sipping her cup of tea and poking at her Cobb salad. Mae looked around the Irish pub. It was a sparse lunch crowd, with only a handful of other customers scattered about the tables. Jill gave her a measuring look.

"Anything wrong?" Jill asked.

"It just seems too…empty, I suppose."

Jill shrugged and turned back to her bangers and mash. "It's probably the weather," she said, attacking her food with reckless gusto. Jill's aggressive eating style always surprised Mae, who had spent most of lunch pushing her food around on her plate, too nervous to eat.

"Mae, can I ask you a personal question?"

Mae bit her bottom lip and nudged her lettuce with the fork. "Sure, I guess."

"What are you scared of?"

"Excuse me?"

"It's just that, well, you're smart, and you're good at what you do. You're liked and respected around the office—"

"But?"

"Do you know Trent is circulating the rumor that you're a lesbian?"

Mae raised an eyebrow. While they had never talked specifically about it, Mae assumed that Jill already knew. "I am."

Jill shrugged. "I figured. I'm just telling you what the office is currently gossiping about. Apparently, you've never shown any interest in Trent's clumsy attempts to flirt or cheesy pick-up lines."

Mae closed her eyes and shook her head slightly. "Back up. There was flirting and pick-up lines? When?" she said, opening her eyes.

Jill laughed softly and turned to her food for a minute, chasing onion-sauce-covered mashed potatoes around, and occasionally off, her plate with her fork. Mae took the opportunity to take a real bite of her food. It was a good salad, but nothing special.

"I'm serious!" Jill said after she swallowed her food. Her face took on a sly smile. "Are you seeing anyone you haven't told me about?"

Mae nearly choked on her salad.

"I'm sorry," Jill said, raising both of her hands in supplication. "I shouldn't pry."

"Jill, we've been friends for over a year. You're allowed to ask a personal question. You just caught me by surprise. That's more of a pre-date question, really, and no, I'm not seeing anyone. I'd tell you if I was."

"So…is this a date?"

"No, it's lunch. Why, do you want it to be?" Mae fired back, Jill's easygoing demeanor and utter lack of table manners setting Mae at ease. "I take it from your familiarity, you've also been on the receiving end of those clumsy attempts to flirt and cheesy pick-up lines?"

Jill rolled her eyes and took a last bite of her food. She nodded her head in an exaggerated manner while she chewed. "Yeah," she gasped out after she swallowed. Jill gave the corner of her mouth a dainty dab with her napkin, an act wildly different from her eating style.

"Would you like a to-go box?" the waitress asked as she cleared their dishes.

Mae looked up at the woman. "No, I'm finished."

The young woman set the bill on the table. On impulse, Mae snatched it up before Jill could make a move.

"Hey, I invited *you* out to lunch," Jill said.

Mae dug through her bag for her wallet, finding it and producing a credit card. The waitress immediately vanished with Mae's credit card and the bill.

"I've got it," Mae said.

"At least let me pay my half."

"Next time," Mae said. She felt some of her earlier confidence fade. "If you want there to be a next time."

Jill reached over and placed a reassuring hand on Mae's arm. "Of course."

Mae felt a pleasurable jolt go through her body. She looked away from Jill, afraid she might be blushing, and tried to find something to change the subject to or at least provide a distraction. She was saved by the return of the waitress with the credit slip. "We should, um, get back."

Mae and Jill stepped out into the cold October afternoon. They started back toward the Government Center, joining the press of pedestrians going about their daily business, Jill chattering on about bits of office gossip.

The ringing of a bell made Mae look over her shoulder. Coming toward her along Fourth Street was one of the big yellow streetcars. Mae gave the pavement a quick glance. There were no tracks.

"Mae?"

Mae looked up at Jill. She realized they were about to cross the street toward their building. Mae was not sure how they had ended up so far down the street without her noticing. "Yeah?"

Jill turned to face her. "Where did you go?"

"I—ah—I was just—" Mae looked over Jill's shoulder at the streetcar passing through the intersection. Faces both beautiful and grotesque peered at her out of the yellow car's windows. Mae shuddered.

"Are you alright?" The concern in Jill's voice was plain.

"Yeah. I was just thinking about one of the cases I'm working on." Mae turned and watched the streetcar continue through the intersection.

The walk sign changed, giving them the right-of-way. Mae took her eyes off the streetcar that should not exist and followed Jill across the street. They made a final dash inside as the winds picked up again, swirling papers and other debris around their legs.

"Thanks for buying lunch," Jill said as they rode the elevator up.

"Thanks for the invite," Mae replied as the door opened to her floor. She stepped off and turned to Jill, who gave her a little wave as the elevator doors closed.

Back at her desk, Mae settled into a quiet routine of reading files for her pending cases and reviewing ongoing issues, making notes on a legal pad, moving from one case to the next for two hours.

A soft tapping at the side of her door made her look up. Her boss, Donald Leftwich, stood in the opening. The cuffs of his white long-sleeve shirt were rolled back past his wrists. He looked tired, all red-rimmed eyes and five o'clock shadow.

"Mae, do you have a minute?"

Mae nodded, filled with unease. Any time Donald asked if you had a minute, it meant trouble. "Sure. What can I do for you?"

Donald slipped the rest of the way into her office and settled his thin frame into the one cheap folding chair Mae kept as a courtesy. He looked around her cramped space, examining everything on the walls. "I want to talk to you about the Arneson case."

Mae made a quick search of her desk, finding the Arneson file, which she had snuck back in that morning. "I think we're in a strong position heading into—"

"There's not going to be a hearing."

"Excuse me?"

"There's not going to be a hearing. The case has been settled. The Arneson child will be returned to the custody of her mother, under the supervision of the court."

Mae went quiet and still inside. "I see."

"I'm sorry about this, Mae," Donald said.

Mae doubted his sincerity. She supposed her look told him that she was having a hard time believing him. Donald lifted his hands in surrender.

"It wasn't my call."

Mae's frown deepened. If Donald was telling the truth and he was not the one who had interfered with her case, then that could only mean the county attorney had made a decision without Mae's input. "You're trying to tell me Backstrom intervened on behalf of the mother?"

Donald gave another shrug. Mae felt the urge to dive across her little desk and take him by the throat. She made a noise somewhere between a growl and a sigh.

"I don't like this, Mr. Leftwich."

Donald straightened in his chair and glared at her. Mae knew going formal on him made him feel his authority was being challenged. She did not care. The safety of a twelve-year-old child was being compromised because her bosses were making backroom deals. Mae was not so naïve as to think that wealth did not matter in situations such as this, but she was damned if she'd be intimidated.

Donald stood and loomed over her desk. "It doesn't matter what you like, Miss Malveaux. The matter is closed. The case is closed. I expect that file to be *closed* and on my desk before you leave the office tonight. Do you understand, Miss Malveaux?"

"Yes, sir. You'll understand if I place a formal letter of complaint in the file, stating that I disagree with the decision made by the county attorney?"

Donald exhaled. "Of course. You should cover your ass in case this all goes bad."

"Sir, I—"

"I don't want to hear anymore, Mae," he said, raising a hand to stop her next outburst. "I'm sorry about this. I know it's unfair. Just leave the file on my desk at the end of the day."

Donald turned and left her office without giving her a chance to argue the matter more.

It took Mae an hour to write her letter and finish closing out the file. As she walked toward her boss's office, she made a detour on impulse. Several minutes and dozens of photocopies later, she left the case file on Donald's desk as ordered.

A copy rested in her bag.

She knew she could be fired for what she had done, but her instincts screamed that it was critical she keep an eye on this girl's welfare, no matter how hard County Attorney Backstrom tried to bury the case. Moving quickly and quietly, Mae slipped out of the building, nervously looking over her shoulder, expecting someone to stop her and demand to search her bag at any moment.

Dear Wall,

Elise did not notice the writing, even when I stood underneath it to make her look. If Elise can't see it, then I'm not worried about Chrysandra or "Mother." Mr. Hodgins is another matter.

I tried to get another message out at lunch. Someone had placed an arrangement of flowers in the center of the table. I hoped they could be my herald, but Mr. Hodgins saw what I was trying to do and threw them into the fireplace.

I hate Mr. Hodgins. I hate him for making me wear Chrysandra's face. I hate him for making me speak in her voice. I hate him for turning me into her twin. I hate that I'm not strong enough to break his magic. Someday I will learn his true name and I will catch him with his iron off of his finger. Someday.

The silverware is real silver. I'm starting to make a connection with it. I could hear a humming sound coming from it, but I couldn't tell if it was because of me or them.

I'm sorry I didn't write earlier, but Chrysandra stayed in my room all morning. We played and I read to her. Chrysandra is funny at times, and much better than being alone all day. She's kind of slow-witted and smells, but it was nice having her here.

They worked on me again. I don't know why they made me eat dinner if they know I'm going to throw up after their little chant sessions. I got most of my vomit on the red-haired woman, right on her shoes. You'd have thought

I'd stomped on the mage's toes, the way she screamed in panic. I'll have to remember that. After, Mr. Hodgins called Elise to take me back to my rooms.

I wish I had a window. I haven't seen the sun, the grass or a tree in weeks, and I'm starting to get sick from being cut off from the world. They know better than to let me outside.

Elise and Mr. Hodgins are ever watchful. I heard them outside the door talking about tomorrow. Elise is supposed to make sure I'm presentable at dinner.

I'd kill Elise and run for it except for the iron ring she wears. I can't get near her if she doesn't want me to. They all wear the rings—rings charged with magic against me. My mother's blood is too strong inside my veins for me to resist their magic.

Chrysandra seems better today. More like a real girl. She seems almost aware, and the smell is not as strong. They must have freshened her up a bit. I wonder why they would use that much magic on her?

I wonder how she died?

MAE DUG AROUND IN the refrigerator, looking for something quick and easy for dinner. She pulled a can of diet cola and a sealed container of leftover lasagna from the fridge, dished the cold lasagna onto a plate and placed it in the microwave. She hit one of the preprogrammed timers and popped open the soda and took a long drink. The microwave dinged and Mae withdrew the plate of heated lasagna.

The high ringing of a bell made Mae look outside. She glanced down from her third-floor window to the street below. Parked in front of her building on Lagoon Avenue was one of the yellow streetcars. As she watched the car, its bell rang twice.

Mae kept her eyes on the streetcar. "I don't think so."

The bells rang again.

Mae frowned. She knew she shouldn't but...

She grabbed her cell phone from the kitchen counter and dropped it into her bag. On impulse, she shoved the copy of the Arneson file into it as well. She shrugged into her coat and picked up her bag. Checking that her pocket was full of coins, she started downstairs.

The streetcar was waiting for her, its red front door open. Taking a deep breath and wondering if she was mad, Mae stepped aboard. She dropped her dime into the fare box and took the slip of paper from the conductor, jamming it into her pants pocket.

Mae turned toward the back of the car, expecting to find an assortment of faerie creatures and animal spirits.

All she found was Death.

Death smiled at her, the universe in his eyes. "Good evening, Maeve Kathleen Malveaux."

Mae licked her dry lips and grabbed the back of a seat to steady herself as the car started rolling. "Death, are you here for me tonight?" she asked, heart pounding.

"No. My business is elsewhere."

Mae was silent, more than a little nervous. She was unsure how to start a conversation with Death. It seemed she needed a better lead-in than something like, "So, how about those Vikings? You think they'll make the playoffs this year?"

As the streetcar passed by the silver shimmer of Lake Calhoun, Mae plunged ahead. "If you don't mind my asking, people die constantly, but here you are, riding a streetcar like you have all the time in the world."

Death smiled. "That is not a question. However, I understand your point. To answer your unasked query, Maeve, I am unencumbered by mortal concepts of time and space. They simply do not apply to my existence."

"Oh." Mae cringed on the inside at her inability to articulate what she really wanted to ask. She gathered herself and made another attempt. Waving her right hand around, she asked. "Why? Why ride on one of these if you can exist anywhere, everywhere, anytime?"

Death's smile grew wider and he leaned toward her. "I do not *need* to ride these cars, Mae. I do it because it amuses me and I enjoy contact with those who I do not have business with."

For what was the first time since she had boarded the streetcar on Hennepin Avenue in downtown, Mae wondered why she could see and interact with the streetcars while other people, like Jill, apparently could not. She glanced out the window and watched the shops along Excelsior Boulevard go by. They seemed dark and alien to her, not at all a part of her normal, everyday life. Mae frowned to herself.

"You are troubled, Maeve Malveaux," Death said.

"I don't understand why I can ride these cars when other people don't even notice them."

Death stood and shrugged. "I do not have the answers you seek, except that the cars are both a part of and apart from the mortal world, and any who interact with them must be as well. That is why the spirits and fae folk are able to use them. As to why they have revealed themselves to you, I do not know. This is my stop, Maeve Kathleen Malveaux. Good evening to you."

Mae saw they were near Methodist Hospital, about to cross Minnehaha Creek, heading into the little suburb of Hopkins. His form disappeared into the darkness when the streetcar rumbled forward again. She looked at the interior. She was acutely aware of how alone she was. Mae sighed. She had not stopped to purchase another can of pepper spray. She settled back into her seat and cursed herself for wandering off unarmed into the night on a vehicle that technically did not even exist.

She watched the night scenery go by. The car traveled through downtown Hopkins, past its string of antique stores and family-owned bars and restaurants, and turned slightly north. Mae realized the car was heading toward Lake Minnetonka.

She withdrew the illicit file from her bag and checked the address listed for the Arneson family. The senior Arnesons lived in Excelsior, just off the lake in a section of the metro where old money held sway. Marie Arneson had returned to her family home, living with her parents after she finished drug rehab.

The streetcar stopped at the end of a long driveway. The back door opened. No one climbed aboard and the car made no motion to continue on its path. Remembering Ellie's statement about the cars getting you where you needed to go, Mae realized this was her stop. Thanking the conductor, she glanced at the name embroidered on his uniform.

Lowry. It was the name of the man who had been the driving force behind the creation of the modern streetcar system in the Twin Cities over one hundred and forty years ago.

She gave him a startled look. He tipped his hat to her and turned back to the front door, ready to greet any rider who might climb aboard. She stepped into the cold night air.

She found herself facing a Victorian-style mansion. Mae realized this was probably an actual Victorian, not one of the replicas that had been cropping up along the lake, built by the new rich. This structure had likely stood on this spot for the last one hundred and forty-odd years.

Mae walked up the driveway, past the elaborate grounds, the snow-covered topiary, the marble statuary. The fountain at the top of the circular driveway was turned off and drained, likely in preparation for the harsh Minnesota winter. Lights shone brightly and Mae took note of the small fleet of luxury cars parked along the drive. She recognized a couple of the vehicles by their vanity plates.

Mae noted the address again as she approached. She gave the huge mansion a sour look. Well, she was here, no sense in not ringing the bell.

The solid-looking front door was answered by a stern, gray-haired woman in a black skirt that reached her ankles and a white blouse that was pressed to razor sharpness.

"Yes?" the woman asked. "May I help you?"

"My name is Mae Malveaux. I'm with Child Protective Services. I wondered if I might have a word with Marie Arneson."

The woman frowned, looking Mae up and down. "May I tell her what this matter is about?"

Mae smiled, hopefully in a winning way. She realized how rumpled she must look. "It's just a small matter that I need to take care of before I can sign off on her case." Mae was lying through her teeth.

The woman stepped aside to allow Mae entry. "If you would follow me, Miss Malveaux."

Mae was led to a sitting room and left alone. She stood, looking at the elaborate decorations and antique furniture. She suspected the contents of this room alone were worth more than an entire year of her salary. She gave herself a quick check in the mirror hanging on the wall, straightening her blouse and smoothing wrinkles from her slacks. She tried to make her limp hair do something besides look stringy and unwashed. It was a failing effort.

The sound of a door opening made Mae turn. She found herself facing Marie Arneson's father, James, and the family attorney, William Hodgins. Both men looked remarkably fresh for late evening, dressed in pressed suits with coordinating ties. Neither seemed to have an end-of-day shadow on their faces, and each man's gray hair was styled and in place as if they had just risen from a barber's chair. It was Hodgins who spoke.

"Miss Malveaux, to what do we owe the pleasure?"

Mae smiled at both men and addressed James Arneson. "I'm sorry to disturb you, Mr. Arneson, but there was one small matter I needed to attend to before I could sign off on your granddaughter's case file."

Hodgins stepped back into the conversation. "I'm sure you're aware this…unfortunate situation has been resolved to the satisfaction of the county attorney's office?"

"Yes, Mr. Hodgins, I understand that, at some point, a deal was reached. However, I cannot close the file until I've done my exit interview."

"I didn't know there was a need for an exit interview," Hodgins said, suspicion in his eyes.

Mae shrugged. She was way off the deep end and knew she was in for it tomorrow at work, but she had come this far. "It's a simple formality. A few questions, then I can complete my paperwork and we can put this—as you called it—unfortunate incident behind us."

"My daughter is at a meeting of her support group," Mr. Arneson said.

Mae nodded in understanding. "I see. Perhaps I could speak with Chrysandra?" She looked at Hodgins. "Under your supervision, of course. That should be enough for me to complete my report." She turned back to James Arneson. "A couple of questions, then I'll trouble your family no more." *At least,* Mae thought, *until I can figure out what's really going on here.*

The two men looked at each other for several moments. Mae felt a little shiver go down her back. The air in the room seemed to cool as the two turned back to her.

"If you will wait here, Miss Malveaux, I shall bring my granddaughter," James Arneson said.

"Thank you, sir. I'll make this as quick as possible."

The man left the room, leaving Mae alone with Hodgins. She turned and grinned at him with false bravado.

"So which one of those rides outside is yours, Bill?"

"What are you playing at, Malveaux? Are you trying to get yourself fired?"

"I'm just doing my job, making sure that little girl is cared for."

Hodgins narrowed his eyes at her. "Your bosses think Marie Arneson is a fit mother. That should be good enough for you. Perhaps I should ask the county attorney to join us?"

Mae shrugged and turned away, pretending to examine a bejeweled egg. Inside, her heart was hammering and there was a ringing starting in her ears. She knew someone like Hodgins could and would get her fired. He could file a complaint with Backstrom, saying that she was harassing the Arneson family.

"It's just a couple of questions, Bill. I'll ask them, and then you and the rest of Arneson's golf buddies can go back to smoking cigars and drinking brandy."

Before Hodgins could retort, the door opened again. James Arneson came into the room, holding the hand of a little girl. The child seemed well fed and clean. Her blue eyes were bright and her brown hair was brushed and tied back in a ponytail with a ribbon. It had a nice healthy sheen to it. Mae smiled down at her.

James Arneson knelt next to the child. "Darling, this nice lady would like to ask you a couple of questions. Will that be okay?"

The girl nodded her head.

"Hello. You must be Chrysandra."

"Yes, ma'am," the child said shyly.

Mae opened her mouth to ask her question, when movement out of the corner of her eye made her glance at the mirror.

The four occupants of the room were all in full view, but where there should have been the reflection of a healthy, well-dressed twelve-year-old child, there was instead a decomposing corpse reflected in the mirror, its hair falling out in clumps, its flesh mostly pale, but in places mottled with red and black streaks. Mae missed a beat as the horrid reflection startled her and bile rose in her throat.

She swallowed, hoping she had recovered before Arneson or Hodgins noticed. She asked the apparently healthy child a series of what she felt were appropriate questions, stopping herself from turning to stare at the mirror.

Mae finished and—giving the mirror the barest glance—thanked Arneson and Hodgins and made her exit.

She ran down the driveway to the street where she bent over and expelled the meager contents of her stomach onto the pavement.

She was just getting control of herself when the streetcar rolled up and the door opened.

Mae rode the car back to Uptown. She rested her head on the cool glass of the window and watched the shadowy world that she knew was her hometown pass by. As they closed on Uptown proper, more passengers came aboard. Mae paid no mind to the parade of faerie and spirit creatures, whether grotesque, beautiful or mundane.

She stared out the window as they reached Hennepin Avenue. Trendy young professionals, hipsters, punkers and goths, and the ever-present teen crowd, filled the area, dressed for each other in their best plumage. Liberally laced in the crowd were what could only be categorized as normals, wandering through Uptown on their way to a particular theatre or restaurant.

This ordinary scene was shattered by the less-than-ordinary participants in the swirling chaos that was the corner of Lake and Hennepin. Mae wondered why she could see them now. Had her encounters with the streetcars changed her, pulled back whatever veil had hidden the fantastical world that seemed to exist alongside the one she had always known?

It was not as if they were *everywhere*, which Mae supposed made them stand out even more. A woman with the lower body of a goat stood in front of The Rainbow Building. Two manlike creatures, one short and decked out in a red cap, the other tall with hair so golden it shone, argued in front of Calhoun Square. Mae saw the bison-headed man, hunched in his heavy winter coat, waiting for the light to change so he could cross the intersection.

Mae closed her eyes. She did not *want* to see this world. She did not want to be a part of this extra reality, not if it meant confronting things like reanimated dead children. She feared it was too late to return to her old life.

Mae shivered as the streetcar turned up Hennepin. She climbed off the car in front of the old Walker Library building, the squat, solid structure that stood across the street from the newer underground complex.

Mae stood on the sidewalk and let the crowds of pedestrians pass around her. She was surprised by how much activity there was for a Tuesday night. Of course, she did not get out much; for all she knew this was perfectly normal.

She was not ready to face her empty apartment after the night's events. Mae wanted something warm to drink and, if not conversation and company, then at least the presence of her fellow humans. She drew her coat tighter around her body and, checking to make sure her bag was closed and secure, decided to walk to one of the local coffee shops.

"Mae? Mae! Over here!"

Mae looked up to find Jill crossing the street toward her, bundled up in her wool coat, wearing a jaunty little knit hat, and looking entirely too put-together.

"How are you?" Jill asked, her breath filling the air with vapor, her eyes and cheeks bright from the night's chill.

"I—um—I was just going to get some coffee."

"Great! Do you want some company?"

Mae considered telling Jill she wanted to be alone, but changed her mind. "Sure."

Mae felt Jill slip her arm under her elbow, locking their arms together. Jill led her the rest of the way through the intersection.

Mae pointed her finger toward Lake Street. "Dunn Brothers is just over there."

"Yeah, and Dunn Brothers is perfectly nice. But Muddy Paws has cheesecake. Many, many types of cheesecake."

"That's quite the walk," Mae pointed out. Muddy Paws was a good six blocks away.

"It will warm us up!" Jill said, dragging Mae along toward her goal.

Mae looked over her shoulder at the slowly receding Dunn Brothers sign. "We could warm up in there."

Jill laughed. "Come on, you."

Mae gave in and followed Jill, heading north on Hennepin Avenue, past the library, the transit station, the goth apparel and gear store, and a dozen small, quirky, independent shops and restaurants, all obstinate resistors against the large corporations swallowing the neighborhood.

"Do you ever go home?" Mae asked as they stood waiting for a light to change, their target in sight at the other end of the block.

"Sure, I do," Jill answered, starting across the street with Mae firmly in tow. "I've changed clothes since we left work, which, it seems, is more than can be said for some of us."

"Yeah, well, there's a story behind that," Mae mumbled as they walked into the coffee shop.

The smell of roasted coffee beans and baked goods filled her nose. Her stomach actually rumbled and Mae realized that she had not eaten any dinner, and whatever had been left of her light lunch was slowly freezing on a street in front of the Arneson mansion.

Jill smiled at her. "Good. Let's order and you can tell me all about it."

Mae chewed on the inside of her bottom lip, considering what to order and what to tell Jill. Mae wished she had kept her big mouth shut.

Mae watched Jill order a large caramel mocha and a slice of turtle cheesecake and wondered exactly where Jill put all the food she ate. Mae ordered a medium cappuccino and a plain piece of cheesecake.

"I'll get us a table," Jill said. "Give me your coat."

Mae considered pleading that she was still cold and keeping her coat on. She also considered making a run for it when Jill's back was turned. Instead, she handed Jill her coat and suppressed a stab of panic.

Jill returned as their order came up, and the two settled at the small wooden bistro table Jill had secured. Mae realized how terribly small the table was. There was barely enough room for all their food and drink. It was tucked into a dark corner of the shop, the kind of table designed for the maximum enhancement of romantic whispers.

Mae took a sip of her cappuccino and watched Jill from over the rim of her cup. She swallowed the hot, frothy liquid and, deciding the best defense was a good offense, she opened the conversation.

"What brings you out to Uptown on a Tuesday night?" she said, looking Jill squarely in the eyes.

Jill shrugged and dug into her caramel and walnut-covered cheesecake. "I was feeling restless, so I thought I'd wander down and see if anything was going on."

Mae nodded. Jill owned a townhouse in the LynLake area. East of Uptown, it was a haven for artists, students and people who lived on the fringe, having suffered less of the gentrification that made the core corner of Uptown looked like an outdoor shopping mall. Mae and Jill were practically neighbors.

"So? Spill!"

"I'm sorry?"

Jill's eyes lit up. "You said there was a story."

Mae looked down at her half-eaten cheesecake. "I think it might be more of a—"

"Third date story?" Jill supplied. "Because if that's the case, then what say we go out to dinner tomorrow night and you can tell me all about it."

Mae frowned. "I was going to say it was more of a 'one year into the relationship' kind of story…and did you just ask me out?"

"That must be some kind of story and yes, I did." Jill scooped up another huge bite of cheesecake on her fork. She paused before popping it into her mouth. "So?"

Mae rested her elbows on the table and laced her fingers together in front of her. She settled her chin on top of her fingers and tried to keep her expression as neutral as possible. She thought Jill was interested in her, but Mae also knew she was lousy at reading signals. "I thought you liked the 'hot, hot boys' down at the Fine Line."

Jill swallowed her cheesecake and gave Mae a little smirk. "I do."

Mae sat up straight in her chair in an attempt to, as a friend from college once said, "Get the girls up where they can draw attention." Mae was not sure if the effort was having the desired effect, but it was the best she could do short of taking off her blouse. She could not stop a slight smile from forming on her lips.

"In case you haven't noticed, I'm not a boy. I mean, I realize I'm a little—"

"Waif-like?"

"I was going to say 'boyish' but that works as well. However, I am *not* a boy."

Jill rolled her eyes and took a drink of her coffee. "Yes, Mae, I realize that. Did it ever occur to you that maybe I like hot, hot girls as well?"

Mae's posture relaxed and she leaned back on the table again. "Oh. Well, then…"

"Or maybe I like hot, hot lawyers."

"I could introduce you to some, if you'd like."

Jill reached across the small table and placed her left hand on top of Mae's right one. "Maybe I like hot girl lawyers named Mae."

Mae gave her a soft smile. "Jill—"

Jill released Mae's hand and leaned back. "This is the part where you tell me you're not interested in me as girlfriend material, and I get to feel like a damned fool, right?"

"Actually, this is the part where I tell you I'm terrible at relationships, and that right now may not be the best of times for me to start something new."

Jill's face broke into a wide grin. "So you are interested!"

Mae looked straight into Jill's pale blue eyes. "Jill, I'm not going to lie to you. There is a lot of…weirdness going on in my life right now." Mae sighed. "There are things I'm not sure I can talk about, not without sounding like a complete loon."

Jill crossed her arms. "Try me. I'm into weird."

Mae looked up as the barista approached their table. "Ladies, I just wanted to let you know we'll be closing in about ten minutes. Do you need anything else?"

"No, thank you," Jill said.

The barista smiled and walked away.

Mae turned her attention back to her cheesecake, devouring it almost as quickly as Jill finished hers. As Mae took her last bite, the voice of Roy Orbison came over the radio playing behind the counter, where before there had been soft Celtic music. Mae turned in her chair and gave the radio a suspicious look.

"Walk you home?" Jill asked, rising from her chair. She checked to make sure the lid on her cup was secure.

Mae stood with her and pulled on her coat. They both moved toward the door, cups of hot coffee in hand. "You don't have to."

"Maybe I want to. I have to catch a bus at Uptown Station, so it's on my way. Besides, you still haven't answered my question." Jill held the door open for Mae.

The cold air grabbed both women with its brutal embrace.

"Shit!" Jill shrieked as the stiff October winds rushed up to greet them.

"Dunn Brothers was closer to the bus station, too," Mae said, laughing at her friend's discomfort.

"Hush, you," Jill said. "Aren't you freezing?"

Mae took a drink from her coffee. "In this? This is nothing. I was thinking about breaking out the grill."

"You're weird. So are we on for tomorrow night?"

Mae gave her answer a moment's thought. She had enjoyed herself tonight and in truth, she needed some normalcy in her life. "Okay. Where do you want to go?"

"I was thinking that barbecue place in Calhoun Square."

Mae gave Jill a faux-horrified look. "Barbecue? This early in the relationship?"

"We've been out together bunches of times, I'm going to hold you to mid-relationship dating rules. Besides, wasn't it you who was just talking about grilling?"

The wind rose up and buffeted them, bending the lightweight maple trees along the avenue dangerously and knocking the lighter Mae into Jill.

As Mae steadied herself on Jill's arm, she heard the faint strains of Roy Orbison's voice singing "I Drove All Night" from a passing car.

She followed the vehicle with her eyes and found herself looking at four figures trailing her and Jill, about a half block behind them.

Mae shivered as she watched them. There was something wrong with the way they walked. Their gait seemed stiff and forced. As she watched, the wind blew back the hood of one of the men.

He had ears, similar to those of a dog, on top of his head. The creature quickly grabbed its hood and pulled it back over its head, but not before Mae saw a long white snout.

"Jill—"

"I see them. Let's make for the transit station. It will still be full of people, even this late, and there might be a transit cop nearby."

Mae knew a transit cop would not be able to handle what was following them, but she did not have a better plan. "Okay," she said softly.

The two women picked up their pace. Mae resisted the urge to look behind her, partially because she knew if she did, she might panic and break into a run, and something told her running would be disastrous. She noticed Jill reach inside her coat and withdraw a metal rod. Mae recognized it as a telescoping baton. She sincerely hoped they did not have to try to fight their way out of a confrontation, the more so because she still had not replaced her pepper spray.

"Cross!" Jill said as they reached the corner at 28th Street, grabbing Mae's hand.

The two women dove into the crosswalk. Mae chanced a glance over her shoulder. Their pursuers had picked up the pace, closing rapidly despite their awkward gaits. They raced along the sidewalk unmindful of the other pedestrians' indignant protests as the four crashed through in pursuit of Mae and Jill.

"They're gaining!" Mae cried.

"The station's right there. We can jump on the Twenty-One bus. It drops off near my place."

They clambered onto the bus as the driver was closing the door. Trying to catch their breath and ignoring the disgruntled looks they were receiving, they fished out their bus passes and paid.

Mae kept a watch out the window. The four figures skidded to a halt at the transit station and watched the bus pull away, red eyes glowing from under their hoods.

Both women were silent for several minutes, content to let the bus rattle along as they waited for the adrenaline rush to subside and their heart rates to return to normal.

"Well," Jill finally said, her face flushed. "That was interesting."

Mae turned to Jill. "They were after me."

"And exactly how do you figure that?"

"You remember that weirdness I was telling you about? They're part of it."

Jill raised an eyebrow as she reached for the pull cord to request the bus to stop. "I think we're going to need to skip the dating part and go straight to the story."

The two women climbed off the bus, looking around cautiously at their surroundings. They made a quick dash down Colfax Avenue to Jill's townhouse. Jill unlocked the door, and both women slipped inside. Jill locked the door, threw the deadbolt and slipped the security chain into place.

Mae gave her surroundings a quick look. Jill's home was an ordinary two-level townhome. A moderately sized living room, complete with fireplace, greeted her on entry, a smaller dining area was set off to one side, and Mae could see the barest glimpse of a kitchen shielded by the long wall across from the fireplace. The staircase in front of the door led up to the bedrooms. Jill's taste in decorations and furniture ran toward comfortable, with oak wood dominating the furnishings. The cushions on the two chairs and the couch were a contrasting red. The entertainment center was modest and the artwork on the walls impressionist, mostly tasteful renditions of the female form.

"Look, Jill, maybe you should give me a ride home. I'm not sure how much you really want to know, or even how much you'd believe, about what's going on. Maybe I should leave."

"Or maybe," Jill said, taking off her coat and favoring Mae with a slight smile, "you can have a seat. I'll make something hot to drink, and you can fill me in on why a pack of two-legged Tindalos hounds are chasing you."

Mae blinked in surprise. "Actually, I think they might have been two-legged Cŵn Annwn."

Jill cocked her head. "Cŵn Annwn?"

"It's Welsh."

"I don't know much about Welsh myth. I'm more of a Lovecraft kind of girl."

Mae stood in the doorway and gave Jill a curious look. "You're taking all this rather well."

Jill snorted. "For your information, I think I might have peed myself a little bit back there. And I've spilled caramel mocha all over my shoes."

Mae chewed on her lower lip for a moment, and then sighed. "I shouldn't get you involved."

"I think it might be too late for that. Besides, I don't think either of us wants to go back out there tonight."

Mae hugged herself. Jill was right. Mae was scared of what might be waiting in the cold Minnesota night. She was afraid to spend tonight alone in her little walk-up apartment. Coming to a decision, Mae took off her coat and kicked off her shoes.

"Okay then. If it's all right, I'll crash on your couch tonight."

Jill smiled. "I'm glad that's settled. I'll make us some tea, and you can tell me all about it."

Five minutes later, the two women were settled next to each other on the couch, steaming cups in front of them on the low coffee table.

Mae decided to start at the beginning. She put her cup down and reached into her messenger bag, withdrawing the illicitly copied file of Chrysandra Arneson. She opened it up on the table and turned to Jill.

"I saw a living dead girl tonight."

Dear Wall,

I killed one of them tonight.

Elise had taken me to the workroom and placed me in the circle. Elise, Mr. Hodgins and the man I'm supposed to call "Grandfather" secured me, then brought in the mage I call Gray Hair. He's the best of them at binding spells, and always stinks of ceremonial magic and blood sport. He walked around me, staring with cold eyes. He frightened me.

They talked a lot. Gray Hair and Mr. Hodgins were look-ing at some papers and passing pictures back and forth, discussing a woman named Mae who they thought could turn into a problem. They had started discussing how to bind my magic tighter when the doorbell rang, startling everyone.

Elise left the room to answer the door and Mr. Hodgins set a series of charged crystals at the edges of the circle to reinforce it. Everyone stepped out into the hallway. I could hear them through the thick door. There was a hur-ried conversation and I felt them drawing up their magic, doing a quick working.

The last time someone came unannounced, it was a teacher from the private school Chrysandra's supposed to be attending. They had to bind me with magic and trot me out to show off. I almost got away that time because they weren't able to stop the woman from giving me her real name. I tried to bind her to my will. It would have worked, but the younger, brown-haired male mage hit her and knocked her out. He and Mr. Hodgins carried the woman to the basement workroom and I never saw her again. Elise nearly twisted my arm off that night when she took me back to my room.

Another of the mages, the black-haired woman who is Chrysandra's minder, came in to make sure I was still bound. She set one of the red-eared hounds to guard me and left the door open, I guess so they could check on me.

They must have sent away whoever it was. Mr. Hodgins and "Grandfather" came back to the room and took down the circle. As Elise and Mr. Hodgins started to walk me back to my room, Gray Hair took out his wallet and opened it.

I never told them just how sharp my eyes are. It's part of my heritage. I read Gray Hair's name off a card with his picture on it, something called a 'driver's license.'

Ernest Parker Slotky II screamed prettily as Death rushed up and collected his due. He screamed until he hacked up blood and collapsed. Untangling something, or even someone, held together by magic is easy, if you know how and you know their true name. After decades of cheating his death from the sickness in his body, I unraveled his existence in less than thirty seconds. He doesn't frighten me anymore.

It was worth it when Mr. Hodgins slapped me across the room. It was worth it when he kicked me into the low table where they had been drinking and looking at papers and photographs. It was worth the blood and lost teeth and broken leg. Those will mend and grow back. I grabbed what I wanted. I have one of the photographs of the woman they were so concerned about.

I wonder who Mae Malveaux is and why they want her dead?

I'd barely healed my leg before "Mother" came to visit me. "Mother" cried and cooed and her breath reeked. Elise finally took her away when "Mother" began to leak uncontrolled magic, making things in the room shake.

Mr. Hodgins and a couple of the others warded my door with their magic so that only Mr. Hodgins or Elise can open it. Then they pounded iron nails in all along the frame and around the knob. They're scared of me. They should be.

Wednesday, 25th of October

MAE AWOKE WITH A start. She had been dreaming about having a tea party with a girl's corpse. They were in a room with writing on the walls, but the words squirmed and twisted like agitated snakes and Mae couldn't read them. There had been a sense of underlying menace, as if something lurked in the shadows, waiting to pounce, waiting to sink its teeth into her throat.

She sat up, disoriented by her unfamiliar surroundings, shaking her head to clear it. Her mouth tasted terrible, like she had kissed a wet dog, and she was on a couch in a strange room. She took a calming breath, remembering how the previous evening had ended. She was on Jill's couch, in Jill's living room, dressed in one of Jill's oversized nightshirts.

After spilling her entire story, Mae had sat holding her breath and waiting for Jill to either laugh at her or offer to pay for a cab to get the loony out of her living room. Instead, Jill had sat silent for a couple of minutes, apparently deep in thought. Then she'd stood and, declaring that they had gone through a difficult ordeal, commanded that they both get some sleep. She said they could take the matter up again over the dinner date Mae had promised her.

Mae rose slowly, careful to make as little noise as possible. She looked around for a clock. The green numbers flashing from the digital video recorder resting on the television read five twenty-six.

After using the bathroom, she moved silently into the kitchen. A quick search yielded a canister of ground coffee and filters for the coffeemaker. Mae started it up and returned to the living room. She found her clothes from the night before neatly folded and stacked in a chair next to the couch. Mae decided that it would be safe enough to change back into her clothes in the living room, planning to duck into the bathroom if she heard Jill coming. By the time she finished dressing and folding the makeshift bedding, Mae was able to pour herself a cup from the not-quite-full coffee pot.

Settling at the kitchen table, Mae checked her watch. If Jill did not make an appearance soon, she would have to find her own way back to her apartment. She expected fallout from her impromptu and ill-advised visit to the Arneson household, and the last thing Mae wanted to be was late for work.

She was trying to decide between waking Jill or leaving her a note and catching a bus back to the Uptown Transit Station, when she heard the sound of a shower running upstairs. Mae was most of the way through her second cup of coffee when Jill appeared, looking fresh, awake, and ready to face the day.

"Good morning," Jill said as she took a travel mug from the cabinet and filled it with coffee. "Sleep well?"

Mae nodded over her cup. "Yeah, actually. I usually don't sleep at all in strange beds, but last night was okay." She decided not to mention the weird dream. She had piled a lot on Jill in a short time last night—there was no need to add more stress, especially since it was only a dream, nothing more.

"Good. I'll drive you home. You shower and change, then we can get scones or something at Dunn Brothers before we head for work." Jill gave Mae a stern look. "I'm not taking no for an answer."

Mae finished her coffee and nodded in agreement. "Okay. It will give you a chance to ask any questions you might have thought of after we went to bed last night."

The two women slipped into their coats and stepped into the unheated tuck-under garage.

Mae gave Jill's vehicle a dubious look. "I'm reminded why you bus everywhere."

Jill gave her a playful scowl. "Hush, you. You'll hurt her feelings." Jill reached out and patted the top of the rusty, red Ford Escort. "It's okay, Maddy. Don't listen to the mean woman, she doesn't know what she's talking about."

"Wait—Maddy?"

"Be nice," Jill said as they both climbed into the cramped interior. "I've had Maddy since I was a freshman in college. She's never let me down." Jill turned the key. The engine whined, coughed and sputtered. Jill pumped the gas pedal and turned the key again. The whole car shook as the ignition finally took and the engine started. The smell of oil filled the car.

"Um...Jill?"

Jill gave her what Mae suspected was supposed to be a reassuring smile. "It's all good. Maddy'll stop blowing smoke before we reach your place."

Mae checked her seatbelt as Jill backed the car out of the garage.

Jill was true to her word. The little car stopped blowing blue smoke out the tailpipe four blocks from Mae's apartment. She smoothly wedged the car into a spot on Humboldt. "Do you think it will be okay if I leave Maddy here for the day and pick her up tonight? I don't want to try to park downtown."

"Yeah, it will be fine."

"You're sure? I wouldn't want something to happen to her."

"I'm sure Maddy will be perfectly safe," Mae said, all the while thinking that no self-respecting car thief would ever touch Jill's rusty heap.

Mae led Jill to the squat, aging brownstone she lived in. Mae struggled with the key in the security door's lock as Jill looked at the building and its surroundings.

"I know I've said this before, but they obviously don't pay you guys enough," Jill said.

Mae gave the key a jerk and a twist. It rotated with a loud snap. She pulled the security door open, the whole time trying to work her key back out of the lock.

"I have simple needs, that's all," Mae replied. In truth, she had found the apartment right out of college and was still living here because she did not want to deal with the hassles of moving.

Jill followed Mae inside. "Well, I need air conditioning in the summer."

"I've got a window unit," Mae replied, starting up the steps to her third-floor apartment. "And how many rooms does that window unit really cool, hmm?"

Mae stopped at the landing to the second floor and peered down at Jill. "It keeps the living room and kitchen cool."

"What about the bedroom?"

Mae gave Jill a wicked little smile, the urge to flirt rising up. "I open the window, turn on a fan and sleep naked."

"Well, that will certainly make things easier."

Mae felt a little shiver, thinking about being naked with Jill. She turned and started up the stairs. "Don't get ahead of yourself, missy."

Jill's snort of laughter was the only reply.

Mae reached her door and started to push the key into the deadbolt.

The door swung open.

Mae took a step backward, bumping into Jill.

"What? Oh!" Jill said, seeing the door standing partially open. "I don't suppose you forgot to close the door when you left last night?"

Mae shook her head. "No. I know I locked it."

Jill took Mae's arm. "Let's go back downstairs and call the cops."

"Yeah. Yeah, I think that's a good idea."

Twenty minutes later Mae watched as Patrol Sergeant Mary Alice Dean of the Minneapolis Police Department frowned and looked up at the building. The sergeant turned back to her. "We'll need you to go through and tell us if anything is missing."

"Okay," Mae said. She did not want to go into her apartment, even with a police escort.

"I'll come up with you. Remember, it's still a crime scene, so try to disturb as little as possible."

Mae hugged herself and pulled her coat tighter against her body. "How long will you need to finish up inside?"

"We should be done soon." The sergeant's face took on a concerned look. "Look, Miss Malveaux, it might be a good idea for you to stay with a family member or friend, just for a night or two."

Jill touched her arm to gain her attention. "Why don't you stay with me for a couple of days?"

Mae exhaled a long breath. "Okay. I'll pack a few things."

Sergeant Dean turned back to the building. "You should have your superintendent change the locks."

"Yeah. That'll only take him a month."

Sergeant Dean looked to Mae, her eyebrows raised. "*I'll* talk to him, let him know that if they're not changed by the time we're ready to leave the scene, there'll be all manner of inspectors from the city coming to visit."

Mae smiled. "Thanks."

"No problem. I'll have someone call to let you know when we're done and the key is ready." The sergeant turned to Jill. "I'll need your contact information."

"Of course," Jill said.

She looked at Mae again. "I'll have a couple of officers drive by your place regularly for a few nights, but honestly, it isn't likely we'll catch whoever did this, Miss Malveaux. So, you think you're ready to go up and see what they took?"

Mae turned to Jill. "Could you call in for me?"

"Sure. Who should I talk to?"

Mae gave Donald Leftwich's direct phone number to Jill. "Tell him as little as you can."

"I'll take care of it."

Mae followed the sergeant and two uniformed officers into her apartment.

The place had been ransacked. In the living room-kitchenette combination, the cushions from the couch and chair were flung into a corner, and tables had been tipped over. The three drawers under the small kitchen counter were opened and her silverware and utensils dumped on the floor.

"They ate the lasagna," Mae whispered, looking at the empty plate.

"I'm sorry?" Sergeant Dean asked.

"Nothing. I was just muttering to myself about the mess."

"Have you noticed anything missing yet, ma'am?"

"No. Not yet."

She gave the tiny bathroom a quick glance. The intruder had ransacked her medicine cabinet, but the small room was not as big of a mess as the rest of the house.

The chaos continued in the bedroom. Her bedcovers were pulled onto the floor, her dresser drawers pulled out and turned upside down. Mae blushed as she saw all her bras and panties lying on the carpet in plain view.

She checked and discovered her emergency stash of cash was gone. She looked through her small collection of modest jewelry. Everything was there, if scattered about the room. It was then that she noticed her important personal papers—her birth certificate, the official transcript from college, a couple of letters from her father, and the only photograph she owned of her mother—were on the bed, arranged neatly next to each other.

"Ma'am?"

Sergeant Dean's voice came from the bedroom doorway. Mae turned to face her.

"They took a little money, maybe a hundred dollars."

Dean stepped closer to her, her frown leaving deep lines on her broad, brown face. "I'll tell you what I think, Miss Malveaux. I think this whole thing was designed to shake you up. Is there someone who would want to scare you or hurt you? Maybe an ex-boyfriend or a coworker who doesn't like you? Anyone you can think of who would do this, anyone at all?"

Mae shook her head. She had her own suspicions, but she could not tell the detective she suspected supernatural forces were trying to stop her from digging too deeply into a case of child neglect she was not supposed to be working on anymore.

"No. No, I'm sorry. I just—I don't know who would do this."

Sergeant Dean sighed. "All right. Why don't you grab some fresh clothes and go with your friend. We'll call you when we're done."

Taking a small travel suitcase from her closet, Mae packed some clothes and her personal papers. Necessities from the bathroom and a few personal items went in next. Mae looked around her apartment as the officers poked through her belongings.

She found Jill waiting for her in the small lobby. Jill took her by the arm and led her past the building superintendent, who gave her an angry glare, no doubt ready to blame her for bringing trouble down on his building.

Mae was quiet on the way to Jill's townhouse. Once inside, Mae took off her coat and shoes and dropped heavily back onto the couch she had been sleeping on only a few hours before.

"What did Donald say?" Mae whispered to Jill, who had settled on the couch next to her.

"He wants you to call him later. He sounded kind of annoyed. Do you want me to stay with you?"

Mae took a deep breath and leaned forward, her hands on her knees. "I know you need to go to work. I'll be fine, really."

Mae knew it was a lie as soon as the words left her lips. She would not be okay. She was in way over her head. Phantom streetcars. Zombie girls. Hounds from hell. Faerie creatures. Death. It was all getting to be too much.

And now someone had broken into her home. They had violated the place where she lived and taken away her sense of security. She knew it had something to do with the Arneson case. She *knew* it, but right now she wanted it all to go away, wanted it to stop and her life to reset to normal.

Mae felt Jill place a hand over hers and give it a little squeeze.

Mae *wanted* it to all go away but knew it would not. Whoever was behind these attacks on her would not stop. She should run, should get as far away as possible. By staying, she was not only putting herself in danger, but now the threat likely extended to Jill, who had seen the creatures chasing them last night and knew the entire story. Mae shivered.

But there was a child who had died, whose body was being used for purposes Mae could not even grasp and she feared that if this one child had met a tragic and unnecessary death, there might be others.

There had to be a reason she was drawn into this. The sudden appearance of the streetcars, the attacks, even the strange behavior of her bosses; these were all connected. She was being pulled into a conflict she did not understand and, God help her, she could not walk away.

Mae burst into tears, crying like a frightened little child awoken by a nightmare, feeling overwhelmed and alone.

Soft arms wrapped around her and pulled her close. Mae let herself be held, let the arms comfort her. Her body lost all of its strength and collapsed. She curled up into a little ball of misery on the couch, lying with her head in Jill's lap. Jill stroked her hair. Mae looked out at Jill's living room through her tears. Her small travel suitcase sat near the door, a solemn reminder of the strange and dangerous situation she was facing. She saw a box of tissues on the coffee table and reached for it.

"Why don't I call in sick?" Jill said. "I don't think you need to be alone right now."

Mae sniffed and smiled gratefully. "Okay."

Dear Wall,

They did not call me to breakfast. They also didn't bring me anything.

I guess Mr. Hodgins wants to punish me for killing the mage. I have a bad feeling that they might not bring me any lunch or dinner, or any food at all for the next couple of days. That's not going to help me as I heal myself, and it is going to be a terrible drain on my magic. I'm not sure how many more days I can hold out before my personal magic runs out.

Most of my teeth have grown back in and the bones have all mended, but I don't think I'll be able to heal myself again, at least not that easily. I miss the lake and it's been so long since I've seen Mother. I wonder if I remember the path home.

I have Mae's picture, so I plan to try to summon her using the same charm I used to try to summon the streetcars. I wish I knew more about who Mae Malveaux is. I wish I was sure my summoning charm would get through the protections on this house.

I have no idea if it will work, and I suspect it will use the last of my magic. I don't know what else to do. There is no way I will be able to escape on my own, they watch me too closely. I will need rescue.

I keep looking at the woman's photograph. She seems familiar to me. I feel as if I should know her. She's not beautiful, not like the Court ladies or Mother. Her hair is too thin and her eyes look like mud, but still, there's something there. I'm hoping it's something good.

I'm also going to need a way to start a fire, as I doubt they'll let me anywhere near a lit fireplace again. Perhaps I can steal some matches, like I stole this pencil.

Do you know how hard it is to sharpen a pencil without a sharpener or a knife? I chipped away at the wood around the lead with my fingernails for some time and then tried to make the lead sharp by rubbing it on my bedpost.

I need more words and maybe a piece of silverware as well, but that will be harder. I'm pretty sure someone checks the silver when they put it away at night.

You're a good wall and a group of good words. You stay hidden and keep my secrets.

Mae gave her apartment a long look. She had decided to move out. After that morning's break-in she could not make herself live here anymore. She would room with Jill while she looked for a new place to live. It had only taken Jill a couple of hours to convince her.

"Are we done?" Jill asked. She and Mae were standing by the front door.

Mae nodded. After the police called to tell her she could return to her apartment, she and Jill had driven back. The two women cleaned, straightening the chaos. Mae packed more clothes and personal items.

"Yeah," Mae said. "Let's get out of here."

Mae locked the door behind her and they walked back to Jill's car, lugging two suitcases, a backpack and a medium-sized box. A large cooler filled with the contents of Mae's refrigerator was already weighing down Jill's little Ford.

"Have you called Leftwich?" Jill asked.

"No. No, I haven't. I'll do that when we get back to your place."

Jill made a quick lane change, driving around a city bus that was loading and unloading. "It's your place too, now. For as long as you need it."

"Thanks. It'll all be good." Mae glanced at Jill as she pulled into the garage. "After we unload, I'll call Donald. Maybe we could get some food?"

"I could call for takeout," Jill said.

"Sounds good."

They hauled the luggage and box up to Mae's new room for the duration. Jill set the suitcase and the box on the futon. She turned to Mae, flush with exertion. "I'll go get the cooler and start unloading it while you call your boss." Jill huffed out a long breath and started down the stairs again.

Mae dug through her messenger bag for her cell phone. She dialed the number. Donald answered on the second ring, his voice sounding somewhere between tired and bored.

"Leftwich. How may I help you?"

"Hello, Donald, it's Mae."

"Mae, Jill called this morning and said you wouldn't be in the office, but she didn't say why."

"My apartment was broken into last night."

"Are you all right?"

Mae felt a small shiver. Something in the way he said it—there was a note of false sincerity. "I wasn't home when it happened. I didn't find out until this morning."

There was a pause on the other end and Mae could tell that Donald was processing the fact that Mae was out all night and that another woman had called on her behalf.

"I see." The disapproving tone in Donald's voice spoke volumes. "Are you planning to come to work tomorrow?"

"Yes, I don't see any reason why not."

"Good, because I need to talk to you about something."

Mae went cold inside. She had a very good idea why Donald wanted to talk to her. She decided to get it over with. If she gave the director an entire day to stew, he would only get madder.

"Donald, why don't I get cleaned up and I'll be in the office in about an hour."

"I think that would be a good idea."

"See you in a little while."

Mae hung up the phone. She took a steadying breath and made her way downstairs. Jill was on her knees in front of the refrigerator, cramming Mae's groceries into the already full appliance.

"Well?" Jill said, looking up.

"You might want to hold off on food. I need to go into the office for…well it could be a few hours or a few minutes. I feel bad about going in when I made you take a day off to help me and all, but I need to do this. Is that okay?"

"Of course it is," Jill said. "Problems at the office?"

Mae gave her a rueful little smile. "Your new roommate may be unemployed after today."

"Ah," Jill said. "I'm in no hurry to evict you, so don't worry about being homeless."

It took Mae fifteen minutes to pull clean clothing from her luggage, shower and dress. On a whim, she grabbed the change out of the pocket of her slacks from the previous night and tossed it into her bag. She trotted to the corner of Lyndale and Lake, where she caught a bus into downtown.

Mae tried to calm her increasing panic as she transferred to the light rail train for the short ride to the Government Center. But she exited the train, walked into her building, passed through security and rode the elevator up to her floor, all without being sick.

"There you are!"

She heard Donald's voice as soon as she stepped off the elevator, as if he'd been standing there waiting for her. That thought did nothing to calm her.

"I got here as quickly as I could."

The instant she acknowledged his presence, she found herself speaking to his back as he turned sharply and made a beeline for his office. Mae got the message. She was to follow him. No side treks, no stopping at her desk. Straight to Donald's office.

Donald opened the door and waved Mae inside. "Come in."

She steeled herself for the worst as Donald settled into his chair.

"So, your apartment was broken into?"

"Yes, sir."

Donald frowned, deepening the lines on his thin face. "Well, I'm glad you're safe." He took a deep breath before Mae could respond. "However, that's not why I've called you into my office.

Miss Malveaux, would you please explain to me *why* you were at the Arneson home last night?"

"I'm sorry. I know I shouldn't have gone..." Mae wanted to cringe and hide as Donald glared at her.

"No, you should not have! The matter was settled and the case closed. Yet this morning, I find myself on the receiving end of an irate phone call from the county attorney, asking me *why* one of my people was out harassing the Arneson family last night."

Mae trembled in her chair. She took a deep breath. She was so certain at this point that her job was forfeit, she decided to at least have her say.

"I wanted—no, I *needed* to see the situation for myself."

"Why?" the director challenged. "I remind you that the case was closed, Miss Malveaux."

"The case was closed in an irregular manner."

"And you put a letter of complaint in the file. You're on record as disagreeing with the decision. Why couldn't you leave it at that?"

"Because there is a twelve-year-old girl suffering from a long history of abuse."

"The county attorney is aware of the particulars," Donald said. "Or are you implying that Mr. Backstrom would purposefully return a child to a dangerous situation?"

"I'm saying, sir, that despite all the evidence and the recommendations of this office, County Attorney Backstrom struck a closed-door deal with the family without consulting the caseworker most familiar with the situation."

Mae sat back in her chair. She decided to lay it all on the table. "Backstrom made a deal in favor of the mother, whose parents are wealthy neighbors of his."

"Mae—" Donald said in a warning voice.

"Yes, sir. I went to the Arneson household last night to check on the welfare of a child whose case was taken away from me for no acceptable reason. Upon arriving, I noted several vehicles, including those owned by Judge Slotky and Backstrom."

Donald leaned back in his chair and gave Mae a long, hard look. "Are you accusing officers of the court of misconduct?"

Mae took a deep breath. "I'm saying there were several irregularities in this case. I'd like to go on the record with that."

Donald seemed to deflate in his chair. "Very well."

She tried not to cringe, expecting the older man to rip into her. Mae was surprised by Donald's next words.

"Mae, when was the last time you took a vacation?"

Mae looked down in thought. "I—I don't really remember," she said, glancing back up at him.

The director looked down at a block of papers on his desk. It was Mae's personnel file.

"Well, I do. Three years ago you took four days off."

Mae frowned, confused as to where this was going. "I suppose that sounds right."

"Backstrom wants me to let you go. He thinks you're unstable."

"I came here prepared to be fired," Mae admitted.

"Well, at least you have *some* sense."

Mae looked at her lap. She'd had her outburst; now was the time to sit quietly.

"I think you're just tired. I want you to use some of your vacation time. Take the next four weeks off. Clear your head. Step away from all this for a while."

"What about my cases?"

"We'll divide them among the rest of the staff."

Mae looked up, straight at the director. She crossed her arms. "What if I refuse to take a voluntary vacation?"

"Then I'm putting you on administrative leave." Donald leaned forward. "It's your choice. You can either go home and get paid, or go home and *not* get paid." He leaned back again. "Or I could just fire you like Backstrom wants."

Mae exhaled. "Then I guess I'm taking a month off."

"Good. Keep your head down and stay out of trouble. No more harassing the county attorney's friends. Spend some quality time with whomever you spend quality time with. Don't make waves, and I'll let you return to work after this blows over."

"Yes, sir."

Ten minutes later, Mae stood in front of the Government Center. She ignored the streetcar parked in front of the building with its door open, and marched directly to the light rail station.

"Miss Malveaux."

Mae turned and found herself facing William Hodgins. It was all she could do not to jump. It was as if he had been conjured. She had neither seen nor heard him approach. She kept her expression carefully under control.

"Mr. Hodgins."

"I see you're leaving work early today. Job problems, Miss Malveaux?"

Mae frowned. "You wouldn't know anything about that, would you?"

He stepped closer to her, forcing Mae to take a step back toward the edge of the platform. "I don't know what you thought to accomplish with that little stunt last night, but I hope it was worth your career."

Mae held her tongue. She realized anything she might say would only worsen the situation. She knew something beyond child abuse was happening in that home, but she had no way to prove it. Worse, she no longer had any real authority to investigate the matter.

"I want you to stay away from my client, Miss Malveaux. If you do not stop your harassment, steps will be taken."

"Is that a threat?"

He leaned into her again. Mae found herself teetering on the edge of the platform.

"You have no idea what you are dealing with, little girl. Go home to your lady-friend and stop meddling in the affairs of your betters."

Behind Mae, the light rail train hissed to a stop, its door opening. She took three tentative steps backward, keeping her eyes on Hodgins as she climbed into the hoped-for safety of the train. She stood in the aisle, watching him through the open doors as he laughed at her. The doors closed and, with a series of short warning beeps, the train rolled away.

Mae settled onto a bench and let the shakes take her.

Dear Wall,

Elise brought me lunch, the first food I've had in almost a day. It was oatmeal, which is terribly bland, but it was hot and it was food.

She told me that tonight I would be having dinner with her and "Mother." Then she reached down and twisted my hair up in her fist and said that if I tried to escape, I would be locked in a cage. She caught me by surprise and I started crying before I could stop the tears. I hate giving them the satisfaction of knowing they've hurt me, even when it does hurt.

"We only need you to be alive, that's all," she said, breathing her smelly stale breath all over me. Then she left Chrysandra with me to "play."

I know Chrysandra tells them about me. I can't blame her for it. But that can't be the reason they keep her as fresh as they do. I wish I could figure out why they keep the poor thing animated. At least she's always up for games and puzzles, and she doesn't complain.

Today she looked at me and I saw something behind her eyes. She's always seemed blank before, but something must have happened after the last time they refreshed the magic holding her together. It was the worst feeling I've ever had, looking into Chrysandra's eyes. I wanted to crawl under my covers and cry, but I didn't. I just asked for the book I've been reading her. She handed it to me, and her fingers touched mine. I knew for sure then. I knew the sickening truth.

She's still in there.

Jill smiled down at Mae, pleased with the way the evening had turned out. The two women were waiting for the bus back to the townhouse from what Jill thought of as their first real date. Mae had tried to talk her out of it, saying that being forced out of her job that morning, no matter how temporary, put her in no mood to be good company. Jill had waved aside her objections, telling her that sitting home brooding would do no one any good. She'd enthusiastically pushed the idea until Mae relented, and they'd had an enjoyable night of dinner and theatre.

"Thanks," Mae said.

"See, I told you going out would lift your spirits."

Mae laughed and nudged Jill with her hip. "Don't make me run you into the boards."

Jill put her hand on the back of the bench they stood by to steady herself. "Run me into the boards?"

"Hockey."

"Are you trying to tell me that a little slip of a thing like you played hockey?"

Mae laughed aloud. "Oh, hell yes. I was an only child living with my bachelor father. In Minnesota. He taught me all the important things. How to field dress a deer, how to fish for walleye and how to play hockey. You want to hit the ice?"

"No," Jill said, shaking her head. "I can barely stand on skates and go forward, never mind doing anything fancy."

"I'll be gentle with you."

"I've heard *that* before," Jill said with a laugh. "Are you still a fan?"

"Yeah. I try to see the Wild play a few times a year. What about you?"

"Men in padded armor with sticks, on ice, engaging in ritual violence? It works for me." Jill peered down the street, looking for the bus. The cold was starting to penetrate her coat, and she wanted to be home, warm and snug with Mae.

"You want to go on a real adventure?" Mae said.

Jill frowned. Mae had a manic look in her eyes. "What do you mean?"

Mae grabbed Jill by the hand and ran, pulling them both into the middle of the street as passing motorists honked their horns and yelled curses at them. Jill tugged Mae's arm in a futile attempt to make her stop.

"Mae! Are you crazy?" Jill screamed.

Mae stopped for a moment, letting a big sport utility vehicle pass her, then leaped up slightly, pulling Jill along with her and forcing Jill to leap as well. She gasped, feeling a jolt as she landed on something solid. A floorboard, she was looking down at the floor of a vehicle.

Mae turned to her, face flushed with excitement.

"Ten cents each, please."

Jill stared around at the impossible interior of an antique street-car as Mae fished around in her pocket, producing two dimes. Mae dropped them into the fare box. "We'll each need a transfer."

The man in the uniform handed Mae two slips of paper.

Jill kept a grip on Mae's arm as Mae led her down the aisle to an empty bench. They found one midway, behind a dozing rab-bit-headed man, ears poking through holes cut in the rounded brim of his hat. They were in front of three small, giggly creatures that looked like miniature teenage girls and glowed like silver-mercury moonlight. Across the aisle sat an elderly Asian couple. The woman kept her hands in her lap, looking straight ahead. The man was read-ing a newspaper. They seemed perfectly normal until Jill noticed the foxtail peeking out from under the woman's dress.

"Here, you'll need this," Mae said, passing Jill one of the transfer slips. "Whatever you do, don't lose it."

"What happens if I do?" Jill asked. She tensed, the evening's pleasantness erased by the impossible, yet obviously real, experience she was having.

"Bad things," Mae said, which did nothing to relieve Jill's fears. She nodded and slipped the transfer into her pocket, mimicking Mae's actions. "Where are we going?"

"I don't know. But we'll get there."

Jill fidgeted in her seat and looked around at the other occupants. She had told Mae she was into weird, and that was not a lie, but this was almost too much.

There had been hints in her life, things her brother Robert had told her, questions he had asked, as if subtly trying to find out if Jill believed in or had ever experienced anything supernatural. She had missed her last self-defense class with Mae to have drinks with Robert. Over lob-ster and wine, after extending her an invitation to a Halloween party with a group of his country-club friends and in between working his charm on the cute little college girl waiting on them, he had bluntly asked her if she had ever made something happen that she could not explain. She had shaken her head no, and he had given her a considering look, as if he did not quite believe her.

It was real, she thought. Magic was real. She had thought once that she had seen a flame appear over her brother's hand as they had sat around talking after a family dinner. He had peered at her over the flame, as if challenging her to ask him questions, but she had decided it was too much wine on her part.

The streetcar stopped two blocks further on and the Asian couple climbed off. Mae sat quietly, occasionally peering at Jill to see her reaction. Finally, Jill blew out a long breath and said with more bravado than she felt, "Well, I said I was into weird. And this is weird."

The car didn't stop again until the corner of Lake and Lyndale. The rabbit-headed man stood and, giving Mae and Jill a polite nod, stepped off the car. "Our stop is next," Mae said, dragging Jill toward the back door.

"How do you know that?" Jill asked.

"Because you live on Colfax."

Jill cocked her head and gave Mae a little smile. "I don't know if anyone's ever told you this before, but you get weirder at night."

"It's the influence of the moon," Mae said. They walked the block to the townhouse, shrugging out of their coats as soon as they entered the building.

"I'm going to go change," Mae said.

"You want anything from the kitchen?" Jill asked. "I figured I'd come up and help you finish unpacking, unless you've got other plans."

"Anything to drink would be fine."

By the time Jill climbed the stairs, two steaming cups of cocoa in hand, Mae had changed into a T-shirt and pajama pants. Jill sat next to her on the futon. "So..."

Mae gave her a crooked little smile. "I just—when I saw the streetcar coming, I really wanted you to see them for yourself."

"And now I know." Jill wondered if she should tell Mae about her brother.

"Are you okay?" Mae looked pensive, as if letting Jill in on her secret might be a deal-breaker in their budding relationship.

"I'm glad you showed me."

"I wanted someone else to know, I wanted you to see. I know it's something out of a fantasy story, but it is real."

Jill nodded. She would have to tell Mae about Robert and his odd questions. Mae seemed to be a part of the magical world Robert apparently lived in. "It's kind of like Halloween came early."

"That was my first thought," Mae told her.

"Speaking of Halloween, do you have any plans for this year?"

"Halloween?" Mae asked.

"Yeah, you know, that night every year when little kids dress up as monsters and extort sweets from adults."

"I think I'll lock myself in my room with the lights off, climb into bed with the laptop, and read email and blogs all night."

"You can deal with phantom streetcars and impossible creatures, but not small children dressed as witches and goblins?"

"Yes. What about you? Are you going to dress up as anything for work?"

"I thought I'd go as a sexy librarian again this year." There was a moment of silence before both women cackled.

"You're mad," Mae quipped.

Jill's smile brightened. "I am. I've actually been invited to a party that my brother is going to, but I'd rather spend the night with you."

"I don't want to interfere with your plans."

"Mae, given a choice between spending the night with my brother and his snotty-ass society friends or spending the night with you, well, that one's easy. You're way more fun and definitely prettier to look at than any of that crowd, no matter how expensive all their plastic surgeries are."

Mae gave her a playful shove with her shoulder, making her shriek and nearly spill her cocoa.

"Were you serious about helping me unpack?" Mae asked.

Jill set her cup on top of a short bookcase. "Yeah, of course."

The two women spent the next hour unpacking more of Mae's belongings, hanging clothes and setting up little personal items that would give the room a bit of Mae's personality. Mae stopped when she pulled a framed picture, wrapped in old newspaper, from one of her suitcases. She sat on the futon, looking at the picture.

Jill leaned over, curious. "Are those your parents?" she whispered.

"Yeah, that's them."

The man in the photograph stood in the middle of a room, his right arm around the shoulders of a blonde woman who was over a foot shorter than he.

"I wish you were in the picture," Jill said, a teasing tone in her voice.

"No, you don't. I was a hideously ugly child."

"Somehow I doubt that." Jill pointed to the woman in the picture. "She's beautiful."

Looking at the faded photograph, Jill saw where Mae had gotten her build. While her father was a bear of a man, standing over six feet tall with sandy brown hair and beard, the woman was his opposite. She was short, probably not even five feet tall. She had a rounded, curved figure and long hair, so pale it was almost silver.

Mae's eyes welled up with tears. "Why did you leave us?" Mae whispered.

"You don't know?"

"No. I wish I could have asked Dad."

Jill placed a hand on Mae's arm. Mae looked up at her. "He passed away right after I started college."

"Isn't there anyone else you can talk to?"

"No. Dad had no living family, and I don't know anything about Mom's side."

"I'm sorry, Mae."

Mae reached over and gave Jill's hand a squeeze. "It's okay."

"Come here," Jill said, pulling Mae toward her. She placed an arm around Mae's shoulder and pulled her close as she began to gently play with Mae's hair.

Jill knew she would tell Mae everything about her family, including Robert. Mae had let her in on a secret, a terrible, beautiful secret. She would be open with Mae as well.

Soon, she decided. But not tonight.

Dear Wall,

They let me eat dinner with the family tonight. I think "Mother" insisted that we meet as a family. They did their best to ignore me, except for "Mother" who talked on and on about going on vacation in someplace called "the Hamptons." She really is insane.

Mr. Hodgins and Elise sat at dinner with us. "Grandmother" just frowned and watched me carefully, as if expecting me to turn into a rabid wolf. If I could, I would.

I realized something tonight. There's a reason they've cast a glamour on me to look like Chrysandra. It's to keep "Mother" as sane as the poor woman can still manage. So that answers who Chrysandra is. Now I need to know how she died. It might be important, and I might be able to use it.

They make me dress up for these family dinners. I hate the clothes they leave out for me. They're all tight and binding. I hate shoes and socks. I miss the grass and leaves underfoot.

I stayed quiet and docile at dinner. I kept one eye on Mr. Hodgins. He seemed pleased about something. Maybe they think they've broken me. Let them think it.

Tonight, the silver answered my call. It's a noble metal. It always knows the truth. Now I have more friends, though you words and the wall are still my best friends in this place. Not like the iron. It buzzes in my head, makes me ill and unable to use any magic. I hate it.

I wonder if I can make friends with Chrysandra before she completely rots?

Thursday, 26th of October

MAE LOOKED AROUND HER new room. It was beginning to take on her personality, even after a day. She still had a few more items to unpack, mostly in the bathroom.

The movers would be at her old apartment the following Monday. It was costing her extra for a short-notice job—more so since she was having them do most of the packing—but it was worth it to get out of her apartment. One of the benefits of living like a hermit for the last few years was that she had a substantial amount of money in her savings. She would pay up the last two months of her lease, drop off the keys and be done with it. Most of her possessions, meager as they were, would be stored in Jill's garage until she found someplace new to live. Mae suspected a surprising amount of her stuff might end up going to a thrift store or in a dumpster.

Once she finished unpacking the last of her clothes and other necessary possessions, Mae decided to spend the first day of her forced vacation wandering around in LynLake and Uptown.

By noon, Mae walked around most of the shops in Uptown. She remembered to replace her empty can of pepper spray. She spent some time drifting around Magers & Quinn, the big independent bookstore on Hennepin, purchasing a couple of books about local legends. She ate a nice, quiet meal at a new seafood restaurant.

Mae hoped a streetcar would appear, had been prepared to interact with the fae and other creatures she had watched in Uptown just two nights before. But the streets were filled with normal humans, not a streetcar in sight. She was bored.

At least until she stepped into Dunn Brothers for a cup of coffee to warm her on the long walk back to the townhouse and spotted William Hodgins, his back to her, sitting at a table, talking to what appeared to be one of the local goths. Strange as the sight was, it was not what caught Mae's attention.

Hodgins was holding a picture of Jill, showing it to the woman in the black blouse and purple skirt. On the table was a photo of Mae and a notebook with neat handwriting in it.

Mae reacted before she could think about the consequences. She smoothly settled into a seat at the table, making Hodgins and the woman both look up, startled. Hodgins slammed the notebook shut, slipping the picture of Jill inside it in the process.

"Bill," Mae said, her voice filled with false cheer. "Imagine running into you here. What are the odds?"

"Mae," Hodgins said. "Enjoying your vacation?"

"It's off to a nice enough start." She plucked the notebook from Hodgins's fingers before he could react. The woman with him reached for the photo of Mae, but Mae slapped a hand down on it first. "I don't think so," she said with a smile at the woman. She turned back to Hodgins. "Could I have a word with you alone?"

"Anything you have to say to me, Ilona can hear as well."

Mae frowned. "I'm not threatening you, Bill. I'm just *extremely* curious about why you're digging into my private life."

Mae watched as Hodgins locked eyes with the woman he had called Ilona. She fingered the cameo choker that hung around her neck, frowning. Hodgins gave her a barely perceptible nod and she stood, glaring at Mae as she shrugged into a black coat and left the table.

"Bye, Ilona," Mae said cheerfully to the woman's retreating form. She turned back to Hodgins, feeling surprised and exhilarated at her own temerity. It felt good, this recklessness welling up inside of her. "She doesn't seem your type. Now, Mr. Hodgins, explain this." She pointed at the photographs and notebook as she set them back on the table.

"And if I refuse? Will you go to the police?" Hodgins had produced a clear crystal marble and was rolling it in his hand with his right thumb and two fingers. Mae had noticed this nervous habit of his before, had seen him do it in Judge Slotky's office, in fact. "Do you think it would matter if you did?"

She tore her eyes from the crystal marble. "You're probably right, Bill. They probably wouldn't do anything, but they might. So why don't you and I sit here like civilized people and talk? You can buy me a cappuccino to make up for getting me suspended."

Hodgins narrowed his eyes. "Mae, you've been warned. Walk away and forget about the Arnesons."

She laughed. "Bill, you're stalking me and my roommate. For all I know, you, or whoever took this photo—" she tapped the picture, "—broke into my apartment. Why should I let it go?"

"Suppose I promise to leave you and your lady-friend alone? I'll give you my personal assurance that no one will bother you if you will promise to stay away from me, Ilona or any of the Arneson family. I'll even refrain from asking County Attorney Backstrom to block your reinstatement."

"Bill—"

"I could even intervene with Backstrom on your behalf. Leftwich will retire in a few more years, perhaps he might even take a promotion to another department—" Hodgins let his offer hang in the air as he nervously worked the marble in his fingers.

Mae frowned. "Bill, are you actually trying to buy me off?"

"Everyone has a price."

"True, but even if I agreed, there's still the matter of Chrysandra Arneson."

Hodgins leaned forward in his chair. "Mae, that matter is closed."

Mae shook her head. "Look, Bill, I understand that the Arnesons are wealthy pillars of the community, and I agree that everyone deserves competent representation, but you know as well as I do what's going on."

"And what is that? What exactly can you prove, Miss Malveaux?"

Mae sat silently glaring at Hodgins. She suspected he had something to do with Chrysandra's case beyond being the family attorney. She wondered how deeply involved he was with her death and whatever was planned for the child's reanimated remains. She glanced at the crystal marble as it caught the light coming in from the window, then looked back to her adversary.

"What's your angle, Bill? Why are you trying so hard to protect the Arnesons?"

He frowned at her. "It is…a personal thing. I'm asking you as a colleague. Leave this alone. I promise Chrysandra will be properly taken care of from this moment forward. Please."

Mae looked at Hodgins's face, using all of her years doing interviews and dealing with people to read his expression. He looked earnest. If she did not know that Chrysandra Arneson was already dead, she might have believed him.

"I give you my word. Chrysandra will be a happy and protected child from this point on." His voice was soft, soothing.

Suddenly, Mae suspected she knew the identity of Chrysandra's unknown father. William Hodgins was a close personal friend of the Arneson family. Marie Arneson, when not drugged out, was a beautiful woman. Both were single. It added up in Mae's head. She frowned.

"I wish I could believe you, Bill."

"Why not?" he asked softly. "Why can you not believe what I am telling you?"

"Because I saw—"

She stopped talking, suddenly aware that she was about to tell him she had seen the reflection of the girl's rotting corpse in the mirror that night. It was enough to snap Mae back to reality. She tore her eyes away from the crystal, not even realizing that she had been staring at it, and glared at Hodgins. He seemed to understand what she was about to say. He lifted the crystal to eye level, and it gave a faint pulse.

Mae's survival instincts kicked into overdrive. Striking before Hodgins could react, she grabbed the notebook and photographs and fled the coffee shop in one swift motion. Behind her, Hodgins swore loudly.

Mae glanced down at what she was carrying, suddenly wanting to be very sure about the items. There was no doubt. Someone had taken this photograph of her on the day her apartment was broken into. She was standing outside, her arms folded over her chest talking to Sergeant Dean.

She turned down an alley, heading south. If she could get out of sight for even a moment, she might be able to hide. She was small and could fit into the most amazing places if need arose, and right now her need seemed all too real.

She burst out of the alley and spared a glance behind her. Hodgins was screaming "thief" at the top of his lungs and closing the distance between them. She looked forward and scanned the area for a place to hide. The messenger bag she carried was weighing her down and flapping against her side.

She made a turn to the right, running full out and around the back of a line of shops, down another alley, hoping to find something, anything that would give her cover.

She heard footsteps and saw a flurry of movement to her side. There was a sudden impact into her back. Mae felt her breath forced out of her body as her feet flew out from underneath her. She hit hard, smashing onto the ground with both of her knees. She flipped and her left elbow hit the concrete as her whole body snapped forward. She rolled once, trying to get away from whatever or whoever had knocked her down, but the person stayed with her, pinning her. Mae made a desperate push, trying to throw off her attacker, but the person was stronger and shoved her back down. Mae's head smacked on the hard pavement and she saw bright lights. She felt a weight lift from her chest, but continued to gasp, unable to catch a breath.

Ilona loomed over her, so close that the woman's black hair touched Mae's face. Ilona threw back her head and laughed, then struck Mae with her open palm. Mae was dazed for a moment, and it was enough for the woman to wrestle the notebook and photographs away from her.

Mae sat up and made a grab, but Ilona touched her cameo and vanished with a shimmer of rainbow light, taking the notebook and pictures with her. Mae shook her head to clear it as she stood to face the new threat approaching her from the end of the alley.

Hodgins was walking toward her, holding the glowing crystal sphere between his fingers. A low buzzing sounded in her ears, and she felt her stomach roil and heave. She scrambled to her feet.

"You were warned, Mae. You were warned, but you would not listen, so I'm going to *show* you what kind of people we are. I am going to show how far we will go, and how easy it is for those with power." He held the glowing stone in front of his face. "Come to me," he ordered her.

Her body went rigid as the glow of the stone increased. She took a stiff step forward, and then another.

The ringing bells of one of the streetcars filled her ears, high and urgent. She kept moving toward Hodgins, who was covered in sweat and starting to pant. He held the glowing stone at eye level. "Come to me," he said again.

Mae gritted her teeth and tried to focus on the streetcar's ringing bell behind her. She forced herself to stop, refusing to take another step. Hodgins stepped toward her. Great rivulets of perspiration were running down his face, as if he were straining against something. Mae tried to tear her eyes away from the glowing sphere but could not. In desperation she bit down hard on the inside of her lip. A burst of blood and pain filled her mouth. She cried out and blinked. The connection between her and Hodgins broke.

She turned and ran, seeking sanctuary in the yellow streetcar waiting for her on the corner, its door open wide. Mae leaped into the car and looked over her shoulder.

Hodgins knelt on the ground, holding his chest and gasping as if he had just run a mile. He looked from Mae to the streetcar, his expression one of shock and, Mae realized, a little fear.

"Ten cents, please."

Mae dropped her dime in the fare box. She watched Hodgins out the window as the red door closed and the big machine rolled away. Once Hodgins was gone from view and Mae was sure Ilona was nowhere nearby, she allowed her body to have its way.

Mae fell to the floor, shaking in fear.

Dear Wall,

They turned the hot water off in my bathroom. I turned on the shower and all I got was cold. What is the point?

I hate them all. I wonder if I could catch a bug and send it down the drain with a message? That might work. Bugs get in everywhere and no one notices. I hope there are still some alive. It's been cold at night. I know this because I don't have any heat in my room.

Elise brought me breakfast this morning. The brown-haired male mage was with her. She called him Robert, so at least I know part of his name, not that it is enough to conjure with. They're being extra attentive now. It must be getting close to time for whatever it is they're planning. Are you words ready? We may have to move fast.

I've finished working with the picture of Mae Malveaux. All I need is to place five drops of my blood on it and set it afire. Of course, the smoke needs to get outside, or the sending will never get past the wards in this house. I'm still not sure how I'm going to manage it since Elise is careful to always be between me and the fireplaces when we leave my room.

I think maybe another day or so and I'll have enough of you words to make the spell work.

MAE WAS MOST OF the way through repacking her two largest suitcases when Jill came home from work.

"Mae! Mae, I'm home," Jill called up the stairs.

Mae wiped her eyes and stuffed more of her possessions into the larger rolling suitcase. She had no plan except to run.

"Mae?" Jill's voice grew louder as she climbed the stairs toward Mae's room. "Are you here?"

"Yeah," Mae called back. She zipped the first suitcase and started filling the other.

"What's all this?" Jill asked from the doorway.

Mae refused to face her. She kept packing the second suitcase, trying to jam as much as possible into it. "I can't stay here. I have to go. I have to go away."

Jill stepped up next to her. "What happened?"

"I have to leave. I have to go before they—" Mae gasped, on the verge of hyperventilating. Tears spilled from her eyes as she sank to the floor and leaned on the futon. She could not breathe or think.

Jill sat down on the floor next to her. "Mae, I need you to tell me what happened today."

Mae shook her head violently. "No. No, the less you know the better. If I go away, they'll leave you alone."

"Mae—"

Mae raised her head and took a deep breath. "Jill, you have to let me leave, and you have to forget you ever knew me."

"No."

Mae grabbed Jill by the shoulders and drew her close, almost nose to nose. "Yes!" she hissed. "You have to. I need you to do this for me."

Jill shook her head. "No. You need to calm down and explain. Tell me what happened, and then we'll talk about this silly idea of yours."

Slowly, over the course of the next half hour, Jill gently coaxed the words out of her with whispered encouragement and understanding touches. When she was done, Mae was calmer, but still determined to put as much distance as possible between the danger she was in and Jill.

Jill was quiet for several moments, digesting what Mae had said. "Bill Hodgins, huh?"

"You know him?" Mae asked.

Jill nodded. "I've seen him in the law library a few times. He's done some work for my family." Jill frowned. "Where exactly are you planning to go?"

Mae sighed and shook her head. All the bravery and recklessness she had felt during her confrontation with Hodgins was gone, washed away by the hard reality of magic that had—if only for a moment—taken control of her body. "I don't know. I thought I'd get a room someplace for a few days. Maybe close my bank account and buy a ticket to a new city. Start over someplace where there are no impossible streetcars, no animated corpses of twelve-year-old girls, no—"

"No what?" Jill asked in a quiet voice.

"No magic," Mae said softly. "But that's not how it's going to happen, is it?"

Jill shrugged. "I don't know. I said I like weird. I never claimed to be an expert at it. What I do know, or at least what I *believe,* is that you can't run from things."

Mae turned her head and looked at Jill. "Even when those things are trying to kill you?"

Jill frowned and nodded. "I think especially if those things are trying to kill you."

"Well, that's just silly," Mae said, looking away from Jill and fixing her eyes on the wall opposite them.

"We are a silly race, we humans," Jill said in a deadpan voice. She straightened and turned to face Mae. "If you're running away, I'm coming with you."

Mae exhaled a frustrated breath and looked up at the ceiling. "That would kind of defeat the purpose of me running away."

"Safety in numbers, I say. Besides, who says I'll be any safer with you gone? They obviously know you're living here and we're at least close friends."

"Jill, I think I like you—"

"Good. I like you too. Maybe it's time I took you home and showed you to my mother."

"Don't interrupt. I think I like you. In fact, I'm pretty sure I like you a lot. I don't want you to be dead."

"Well I don't want to see you dead either. In fact, I vote that if anyone is going to do any dying, it be the other guys."

Mae blew out a long breath. She sat up straight and looked at the floor. "Tell you what. I promise not to run and hide in a deep hole, if you promise to come away with me this weekend. We can go someplace out of the Cities, put some space between us and Hodgins, and think about what we want to do about this mess. Maybe we can stay at a bed and breakfast in Stillwater or Red Wing. It would be a good way for both of us to fall off the radar for a couple of days."

"Okay, it's a deal." Jill regarded her. "Does that mean I can change and clean up without worrying that you're going to disappear while I'm in the shower?"

"I promise I'll be here when you're done."

"Good. I was worried that I was going to need to handcuff you to the plumbing or something while I tried to talk some sense into you."

Mae raised an eyebrow. "You have handcuffs?"

Jill stood. With a smirk on her face, she reached down to offer Mae a hand up from the floor. "That's kind of personal for this stage in the relationship, don't you think?"

Mae took her hand and stood. "You're the one who brought it up." She looked down at the mess on the floor. "Damn. I'm going to have to unpack *again*."

"You cook dinner while I wash up, and I'll help you with this mess later."

Mae laughed. It caught her by surprise. She thought she would never laugh like that again after this afternoon. "You just want an excuse to paw through my underwear."

Jill lowered her head, letting her black hair fall forward after releasing it from its ponytail. She gave Mae a come-hither smile. "Damned straight. And Mae, my handcuffs are lined with faux-leopard fur, just so you know." She turned sharply on her heel, hair fanning out on her shoulders as she swished toward the bathroom.

Mae laughed again and walked downstairs to the kitchen.

Dear Wall,

Tonight, Chrysandra held out her hand and said, "Pull my finger."

Chrysandra never speaks, but today she did. It was rough and raspy. I think she doesn't really breathe, so she has to remember to inhale and exhale if she wants to talk.

Her voice caught me by surprise and I knocked over my chair trying to get away from her. She just sat there, holding her discolored hand out to me. She smiled at me with her yellow teeth and black lips. I wonder if they could be using her to keep me in line. You know, something like, "Here is how you will end your days if you don't do as we say." It could be that kind of thing, but I doubt it.

I started to reach out and do it, then I realized her finger would likely pop off in my hand. I shook my head and told her I didn't think it was a good idea.

She laughed. It was croaky and wheezy, but it was a laugh. Then she looked at me with her milk-white, washed-out eyes and would not stop laughing, even after she forgot to breathe and the laugh became a choking gurgle.

It seemed like ages before Elise came and took her away.

MAE FELT JILL LEAN over her shoulder as she loaded the last of the plates into the dishwasher. Jill's breath was on her neck, tickling her ear and cheek. Mae smiled up at her.

"This is really why I want you to live here," Jill said.

"You invited me to live with you for my mad domestic skills?"

Jill wagged her eyebrows and stood back. "You know it."

Mae closed the dishwasher door and set it to start in four hours, long after both of them would be in bed. She followed Jill, who had picked up their wine glasses and the half-empty bottle of chardonnay from the dining table, to the living room.

"I think," Jill said as she set the glasses and bottle down, "we should change into comfy clothes, turn on a trashy movie and ignore the world outside."

Mae nodded. "I like it."

"Cool. First one back to the couch picks the trashy movie."

Mae did not bother rushing. She knew Jill, manic to pick the worst movie on-demand had to offer, would find a way to reach the couch first. In fact, Mae realized Jill might make it back to the couch before Mae made it upstairs to change.

"That was your cue to squeal and run for the stairs," Jill called down from her room.

Mae laughed as she reached the landing. Jill was already changed into a pair of red and green tartan pajama pants and a T-shirt with the fading words "Storm Chaser" across the front.

"I concede," Mae said.

"You're no fun. I'm going to pick something truly awful to watch as your punishment."

"You do that. I'll be right down."

Mae dug through the clothes on the floor and found her favorite sweatpants, all faded gray with the elastic at the ankles pulled out. She grabbed a white T-shirt off the floor and changed into it. The sound and smell of popcorn being prepared reached her as she started back down the stairs.

"Ready?"

"Sure. What did you pick?"

Jill nodded toward the television screen.

"You spent three ninety-five on a slasher flick with a pirate?"

"Undead, revenge-seeking, zombie pirate. Don't worry, it will be awful. That's the point. Get the lights."

"Uh-huh," Mae said, turning off the lights and settling on the couch next to Jill. She reached for the popcorn. It was hot and smothered in something resembling butter.

"Napkins?" Mae asked, looking for something to wipe her greasy hand on.

Jill raised an eyebrow. "That's why God made cheap pajama pants."

"Fine." Mae reached over and cleaned her hand on Jill's pants.

Jill laughed like a loon and pushed the button on the remote to start the movie. Listening to her laugh made Mae determined to make the best of the movie no matter how bad it was.

An hour and a half later, she knew it had been a futile effort.

"The problem was," Jill said, stretching and shifting position, "if the entire pirate ship's crew settled down in that village and their descendants all still live there, they must have been an inbred lot. That's why they were all too stupid to survive. No branches on the family tree."

"The problem," Mae corrected, "was the producers and director were just looking to make a fast buck off the pirate craze and apparently hired some random high school film class to make a movie. But you know what the real problem is?"

"What's that?"

"Neither of us will ever get that time back. And you're out three ninety-five."

"Actually, half the cable bill is yours now."

"I'm sure I shouldn't be made to pay for that. In fact, I think I've already paid enough. What are you planning to do for the rest of the evening?"

Jill shrugged. "I could paint your toenails."

Mae laughed. "Why?"

Jill wiggled her own toes with their burgundy-colored nails. "Because it would make you feel pretty, oh so pretty."

Mae turned to look at Jill. She rested her right arm on the back of the couch and laid her head on it. "Could I ask you a personal question?"

Jill's pale blue eyes held surprise, but she nodded. "Sure. I guess there are a lot of things you don't know about me. Ask away."

"Tell me about your family."

Jill drew a deep breath. "Well. You really went for the big one, didn't you? Is there anything left in that bottle?"

Mae lifted the wine bottle. "No. We drank it all to numb the pain of the movie. Should I open another?"

Jill smiled, all lopsided and melancholy. "Yes, please. Get the merlot out for this."

Mae returned with an open bottle and two clean glasses. She poured for both of them and passed a glass to Jill. "You don't have to—"

"No. It's okay." Jill took a long sip of her wine then began to idly play with a bit of loose thread on the back of the couch. "When I made that little comment about taking you to meet my mother, well, it would be more to horrify her than anything else. You don't deserve that, and you never have to meet my mother or my father, unless you feel a deep burning desire to do so."

"I take it they don't approve of your life?"

Jill raised her eyebrows and nodded. "You could say that. My father does something in real estate. Buying. Selling. Leasing. Something. He's been quite successful at it, as was my grandfather and, if the stories are true, my great-grandfather."

"Your family has money?"

"My family has *a lot* of money. My family lives in one of those big houses in Edina. My parents and brother belong to the country club. They own vacation property on Lake Minnetonka and back east in the Hamptons. There's a hunting lodge in Montana. Please don't hate me."

"You can't help your upbringing," Mae said, her face completely straight.

"No, but you can rebel against it." Jill took another, deeper drink of her wine. "I just don't want to come across as being all 'oh, the poor little rich girl' or anything, you know?"

Mae nodded and refilled Jill's glass. Jill nodded her thanks and continued, "My mother is very active socially. She sits on the board for a major local charity. She manages fundraising events and gives generously to the local arts. She drives her Jaguar to shop at the trendy shops. She throws extravagant parties, and she attends all the best social events and *she* is loved by all. My mother is very conscious of her position."

Mae took a small sip of her own wine. "I see. And she expected her daughter to follow in her footsteps?"

Jill nodded shakily and drank half her glass of wine in one gulp. "Oh, God yes. And anything I took an interest in that might not fit the little round hole I was to slip into was frowned upon. Sports of any kind. Books, music, clothes and friends of the wrong sort. As a rule, curiosity was not rewarded. I was to conform to an ideal." Jill smiled a nasty, humorless smile. "My mother frowned a lot, at least at home."

Mae peered at Jill over her glass. "Then you were the rebel child."

"I had to be. My brother, you see, is the oldest. The boy. The heir to the empire. The one with the penis that will provide more little Halls to carry on the noble bloodline. Nothing but the best for him. The best tutors, the best private school, a spot at Yale waiting after graduation. Robert Coleman Hall the Stinking Third was groomed from conception to play his part."

Jill held her glass out for a refill.

"Are you sure that's a good idea?" Mae asked.

"All I have to do is make it up the stairs and fall into bed."

"As long as you don't fall on the stairs."

"Never. Now top me off, sister."

Mae refilled Jill's glass and sat back to let Jill finish her tale.

"I, being the girl, was held to a different set of obligations and expectations. My every bit of schooling was geared toward making me the perfect little upper-society trophy wife." Jill leaned forward conspiratorially. "My sixteenth birthday was the social event of the season."

"Like a debutante ball?"

"Exactly. Oh, it was technically an event for some charity or other of Mother's, but everyone knew what it was in reality. It was my mother's way of saying, 'Here is my daughter, meticulously groomed to be a model bride and the quintessential rich man's wife. She will be educated and ready for marriage soon, so you young gentlemen start considering the possibilities.'"

"Seriously?"

"Seriously."

Mae noticed that Jill was starting to slur her words. She was about to suggest that they call it a night when Jill suddenly shifted position, ending up on her knees on the couch, mere inches away from Mae. Some instinct made Mae reach out and take Jill's not-quite empty glass and set it on the table.

Jill's eyes lit up as she leaned closer to Mae, so close that they were almost touching. "So you know what I did? I had sex with Mindy Johnson—one of the other potential young trophy wives on display—in the coat closet. Loud, vigorous, 'everyone for two city blocks can hear it' *sex*." Jill burst into wild laughter and fell backward. Her voice stilled suddenly.

"Jill? Are you okay?"

"It was a stupid thing to do, really," Jill whispered, a sad, faraway look in her eyes. Her smile returned. "Anyway, after that my mother and I tried to ignore each other. I became progressively wilder and she got a little drunker every day. They had intended for me to attend the College of St. Catherine, because a proper lady should be well educated, you know. I decided I wanted to be as far from them as possible. I told them to keep the damned trust fund and I moved to Madison. I enrolled at UW, majoring in alcoholic binges and library science."

Jill grinned up at Mae from where she lay. "By my junior year I started hating the hangovers, but I loved books. I sobered up and got a master's degree. When I graduated, I realized I missed Minneapolis, so I moved back. And here we are!"

"And here we are," Mae said softly.

Jill giggled in reply. "Now, if you will help me up from this couch, I need to pee, and then fall on my nose in the bed. Because some of us are indeed a little drunk and some of us have to work tomorrow and you, my dear Mae, are neither of those people."

Mae reached down and took both of Jill's hands, helping her up off the couch. She steadied Jill as she climbed the stairs, then waited patiently for her to use the bathroom, making sure Jill did not pass out or need to throw up. When Jill was safely tucked in bed, Mae went back downstairs and cleaned up.

Once back in her own room, she gave the clothes on the floor a tired look and decided they could wait until tomorrow. Besides, Jill was supposed to help her, and who was she to deny her friend the opportunity to play with her underthings?

Dear Wall,

It's hard to write in the dark, but I can't sleep and I don't want to turn on the light. I don't want to look at her.

I'm scared. For the first time since they brought me here, I'm really scared. In truth, I've been scared the whole time, but I've been able to deal. I knew someone would come for me, or I'd be able to trick someone or sneak my way to freedom. But now I realize I am alone in this, with only you words and the wall for comfort.

I can't get the smell of Chrysandra out of my nose. It's into everything. My bedding, my clothes, my hair. They brought her back into the room as I was going to bed. She is just sitting in the chair, smiling at me with her ugly black lips, staring at me with her dead eyes. She's starting to ooze. It's nasty.

Is that how I'm going to end up? Some rotting piece of meat kept alive for some secret reason?

Chrysandra's making little wheezing noises. I think she's trying to cry.

I hate them all. I hate them for locking me away. I hate them for what they've done to Chrysandra. I hate them for what they've done to the Hounds.

I wish Chrysandra wouldn't try to cry. It sounds like the whimpering of a dying animal. I wish I could do something for her. I can't stand listening to her. I can't stand looking at her. I can't stand smelling her.

I can't leave her alone. No one deserves to be alone.

I'm going to turn on the light now. I'm going to try to do something to help her. You have to hide.

Jill sat up in bed, the sharp scream coming from her throat cutting off as she surfaced from the nightmare. At some point she had kicked all the covers to the floor and now she was cold. She drew her knees up to her chin and rocked slightly on the bed, sniffling and waiting for her heartbeat to return to normal.

Her door opened, letting in light from the hallway. Mae walked into the room slowly, probably trying not to startle Jill with her presence. "Jill? Are you all right?"

Jill swallowed and nodded. She reached over and turned on the bedside lamp. "It was just a bad dream."

Mae settled on the edge of the bed. She did not seem convinced. "You want to talk about it?"

Jill shook her head. "I don't think I can."

Mae put a hand on Jill's knee. "Because sometimes it helps. Sometimes it's better to talk or do something than to brood. You know, like when you've been forced into an unwanted vacation by your boss."

Jill sniffed hard and wiped her nose with the back of her hand. Mae grabbed the box of tissues from the nightstand and passed it to Jill. She pulled five pieces out and blew her nose.

"Why don't I make us a pot of green tea?" Mae said.

"That would be great. I take mine with honey."

Mae stood. "You want to come downstairs or should I bring it up?"

"Up here, if that's okay?"

Jill drew a long breath and steadied herself. She stood on shaky legs and went to the bathroom, splashing some water on her face. By the time Mae returned, a tray with two cups and a teapot in her hands, Jill was back in the bed, sitting up against the headboard, pillows behind her to cushion her back. She had pulled the duvet and sheet onto the bed.

"Join me?" she asked Mae.

"Trying to get me into your bed, Miss Hall?" Mae teased lightly. Jill gave her a smile and patted the empty spot. She took the offered cup as Mae climbed into the bed and pulled the covers up around them both.

Jill shivered again. "I should have asked you to turn up the heat."

"I did. It should kick in any minute. It's snowing outside, by the way."

Jill raised her steaming cup to her lips. "Well, it is Minnesota in late October. What else can you expect?" She took a sip and closed her eyes. "Good stuff. Thanks."

Mae settled next to her. "So?"

Jill shrugged her shoulders and looked down at the bed. She set her tea on the nightstand and picked nervously at a stray thread. "It's nothing really. It's just a stupid nightmare I have sometimes."

"Honey, you were screaming at the top of your lungs. People down in Eagan heard you. It's more than just a nightmare."

Jill sighed and leaned forward, covering her face with her hands. "I was so fucking stupid. It was a long time ago. I was just a stupid kid and most of the time I don't even think about it anymore, but sometimes the—sometimes what happened after comes back and—" Jill closed her eyes and began to cry again. "And sometimes I really hate myself."

She did not resist when Mae pulled her close, letting Jill lay across her lap. Mae reached over to the nightstand and grabbed the tissues again, setting the box in front of Jill.

Mae began slowly rubbing her hand up and down Jill's arm. "Tell me."

Jill sighed in resignation. "I was a stupid girl."

"Um-hmm. What makes you think you were stupid?"

"Remember what I told you about my little coming out party?"

"I'm guessing we're talking about the loud sex in a coat closet part?"

Jill snuggled closer to the soft warmth that was Mae, curling up into a tight little ball. "Yeah."

Mae stroked Jill's hair. "I take it your parents weren't happy."

"Mother was furious. I was going to be a horrible scandal, and we couldn't have that could we? No, appearances had to be kept up. Something had to be done to hide 'Jill's little perversion.'"

"What did they do to you?"

"They sent me to a camp in SoCal. It was supposed to help confused young people sort out their sexuality. Basically, they were trying to cure me," Jill said. Her chest felt tight, as if she were being squeezed.

Mae continued to stroke Jill's hair, soothing her. "So what happened?"

"I hated the camp, hated California, hated my mother for sending me away from everything I knew. So like any dumb, headstrong teenager, I compounded my mistakes. I ran away. I made it all the way up to Seattle, and I let the cops pick me up for shoplifting."

Mae chuckled. "Clever."

"Thanks. I made sure the cops knew who my parents were and how to find them. Mother and Father were forced to fly out and pick me up." Jill paused her story to grab a wad of tissues and wipe her eyes. "They didn't understand that all I wanted was to *come home*. No, that was totally lost on them. They just knew their useless daughter had forced them to drop everything to come and get her, and then their useless daughter put them in an awkward position with the local authorities. They were embarrassed and angry. Once the police released me, my parents took me back to the hotel. We fought."

"Bad?"

Jill trembled, remembering. "Mother slapped me a couple of times. Then Father proceeded to tell me exactly what I was going to do when we got home. That they were going to check me into a center so I could 'get my damned head on straight' before I damaged the family reputation any further. The next morning, we flew back to Minneapolis."

Mae's arms held her tight. "It's okay. It's okay," Mae whispered. "Tell me."

"The first night back, my brother, Robert, cornered me in my room and told me—Mindy, the girl I'd had sex with—her parents didn't react any better than mine. Robert told me that the day I left for camp they found Mindy hanging in her closet. She had killed herself. Mindy was dead. I decided it was my fault."

"Oh, Jill."

"I took every goddamned pill in Mother's bathroom and washed them down with half a bottle of scotch. Let me tell you, that is *not* the way to kill yourself. I threw most of it back up. I don't really remember much else about that night. I passed out, of course. Two days later I came to in the hospital." Jill let out a long breath and lay still. Mae began to gently play with her hair.

"I'm so sorry, Jill. I'm so sorry. But honey, you were just sixteen. That's not an age for making good choices, especially not when the people around you are making matters worse."

"I know I was young and stupid. It's not that I'm sorry I lived, it's just that I feel so—I feel like a terrible excuse for a human being. There it is, nothing to be done about it."

"Of course there's something to be done," Mae whispered. "First, you forgive yourself for your mistake. Then you live the best life you're able. You'll never forget, but what you *can* do is live."

"You sound like the voice of experience."

"I am. But *that* is a story for another night."

Jill nodded and closed her eyes. She shifted into a more comfortable position, but did not leave Mae's lap. "Mae? Will you stay with me, at least until I fall asleep?"

"Of course."

Jill closed her eyes and took a contented breath. After tonight, she hoped it would be easier to tell Mae about Robert. She relaxed as Mae continued to gently stroke her hair.

Friday, 27th of October

Dear Wall,

They took Chrysandra away this morning. I think the plan is to exhaust me, because Elise keeps coming into my room, checking to make sure I'm not asleep.

It stinks in here.

Poor Chrysandra. She knows what she is. I can't even begin to imagine what that would be like. I got her to talk to me last night, in her wheezy voice. I had to constantly remind her to breathe. She doesn't remember much about what happened to her, only that it had something to do with Mr. Hodgins and "Mother." She thinks she may have died in a magical accident.

I took a chance and confided in her. I'm never going to get out of here on my own. You words and the wall have been great, but I need a friend who can help me escape. I hope she doesn't betray me.

Last night I placed five drops of my blood on the under-side of Mae Malveaux's picture. I couldn't find anything to cut myself with, and was getting frustrated, when Chrysandra grabbed my arm and slashed me open with her thumbnail. For an undead girl, she's pretty bright.

I think I worked the summoning right. Now it's all up to Chrysandra. She rolled Mae's picture up and hid it in her clothes, promising to burn it as soon as she can. Chrysandra pointed out some writing and numbers on the back of the picture. She said she might be able to contact Mae Malveaux if she can slip her minder, Ilona, for a few minutes.

I wish I knew more about mortal magic. I'm starting to understand some of this. They've corrupted the Cŵn Annwn, so I'm guessing it has something to do with Gwynn ap Nudd or with the Courts. Mother would have figured this out weeks ago. Of course, Mother would never have gotten caught.

She told me to stay out of the human realm. She warned me, but it kept calling to me. I had to see the place where I was born. Stupid, really. I hadn't gone more than ten steps before they captured me.

I'm going to lie down before Elise comes back. I need to rest. I need to cry.

MAE OPENED ONE BLEARY eye. The room was cast in shadows, the barest amount of light bleeding through the window blinds. She was lying down, stretched out on her side in bed, warm and relaxed. This was, to her sleep-muddled mind, a vast improvement over the uncomfortable propped-up position she had been in when she drifted off to sleep, Jill's head still in her lap.

Thinking of Jill made her remember last night's rather intense conversation and she wondered groggily what state Jill would be in when she finally awoke. Mae had a vague, dreamlike recollection of Jill sitting up and a soft rustle of clothing in the dark as she slid down into a more comfortable position and drifted back to sleep.

Mae came fully awake when she heard Jill's soft snores and felt the warm pressure on her back. Jill was spooned up against her, right leg on top of Mae's legs, right arm around Mae, right hand on Mae's breast on the outside of her T-shirt. She could get used to this, she decided.

Mae raised her head from the pillow, seeking a clock. There was not one this side of the bed and she had removed her watch when she changed clothes before the movie. She laid her head back down and considered her next move. The thin light peeking through the blinds told her Jill was probably running late for work.

She lifted Jill's arm, intent on rolling out of her grasp.

"Um-mm," Jill murmured, shifting toward Mae and attempting to pull Mae back to her with her leg. "Stay."

Mae managed to wiggle out of Jill's embrace. She sat up and looked at the alarm clock. "Jill. Jill, you need to wake up."

"Don't wanna. Lie back down."

Mae gave Jill a little shake. "Jill, you're already ten minutes late for work."

Jill pulled the covers up over her head. "Then it doesn't matter. Late's late. I'll call in sick."

"You've taken a day off this week already."

Jill flipped the covers down and glared at Mae. "Being an adult sucks. Could you start some coffee while I hit the shower?"

Mae stood up. "Sure. You need to hustle. Come on! Up!"

Jill sat up and rubbed her face. "You're a completely different person in the morning. An evil person to be exact. Go make coffee."

Mae marched downstairs, stopping off at the bathroom on her way to the kitchen.

While the coffee dripped into the carafe, Mae searched the cabinets for something Jill could eat on her way to work. Faced with the choice between granola bars and frosted strawberry toaster pastries, she chose the latter. She coaxed a cup of coffee from the gurgling machine, spooned in some sugar and started back up the stairs. Jill exited the bathroom, wrapped in a bathrobe and furiously toweling her long hair.

"Coffee," Mae said, handing her the cup.

"Thanks. Do me a favor?" Jill asked, releasing her wet hair from the towel. She took a slurp of coffee and reached for her comb. "Can you drive me into work? I hate letting other people behind Maddy's wheel, but I think this constitutes an emergency."

"Um, actually, I can't."

Jill hesitated with the comb. "You can't drive a stick?"

Mae shook her head. "No."

"Okay then." Jill twisted her hair into a bun. "Well, I'm not paying to park downtown, so I'll just be a little later. Can you grab something I can eat on the bus?"

"I've got a packet of toaster pastries for you."

Jill dived around Mae and into her closet. "You rock," she called out.

"You want me to fill your travel mug?"

"Yes, please. I'll be right down."

Mae dashed down the stairs and filled Jill's mug with hot coffee. Within minutes, she heard Jill near the door, putting on her winter gear. "Here you go," Mae said, passing a frazzled Jill the mug and the shiny packet of pastries.

"Thanks," Jill stuffed the packet into her coat pocket and grabbed her small purse. "Mae, promise me you won't go off on any adventures until *after* I get home."

"Promise."

Jill opened the front door. "I'll see you tonight."

Mae started to wish her a good day at work when Jill suddenly leaned forward and kissed her on the cheek.

"Thank you for last night."

Jill vanished out the door into the falling snow before Mae could react.

Faced with the pleasant prospect of a day inside, Mae decided not to shower or change until an hour or so before Jill was due to come home. She made herself toast, fruit, yogurt and coffee for breakfast and climbed upstairs.

Sitting on the edge of the futon, Mae considered the mess in her room. Two hours later she was almost done cleaning up. She was putting her underwear in the small dresser when her cell phone rang. Mae did not know the number. She considered letting the caller leave a message, but realized it might be Jill calling from work. Mae pressed the talk button.

"Hello?"

There was a loud hissing, as if the caller were standing outside in a stiff wind.

"Hello? Is anyone there?"

"They have her."

Mae felt her body grow cold. "Who is this?"

"They have her."

Mae thought the voice might be a woman or even a girl. She could barely hear it over the blowing and hissing. "Who do they have? Who is this?"

"Hurry. She won't last." The voice faded out with a wheeze and the connection died.

Mae dialed the number for the Government Center's central switchboard. She waited impatiently for the operator to answer and barked out her request to be connected to the law library before the woman could finish her greeting. The office answering machine picked up. Mae left a message asking Jill to return her call on a matter regarding a volume she wanted to check on. Mae hoped Jill would understand the urgency in her voice.

Mae waited for a few minutes, and then dialed Jill's cell phone. It rang twice before the mechanical recording spoke over the phone.

"The voicemail box of the customer you are attempting to reach is unavailable at this time or the customer is out of the service area. Please hang up and try your call at a later time. Thank you."

Mae hung up and decided it was fine to panic, at least for a minute. She tried Jill at work again, with no answer. Dropping the phone into the pocket of her sweats, Mae raced to the bathroom, stopping long enough to splash water on her face and tie her hair back into a short ponytail. She dashed back to her room and changed into jeans, a Navy blue cable sweater and heavy wool socks. She scooped up all of her loose change and dropped it into her pocket. Her keys and her wallet went into the messenger bag. Mae bolted downstairs, grabbed her heavy coat and ran out the front door.

Mae jogged through the deepening snow toward the bus stop. She shifted through the people bundled up against the cold, pushing her way to the corner to catch the bus into downtown, reaching the stop seconds ahead of the bus. Settling on a bench as the bus bounced and swayed along, she opened her bag, looking for her phone. After a moment of fruitless searching, she realized she had left it in her sweatpants and swore softly to herself.

Transferring to the train, a short ride brought her to the Government Center. Mae hesitated. If she was spotted by Donald or any of her office mates, there would be questions. Mae decided there was nothing for it. She walked in the front doors. At the security checkpoint she nodded to the guards, put her bag on the belt and walked through the metal detectors.

"Ma'am? I'll need you to step over here, please."

She turned to the guard who spoke. "Is there a problem?"

The guard took her bag and pointed. "If you could step over here, please?"

She followed the guard to a folding table. He opened her bag and withdrew the pepper spray. "I'm sorry, ma'am, but this item is prohibited inside the building."

Mae sighed. She had forgotten she was carrying it. County policy allowed for personal defense sprays, but you had to check them with the guards. "I'm sorry, I forgot. Can you store it, and I'll pick it up after I'm done?"

The guard gave her a sour look. He placed the little can in a box and passed her a numbered receipt.

"Thank you. Is there anything else?"

The guard gave her one more suspicious look. "No, ma'am."

Mae walked to the elevators, resisting the urge to look over her shoulder. She could feel the man watching her. She pressed the up arrow and waited patiently. When the elevator arrived, she squeezed aboard. At the top floor she was the last person riding.

It took only a moment to find Jill. She was bent over her desk, but looked up at Mae's approach. "Did you get my message?" she asked, looking concerned.

"No. I ran out of the house so fast I left my phone." Mae took a steadying breath. "I was worried about you."

Jill looked around as she steered Mae to a corner. "What happened?"

Mae told her about the phone call.

"Well, I'm fine. So your mystery caller must have been talking about someone else." Jill paused. "Unless it's an attempt to draw you out into the open for some reason."

"Shit," Mae whispered. "I have to get out of here. I'm supposed to be on vacation. If someone sees me—"

"It's a public building," Jill pointed out.

"Yeah, but I don't want to draw attention."

"All right, go home. I'll bail out of here as quickly as possible."

Mae turned to leave. She saw her supervisor enter the library and spun back around, facing Jill and placing her back to Donald. "Shit. That's Donald. What's he doing?"

Jill glanced over Mae's head. "Coming this way. You know, he's been trying to get under my skirt since I started working here."

"I'm pretty sure he's in bed with the people who wanted me to drop the Arneson case. He'll want to know why I'm here. He'll probably report it to Backstrom. What am I going to do?"

"Follow my lead."

Jill smiled broadly as Mae felt Donald's presence at her elbow.

"Mae? What are you doing here?" Donald asked.

Mae turned to face him, trying to think up something plausible.

"She brought me something from home," Jill said. "You know, something…necessary."

Donald glanced from Mae to Jill, confusion plain on his face.

Jill turned back to Mae. "Thanks again. I know it's damned cold, and the snow's coming down in buckets but, well, I didn't expect to start a week early, and the ladies' room was out again."

"Oh, not a problem," Mae said, picking up on Jill's approach. Most men would rather strangle themselves with their own ties than discuss feminine hygiene products.

"Um…" Donald said.

Jill flashed a winning smile. "All right then, I need to get back to work." Jill reached out and grabbed Mae's hand, giving it a little squeeze. "I'll be home on time tonight, assuming the buses keep to schedule. Do I need to stop at the store for anything? Bread, milk, Halloween candy?"

Mae gave Donald a quick glance out of the corner of her eye. He looked like someone had walked up to him and smacked him with a dead fish. The same recklessness she had felt during her confrontation with Hodgins welled up inside of her. She decided to press the advantage. Maybe he would be too stunned or embarrassed to question her further.

"No. We should be set for a few days." Mae stood on her tiptoes and gave Jill a quick kiss on the cheek. "See you tonight."

"Bye," Jill said, her eyes alight with mirth. She turned to Donald. "Sorry about that. What can I help you with?"

Mae used Donald's momentary confusion to make her exit. Slipping out of the library, she made herself walk and not run back to the elevators. She retrieved her pepper spray from the guards in the lobby and stepped back out into the freezing late-October afternoon.

She climbed aboard the train and took a seat, shivering from her short exposure to the outside temperatures. She looked around, surprised that she was the only person in the car. The snow was falling in heavy sheets, and the train was moving slowly along the track. A burst of cold air swept through the train, making the hair on the back of Mae's neck stand up. Three figures wearing hooded sweatshirts had entered the train. One of them sat down immediately while the other two walked toward her. Mae shifted, placing her back to the wall of the train car. She fumbled in her bag, grabbing the can of spray. She kept the can in her bag where they could not see it, but she could draw it out in an instant. The figures walked past. One sat on the bench nearest the exit. The other turned and looked at her, red eyes standing out against the white, dog-like face.

Mae realized they had neatly cut her off from the exits.

A fourth figure entered the car and settled across from her. Screwing up her courage, Mae looked up at the person. William Hodgins regarded her with cold, gray eyes.

"Hello, Mae."

Mae looked forward, unwilling to meet the man's gaze, afraid he would trap her again. She swallowed back the fear-induced bile rising in her throat and took a shaky breath.

"Nothing to say, Miss Malveaux?" Hodgins's voice came harsh and raspy.

"Are you here to kill me?" Mae asked in a soft voice.

"Yes. I'm sorry, Mae. You've left me with little choice. You're too inquisitive. You know too much. I cannot allow you to oppose us."

"How do you plan to do it?" Mae reasoned that the longer she kept her opponent talking and distracted, the higher her chances of something happening in her favor.

"I promise it will be quick and relatively painless."

"Well, that's a mercy." Mae looked past the two hounds in front of her, watching with their glowing red eyes. She knew she was going to die, but she would not make it easy for any of them. She found the trigger of her pepper spray and withdrew the small can from her bag, keeping it from sight.

"It's time." He stood, drawing the round crystal from his pocket. One of the hounds stepped forward. "Goodbye, Mae."

Mae exploded out of her seat, letting all the aggression she had learned playing hockey with the neighborhood boys come to the fore. She hit Hodgins hard with her shoulder, lifting the man from his feet and slamming him into the opposite wall. There was a sharp cracking noise and a raspy exhale.

Mae turned to the hounds in front of her. They were between her and the nearest exit. The one standing rushed her as the others left their seats. Mae pulled the pin from the can and aimed at the hound closest to her, squeezing out a stream of chemicals. She rushed forward, holding her breath and squinting her eyes.

The first of the two-legged Cŵn Annwn fell to the floor of the train car, writhing in pain and trying to cover its face. The second creature was on her as she changed the direction of her spray. It caught her arm with its claw-like fingernails, ripping into her heavy coat. Mae twisted and struck with her knee, as she had been taught in her self-defense class. The thing gave a short bark and stepped backward. She jabbed the can of spray into its face and held the trigger down. It backed away, howling, covering its eyes. She pushed past it as her spray ran out.

The train stopped and the exit door opened. Mae could see safety, a snowy platform full of pedestrians, only a handful of feet away. Another of the hounds came in behind her. It caught her around the waist and bore her backward. She stumbled, slamming into the side of one of the benches. The hound's face contorted into a dog's head.

The train door hissed shut and the machine started moving again.

Mae lashed out with her arms and legs, trying to force the creature off. She raised her arm to cover her face and it bit down. Teeth sank into her coat, driven by powerful jaws. They punctured the fabric and tore into Mae's arm.

Mae screamed. She brought her other hand up and raked the creature across the eyes with her nails. It released her arm. Mae tried to twist away, seeking the door, wanting to get out of the car. She braced a foot against the side of a bench and pushed hard, driving the creature back. There was a snapping noise as they hit the edge of the opposite bench, and the creature yelped once before it went limp and slumped to the floor.

She straightened as another of the dog-men lunged at her. Mae swept her bag off her shoulder and swung down with it, catching the hound across the side of the head. The creature fell, stunned. Mae caught a glimpse of William Hodgins, sitting on the floor, holding his left arm close to his body.

The train stopped. Mae lost her footing and crashed to the floor. She crawled and dived toward the door as it swung open. Leaping forward, Mae fell into the packed snow and ice on the platform at the feet of a group of waiting commuters.

Mae rose to her hands and knees, looking up. The two surviving hounds exited the train and turned toward her.

She scrambled up as the shocked group of waiting riders backed away. Sprinting up the street toward the warehouse district, she ran hard and screamed for help, hoping to draw attention. She heard a shrill scream behind her and realized that someone must have climbed onto the train and found the dead body.

Mae saw two more shapes come from between buildings in front of her. She turned right and dived into the crosswalk against the light. She heard horns and what might have been a car riding up onto the curb and striking a pole, but she kept her focus on getting away. She chanced a glance over her shoulder. There were five hounds now, and they were closing in on her. Mae tried to put on a burst of speed, desperate to reach the police station only two blocks away, but her feet lost their grip on the icy sidewalk. She tumbled and rolled forward. The hounds surrounded her.

Mae rose to her knees. Her coat sleeve was soaked through with blood and she was starting to lose feeling in her arm. She looked around for help, but the street was strangely devoid of traffic. She could hear sirens in the distance.

Mae knelt in the dirty snow and glared at what she suspected was the lead hound. Her breath came hard and raspy after her run.

"Do it!" she cried. "Get it over with!"

The presumed pack leader lunged at her, his mouth morphing into a long, tooth-filled muzzle. Mae closed her eyes.

A surprised yelp of pain made Mae open her eyes again.

Kravis ap Thimp, the ugly man-like thing who had greeted Mae on her first streetcar ride, stood in front of her. His right arm was wrapped in heavy bandages and his left wielded a wicked-looking curved blade. Kravis made quick work of the first hound, leaving it dying on the sidewalk, bleeding black on the snow. Mae rose to her feet as the bell of a streetcar rang out urgently.

"Get on the car, Mae!" Kravis yelled, using his weapon to hold the other three hounds at bay. Mae realized he had lost the element of surprise and the hounds had regrouped.

Mae started for the car when two of the hounds attacked Kravis from opposite sides. He stabbed one in the chest, but the other was on his back, tearing into his neck. The last hound rushed forward.

Unthinking, Mae charged, placing her slight frame between the hound and Kravis. The larger, heavier creature crashed into her. She lost her footing again and fell on her back with a hard thud.

"Police, everyone stay where you are!" a voice above Mae commanded.

Mae fought back the pain, resisting the urge to either pass out or throw up. She managed to get two shallow breaths, followed by a slightly larger one. She tried to sit up, but her back felt on fire. Mae twisted around to see a woman holding an automatic pistol in one hand, a badge in the other. The woman held her weapon like she meant business. Mae recognized Sergeant Dean, even in her street clothes.

The hounds turned and rushed the police woman. Mae heard gunfire and a scream as she rolled, scrambling to reach the waiting streetcar. Kravis was lying across the steps of the car, blood oozing from the back of his neck. A second burst of gunfire sounded. Bullets ricocheted off the buildings. Mae screamed in pain as something hot slammed into her middle. She was pulled through the doors of the streetcar. Behind her there was a wet ripping sound and a short, gurgling scream. The door of the streetcar closed.

"Ten cents, please."

Mae stumbled to her feet and reached into her pants pocket. Fumbling, she withdrew a handful of coins. They were covered in blood. She looked stupidly at the sticky red liquid smeared on her hand before dropping the coins on the floor. Mae blinked to clear her blurry vision, looking down. Blood was spreading across her stomach, running down her pants and to the floor. At her feet lay Kravis, his eyes closed, his breathing labored and unsteady. She looked up for the conductor and found herself facing a disheveled William Hodgins standing in the aisle before her, still holding his injured arm awkwardly against his body.

Hodgins raised the glowing crystal in his good hand. "Goodbye, Mae."

"You are not welcome here," the conductor said, stepping up behind Hodgins and placing a hand on his shoulder.

Mae slipped on the bloody floorboard and fell. Her face on the floor, she looked out the door windows. A pack of the Cŵn Annwn were shadowing them, pacing the streetcar despite the breakneck speed at which it was moving, running in the gray mists outside. Mae knew she should have felt afraid, but all she felt was cold and weak.

She looked up at Hodgins and the conductor. They were struggling. Several creatures, some winged, some with animal heads, some who looked almost human, surrounded the combatants, reaching for Hodgins. As they started to wrestle him down, he dropped the clear crystal marble to the floor and—with a harsh curse—stamped down on it.

There was a brilliant flash of light, and Mae felt the streetcar began to tip. She heard the high whine of the brakes. There was a moment of silence, and then Mae was flung like a rag doll around the inside of the car as it rolled over and flipped. The tortured screech of the wooden car breaking into pieces was overlaid with the terrified screams of the car's occupants. The car tumbled twice more, breaking in half before coming to rest in the shadows.

Mae landed with a painful crash halfway out a window. Through swollen, unfocused eyes she watched the white hounds close in on her. They gripped her coat with their teeth, dragging her wounded body out of the broken window and away from the wreckage of the streetcar, into the gray mist beyond.

Mae blacked out.

Dear Wall,

Something has happened. Everyone is running around in panic. I can hear them outside my door. Every so often someone, usually Elise but sometimes "Grandfather," looks into the room. Someone must have changed the binding magic on the door.

They're nervous. The last time they opened the door I could feel something different. The magic in the house was weaker. Not weak enough for me to break, but weaker.

"Mother" came and checked on me once. She was frightened. I could feel the fear on her. She kept trying to hold me in her lap and pat my hair. She was crying a lot and bright with barely controlled magic. I thought for a minute she might do something rash, but Elise came and took her away.

I wonder where Chrysandra is? I hope she managed to send my message. I hope she didn't betray me because I'm pretty sure I've got enough power left in me to hurt her—undead or not.

I really want something to eat, but I have a bad feeling that what I want is not something they are concerned about at the moment.

They're at the door, I can hear them taking down the magic to get inside. I can hear three or four people arguing.

How long she was unconscious, Mae did not know. When she opened her eyes, she found herself lying on her back, snow falling on her face. She sat up. The hounds lay in the snow, encircling her. They watched her with blazing silver eyes, their tongues lolling out of their mouths and over their wicked, yellow teeth, panting from their exertion.

She looked down at her wounds. Her coat was soaked with blood, completely ruined, but she could find no evidence that she was still bleeding. Mae unbuttoned her coat and shrugged out of it, being slow and careful in case she ripped or tore something.

The bullet had gone in through her stomach; that was obvious by the location of all the blood. Shivering from the cold and frightened expectation, Mae lifted the bottom of her dark blue sweater. The wound looked bad but was no longer bleeding. She checked her arm where the hound had bitten her, pulling back the sleeve. One of the creature's long canines had punctured her arm, but as with the bullet wound, there was no active bleeding. This did nothing to set Mae's mind at ease about her situation.

"Hello, Maeve Kathleen Malveaux."

Mae turned and looked into the eyes of Death. He was dressed in a tailored business suit, complete with a deep maroon tie.

She scrambled to her feet, causing the hounds to come to attention as well. "Death."

"Welcome to Annwn, Maeve."

Her ponytail had come loose at some point, and she brushed the hair out of her eyes with a blood-covered hand. "No one calls me Maeve. I'm just Mae."

"As you wish."

She looked around. "So, this is Annwn." Mae paused and frowned. She turned back to Death. "Would you care to explain why I'm in the mythological Welsh afterlife?"

"The hounds brought you here. With their pack leader dead and their Master incapacitated, they had no direction. They looked deep into their memories for guidance and brought you to this place."

"Then…am I dead?"

Death looked down at her. "Not yet."

Mae looked around and sighed. The landscape was all frozen winter. Snow fell and drifted on the breeze, trees were barren and sagging with large icicles. There were no signs of life, or at least of anything animated. "This looks like a miserable place to spend eternity."

"It was not always so, Mae. Once, this was a place of eternal youth, free of disease. Once, this was a place of abundance where the dead were rewarded with a pleasing and painless afterlife. It was a splendid place for the souls of the departed to rest while awaiting rebirth."

"What happened?"

"The death of Bebhinn."

Death began to walk forward, toward the frozen trees. Mae fell into step next to him. Around them the hounds spread out, flanking Mae and her companion. As they drew nearer the frozen forest, Mae could see how each tree was thick with ice, encased in a silver embrace.

Mae frowned. "I thought Bebhinn was Irish."

"Perhaps she was Irish or Welsh. Perhaps she was a goddess of the Underworld and of pleasure. Perhaps she was a giantess, or the queen of the fae, or even a mortal Viking princess. Those are imposed labels. They are not important. What *is* important is that she was a daughter."

Mae searched her memory. It had been years since the two mythology classes she took in college. Even longer since she had heard the stories her father told her as a child. Still, she was willing to hazard a guess.

"Arawn had a daughter? Bebhinn was the king of the Underword's child?"

Death smiled down at her as they walked through the icy landscape. "Not Arawn, but the later Lord of Annwn, Gwynn ap Nudd."

Mae nodded. She remembered a bit about Gwynn ap Nudd. Master of the Wild Hunt, king of the Tylwyth Teg, as the Welsh fae were called. At some point he became ruler of the Underworld, though Mae did not remember the circumstances, if she ever knew them. She had not realized he was also a father. She gestured at the world around her. "Is this caused by his grief?"

"Indirectly. He fell into grief and began to let his duties go. Like the Tylwyth Teg fae of which he was lord, Gwynn was prone to melancholy. His grief weakened the Fair Ones, making them vulnerable to outside manipulation. Without their Lord and Champion, they were at risk of being subjugated by stronger forces."

Mae and Death entered the frozen forest, crossing through the tree line. Mae looked closely at the hanging icicles. They were creatures. There were small, brown men and tiny, golden-haired women. Winged creatures hung like Christmas ornaments from the white branches. There were others on the ground, at the base of the trees— white cattle and hunched, hag-like women, encased in clear boulders of ice. Mae looked closer. There were human figures scattered among the fantastical creatures.

"Like Hodgins?" she asked.

Death nodded. "The children of the mortal world took advantage of the son of Nudd's weakness, promising to retrieve his child's spirit and return her to his forest. They corrupted him with their lies and bound him to their will. He was the first to fall."

Mae looked up at Death in confusion. "But if Bebhinn was dead, wouldn't her spirit dwell in Annwn anyway?"

Death gave Mae a sad look. "Remember, Mae, for the departed to reach the realm of Annwn, Gwynn ap Nudd was forced to ride out with his hounds and collect the spirit."

"He couldn't collect his own daughter," Mae whispered.

"To do so would have been to admit the death of his only child."

"But—but she would be reborn again, right?"

"Yes, Mae. Bebhinn would have, as any spirit in Annwn, been reborn to another life after a time. But she would have no longer been Bebhinn. Her father could not allow her uniqueness to be lost. Like any parent, when faced with the death of his child, he could not give her up willingly."

They stopped in front of a large oak tree. Encased in the clear ice was a figure upon a rough-hewn throne that seemed to grow from the tree itself. Mae walked closer, placing a hand on the ice. It was a man wearing antlers, or at least an antlered helmet. His clothing was the rough leathers and furs of a hunter. A bow and spear lay near his right hand, a horn around his neck. At his feet lay two frozen white hounds, creatures twice the size of any Cŵn Annwn Mae had encountered.

She looked through the ice at the man's face. His cheeks were shrunken, his hair unkempt. His open eyes were fields of stars at midnight

Mae turned to Death, who stood a few feet away, watching her carefully. Several things clicked together in her mind. Gwynn ap Nudd, Thanatos, Anubis, the Valkyries, the archangel Gabriel, Charon, the grim reaper.

Death.

They were incarnations of the same concept, a being who collected souls and carried them to the appropriate afterlife.

"I'm sorry," Mae said. "What happened to her?"

Death stared at her for several moments. Mae waited patiently.

"I do not know. I suspect Bebhinn's essence roams lost, and shall do so until her father rides out and brings her home to Annwn."

Mae shook her head. It was a sad tale, though she was not sure how it pertained to her situation. She decided to bring the conversation back to the human mages and the hounds. That, she felt, was where the answers to her questions lay.

"You said Gwynn was the first to fall. I see all these others imprisoned in ice. What's happening to this place?"

Death walked closer to Mae, standing so close she could feel him, though their bodies did not touch.

"William Jefferson Hodgins and his allies have bound the son of Nudd to their will. They are draining his power, draining the spark of his existence from his physical form and his domain for their own ends. As they siphon off more and more of the magic of Annwn, the landscape changes, becomes the opposite of what it should be. The creatures that dwell here are as trapped as their master. But the power, the magic, is not limitless, and the mortal mages have nearly exhausted the energies of this place, so they have begun to seek elsewhere for power."

"Are they trying to take over another spirit world?"

Death smiled. It was the kind of smile you did not want aimed in your direction. "No. This was a unique set of circumstances. They shall not catch another of us in this manner. Instead, they send the hounds out to hunt down any of the Tylwyth Teg fae who still dwell in the mortal world. When they find an enclave of the Fair Ones, they move into their area and begin capturing them, bringing them here to drain their small magics and life forces. A large enough group of Tylwyth Teg can take years to hunt down."

"The mortal mages, Hodgins and his people, are they using the magic to live forever? To gain wealth? To take over the world? I mean, what exactly are they doing with all that power? And how long has this been going on?"

"These mages have been creating havoc for centuries. As for what they do with the power they steal, it is the same that any mortal does with power, be it magical, physical or political. They extend their lives. They force their desires and their influence on anything weaker than they."

Death paused and stepped even closer to Mae. She took an involuntary step backward. "They cannot, however, live forever. They are able to extend their mortal span past the norm, but in the end, they are still mortal. Accidents, sudden violence, any number of things can cause their demise." Death flashed Mae a wicked little smile. "I admit to taking an unseemly bit of pleasure when I come for one of them."

Mae nodded. It was all making sense to her, and if she could get back to the mortal world, she would be better armed to fight her opponent. Assuming that she was even still alive. There was one more thing she needed to know.

"Why am I still here? I understand that this is the default place the hounds bring their prey, but I'm not a faerie creature. I don't have any magic for these mortal mages to strip."

Death's smile changed. It was not a sinister smile, or a sad smile. It was the kind of smile that said, "I know something you don't." It was the kind of smile that made Mae wonder if she had missed something important during the conversation. It was the kind of smile that made her realize she might not have asked the right question, and time was up.

"I swear to you, Maeve Kathleen Malveaux, you are indeed in the correct place. It is time for you to begin the next part of your journey."

Mae opened her mouth to protest. Before the words could spill over her lips, Death reached out with his right hand and gently, tenderly, brushed his fingers across her cheek.

Mae's perceptions of the world around her turned bright, too bright to bear, for what might have been a heartbeat. There was a sudden explosion of sounds and smells and sights and tactile sensations and tastes on her tongue.

She felt her body rising from the ground, being lifted up by two strong hands. Mae thought she might have laughed.

There was a sharp pain in her chest.

Maeve Kathleen Malveaux was plunged into a world of freezing cold and darkness.

Dear Wall,

Chrysandra managed to burn the picture in a fireplace! If I did everything right, the smoke should carry the message. All I can do now is hope my summoning worked.

I hope this Mae Malveaux woman is tougher than she looks in the picture. I think that I've seen her somewhere before. She seems so familiar to me.

Chrysandra told me Mr. Hodgins was injured, but she did not know what happened.

He wasn't at dinner. Afterward, Elise took me to their little magic workshop. "Grandfather," Ilona and Robert cast the bindings on me. They're weaker than Mr. Hodgins, but still too strong for me to fight alone.

They performed a ritual, chanting for the aid of some creature whose name I didn't recognize. Then "Grandfather" cut my arm and took some of my blood, putting it in a silver bowl. I felt the silver quiver and reached out to it, letting it know everything was okay.

Elise bandaged my arm while the two younger mages kept watch. I can tell I make them nervous. Not Elise though, she never shows any emotion. She's weird like that.

On the way back to my room, there was a scream. Chrysandra and "Mother" were standing outside my door. Chrysandra must have gotten away from wherever they keep her. Elise rushed forward and grabbed "Mother" by the elbow and turned her to look at me while Ilona took Chrysandra away. That calmed "Mother" down. She hugged me and smoothed my hair a lot before Elise put me in my room and took "Mother" away.

Chrysandra has the scariest rotten corpse smile I've ever seen. Then again, she is the only undead I know.

I think my summoning and Chrysandra's burning worked. I can feel something coming. Something awful and power-ful. It makes me happy.

Jill sighed as she rode the elevator down. Her intention to leave work early had evaporated through no fault of her own. At least she had not been held late.

She struggled through the snow to the train platform, but found herself facing not the light rail train, but a bus with the number fifty-five on its front parked on the street next to the tracks. She climbed aboard and settled into a seat near the front.

The bus stopped at Nicollet, a block before Hennepin Avenue, the driver telling people there was a "problem" at Fifth Street Station and that they should catch their transfers at Seventh. Jill disembarked with the rest of the passengers and struggled through the snow to Hennepin.

The light rail train sat at Fifth Street Station, surrounded by police cars. The street was closed past Hennepin and the police were waving people away from the scene. Jill quickened her pace, crossing Hennepin at Seventh just as her bus pulled up to the covered stop.

She rode surrounded by silent strangers. The mood on the bus was somber, as if the combination of ever deepening snow and frantic police activity had sucked the spirit from the usually animated riders on this route.

When the bus reached Lyndale and Lake, she was the first out the back door at the busy stop. Jill struggled to run in the calf-deep snow, reaching the door of her townhouse, gasping for breath and sweating under her coat. She fumbled with gloved hands, finally pushing the brass key into the lock. She burst through the door, kicking it shut and shedding her coat in one motion.

"Mae! Mae!"

Jill gave the living room and kitchen a quick glance. Nothing. She checked the downstairs bathroom. There was no sign of Mae. She started up the stairs.

"Mae! Mae, answer me!"

Jill turned the corner on the landing at a run and took three quick steps into Mae's room.

She could see where Mae had begun replacing the clothes she had dumped last night. A small blue suitcase was on the futon, unpacked and open. The clothes Mae had slept in last night were on the floor. There was a soft beep from the sweatpants. Jill picked them up and found Mae's cell phone.

Jill let out a frightened breath. Mae never made it home.

She ignored her first impulse. Dashing out into the gathering gloom and blowing snow would do no one, especially Mae, any good. She needed to think this through.

Jill gathered every phone in the house and carried them with her from room to room. She changed into a black pair of jeans and long-sleeved T-shirt. She carried her boots, a heavy sweater, and her warmest socks downstairs, prepared to venture into the freezing Minnesota winter at a moment's notice.

She put on a pot of coffee, suspecting it was going to be a long night. Food, Jill decided. She needed to eat now, in case she needed to…she was not sure what, but in case she needed to do something.

Ten minutes later she was sitting at the kitchen table, a cup of hot coffee with extra sugar and a microwave dinner in front of her. The three phones were arrayed around her on the table.

She was staring at her untouched dinner when Mae's phone rang. She grabbed for it, knocking her coffee cup onto the floor.

"Hello? Hello? Who is this?"

"They have her."

"Mae? Who are you? Who has Mae?"

"They have her," a female voice said again, then there was a soft click.

For a moment she thought she heard the soft chime of a bell through Mae's phone. She listened closely. There was silence. She checked the phone, trying to see the caller ID. There was no number, just the word unknown. She tried the call-back feature on Mae's phone, but was redirected to a message telling her the number she was trying to reach was blocking calls. She set the phone back on the table and swore.

Jill settled into a chair by the window, staring at the falling snow, thick flakes stacking up like little moments in time, shutting down traffic on the street below. She shivered. *Mae,* she thought. *Mae, where are you?*

The silence was unsettling. She turned on the television and flipped to the cable radio channels, picking one at random. Roy Orbison sang "Pretty Paper" at her. She switched the channel. The same song sounded from the speakers. She did it again with the same result. Unnerved, Jill turned the television off.

Glancing at the phones again gave her an idea. The voice on the phone had said they had her. She had to assume the caller meant Mae, and the only people who would be after Mae would be Hodgins and the Arnesons. She knew where they lived and could probably manage to get inside their home. How she would get Mae out was another matter, but she would worry about that once in the mansion.

She stepped back to the window in time to see one of the streetcars, its yellow frame nearly obscured by the heavy snow, pull up on the street below. She watched it, hoping she would see Mae climb off, safe and alive. She did not. Instead, the red doors opened and the bell rang twice.

Jill let out a shaky breath. She hoped she knew why the streetcar was here. She started to tremble. This business with magicians and faeries and anthropomorphic hounds was dead serious. Her gut was telling her that to save Mae, she needed to be prepared to travel right to the edge of everything, and then step off.

Jill looked around her townhouse, trying to decide what she might need. She put her baton and cell phone in the inside pocket of her coat, adding Mae's phone on impulse. She grabbed a pair of granola bars from the cabinet and filled a water bottle. She climbed the stairs and added another pair of socks to her feet and coins to her pocket.

Keys and wallet vanished into the inside coat pockets, making them bulge. She took another steadying breath and walked outside, through the deepening snow to the patiently waiting streetcar.

Jill climbed aboard. The door closed and she turned to find the conductor.

"Ten cents, please."

Jill gave him a dime, taking the offered transfer slip. She walked to the back of the empty car and looked out the window, searching the darkness. The streetcar bell rang twice and the machine lurched forward. Jill took a seat and stared out the window into the snowy Minnesota night beyond.

Wherever you are, Mae, hang on, she thought. *I'm coming. I'm coming to bring you home.*

Saturday, 28th of October

Dear Wall,

I can't sleep. My arm keeps throbbing and I'm all nervous with anticipation. I'd heal the cut, but I don't want to waste any more magic.

I keep hearing noises, something in the walls. I hope it's a rat, drawn to the room by Chrysandra's smell. Rats make good messengers, if you can offer them something to make it worthwhile to them, like meat or a bit of shiny for their nests. I'd turn on the light and read, but I don't want anyone coming into the room. Some Champion of my people I turned out to be, trapped and helpless, my only friends you words and a dead girl.

I'm not going to cry. I'm not.

I'm not going to die here. I'm not going to let them suck me dry and toss me to the hounds. I'm not going to let them use me to hurt my mother or anyone in the Court. I won't.

I'm going to escape and go home to Mother. I'm going to throw snowballs at the old Cyhyraeth hag who prowls the lakeshore, and when summer comes, I'm going to play in the sun and swim in the lake. I'm going to learn the names of the squirrels, and I'm going to coax the crows into a chorus.

I'm going to help Chrysandra. No one deserves to suffer, not like that.

I'm not going to venture into the human world again until I come to my full power. When I do, I'm going to come back to this house, and they will pay for everything they've done to me and to Mother and to my kin. I hope you words are still here to bear witness.

JILL RODE IN SILENCE. She hoped that her previous experience of the streetcar stopping where she needed to get off would hold true for this trip. It was hard to see outside the window, but as the car moved through the dark night, the city faded, giving way to forests and grass.

The streetcar parked and the red doors opened.

Creatures from imagination and nightmare climbed aboard. Jill sat up and watched the strange procession. Most of the fae creatures—for with their pointed ears, earth-toned clothing and antique weapons, Jill was sure they could be nothing else—seemed to be injured. Several bore head wounds. Most were bleeding or covered in blood, and not a few held limbs that were obviously dislocated or broken. After a few minutes, some of the more ambulatory creatures began carrying the seriously injured onto the car.

Any other night and Jill might have sat gazing in fear and wonder at the parade, but tonight she was focused on one thing. Mae. When she could finally no longer sit still, she climbed off the car, stepping into a gray twilight.

She was greeted by the sight of one of the streetcars lying wrecked, torn into pieces, its wooden body splintered and scattered about the landscape. There were ominously still shapes on the ground. Jill took a step forward, fearful of whom one of those still forms might be.

"You'll not find her here, Jill Hall."

She turned toward the voice. The creature who addressed her was short and squat, wearing the remains of a floppy brimmed hat. He had a heavy bandage on one arm and a deep scowl on his gray, warty face. There was blood on his shirt and a deep, oozing gash along his neck. "The hounds took her. They dragged her into the mists."

Jill looked around. All the landscape looked the same to her. "Which way did they take her?"

"There's no point in following," the wounded faerie said.

Jill rounded on him. "I'm going to find her, and I am going to bring her home. Which way did they take her?"

"You don't understand. No living mortal can find or enter Annwn. If they've taken Mae to Annwn, then she's lost to the mortal world."

Jill stared at the squat creature for a moment. "You're Kravis, aren't you? The one who met Mae on the streetcar the first night she was attacked by the hounds?" Mae had told Jill everything about that night after their own encounter with the Cŵn Annwn, giving Jill a vivid description of Kravis, Ellie and Death.

He squirmed. "Yes."

Jill walked up to him. "I need to know how to find Mae."

"Are you deaf? I just told you—"

Jill grabbed him by the front of his raggedy shirt. "If the hounds took Mae to Annwn, there must be a way in." She gave Kravis a shake, making him gasp in pain. "You are going to lead me there."

"There is a door," a tiny voice said. "There is a door to the place you seek."

Jill turned to find herself facing a winged woman, all long blue hair and so short the top of her pointed ears did not quite reach Jill's waist.

"Lady Elliefandi! No!" Kravis snapped.

Jill spun on the wounded creature, furious. "Quiet!"

"You can't get to the door," Kravis said. "It is in our realm. Even if you were allowed to travel through to the Court, the door is locked."

"Locks can be picked. Locks can be broken. I'll deal with that when I get there. Take me there. Now."

"If you don't, I will," the winged woman said, her face stern.

Kravis frowned at her, but stood and limped toward the streetcar. "You're going to get us both banished, you daft thing. No one will stand for bringing a mortal into our hold and hall."

Ellie grinned at him. "Then we'll have to make sure no one knows, won't we?"

The three climbed aboard the waiting streetcar when its bell rang out twice in warning. As Jill stepped through the streetcar's door, she looked over her shoulder at the wreckage of the first car. She was not sure how Mae could have survived the accident, but others had, so it was possible. She reached the bench where Ellie was standing next to Kravis.

"We can slip her past the guards in all the confusion," Ellie said. "They'll be overwhelmed with trying to help everyone to safety."

"It's fine for you to make wild plans," Kravis snorted as the car lurched and started rolling along. "You've protection and kin."

"You don't?" Jill asked squeezing past Kravis and into the seat next to the squat faerie.

"No. The Dark Ones were the first to fall into shadow. We tried to save ourselves by aligning with mortal mages. It was our doom. A few survivors claimed sanctuary with our Light cousins, but they have little use for us. They host us because courtesy and blood demand it, but they do not trust us."

"And justly so, for the most part," Ellie said softly.

"And justly so," Kravis echoed in agreement, a small smile on his weathered face.

"Mortal mages?" Jill asked.

For the rest of the ride, Kravis and Ellie took turns explaining to Jill about the death of Bebhinn and binding of Gwynn ap Nudd. They told her how the mages, who had bound the faerie Lord and Champion, drew their power from the lands and spirits of the Tylwyth Teg, and how they were all being hunted and taken, stripped of their magic to feed the power of mortals.

"We're the last great Court of the Tylwyth Teg, come over the seas and hiding in this new world, and we are but a shadow of our people's former glory," Ellie said. "Most of our numbers have been captured and taken to the horror Annwn has become. The survivors of the lost Courts live in exile in the great Courts of our distant fae kin."

Jill reached over and placed a hand on Ellie's arm. "I'm sorry." She looked at Kravis. "Show me the way to get into your realm, and I'll go in alone."

Kravis sighed. "No. I was charged with guarding Mae and I've failed. I'll help you because I must and because I need to."

Jill gave him a critical look. "I'm not sure you're in any shape to be fighting hell hounds and who knows what else."

Kravis smiled at her, all sharp and crooked green teeth. "Would you *prefer* to go alone?"

"Not really."

"Then it's settled," Ellie said. "We'll sneak you into the hold, talk to our *swynwraig*, and convince her to open the door."

"*Swynwraig?*" Jill asked.

"A wizard," Ellie said absently.

Kravis snorted. "You make it sound like a flower gathering trip."

"And what would you know about gathering flowers, Kravis ap Thimp?"

"Nothing, I'm afraid."

The streetcar stopped and opened both its doors.

"This is it," Ellie said, looking over the seated Kravis at Jill. "Take one of Kravis's arms, I'll take the other, and we'll blend in with the injured."

"I *am* one of the injured," Kravis said.

Ellie nodded. "That will make it all the more convincing. Now moan like you've lost your lover and stagger around a bit when we lead you."

"Won't I be noticed?" Jill whispered, standing up and taking one of Kravis's arms.

Ellie shrugged. "Turn your coat collar up and let your hair cover your face. Keep your eyes down and look at the ground. Maybe they'll think you're a hag or giantess. If anyone asks questions, I'll speak to them."

"Right," Jill muttered. "No eye contact and no talking."

They stood in the line to exit the car, Kravis leaning heavily on Jill, with Ellie walking slightly ahead of them and Kravis keeping one hand on Ellie's back, between her wings.

"Don't overact," Ellie hissed.

"I'm not. I'm really quite injured."

In front of them was a frozen lake. The line of injured and those giving them aid were moving steadily through the falling snow toward a large old tree. Jill gasped in surprise. She recognized this place. It was the tree that hosted the fairy door at Lake Harriet. Apparently, it was more than just a bit of local color. As the fae reached the door and passed through, the door was either expanding or the creatures were shrinking.

"Ellie," Jill said softly, "am I going to fit through that door?"

"It will be fine. You'll pass through as long as you hold onto Kravis and he holds onto me."

Jill wished she felt as sure about the situation as Ellie did, but there was nothing for it but to continue on. They reached the little wooden door, trailing behind two knee-high nut-brown creatures that looked like they had just left a mine. Jill closed her eyes and stepped forward, clutching Kravis's arm.

The smell of wildflowers and rainwater filled her nose, causing her a moment of confusion. Jill opened her eyes, giving her surroundings a quick glance through her hair before looking down again.

It was night in the realm of the fae. Softly glowing orbs floated in the tree, illuminating a pathway that everyone seemed to be walking down. There were guards guiding the wounded farther down the path. Jill could see the occasional glint of light off polished weapons—weapons so bright and pale they could only be silver—held by pale-haired warriors. The sound of a small waterfall reached her ears, just underneath the continual groans and moans of the injured and the orders of the guards.

"Steady now," Kravis whispered as they approached the first of the guards.

"Lady Elliefandi, are you injured?" the guard asked.

Jill kept a careful watch from the corner of her eyes. The guard ignored both her and Kravis in favor of the winged woman.

"No. I'm helping this one," Ellie nodded toward Kravis.

The guard frowned. "Shall I summon an escort for him?"

"No, we can handle it." Ellie started to move forward.

"Hold, Lady Elliefandi," the guard said. Jill saw him nod toward her. "This one is unfamiliar to me." He moved in front of her. "Who are you, come to our realm?"

Jill's heart started to beat wildly. She knew if she looked up, he would recognize her for what she was.

"She's a hag, banished from the unseelie and under protection of Lady Rhyania's Court. I know her from my visits." Ellie leaned forward. "She is mute, but she helped me carry Kravis this far. Uncommonly strong, that one."

The guard stood in front of Jill. She kept her head down, looking at the guard's boots.

"You vouch for her, then?" he asked Ellie.

"Indeed. I will see her home when this is done."

"You should call for an escort. It is too dangerous to be about in these times, Lady Elliefandi."

"I shall."

Kravis gave a small moan. Jill hoped it was enough to get the guard to send them on their way. She was not disappointed.

"Very well, my lady. If you have any need, I am at your service."

Ellie led Jill and Kravis further down the path, away from the watchful gaze of the guard.

"Here," Kravis said in a low voice. He guided them into the rich, fragrant foliage that lined the pathway.

"Where are we going?" Jill wanted to know, releasing Kravis's arm and falling into step next to him. Ellie did the same on the other side.

"Our *swynwraig* lives not far from the door. Hers is the task of guarding the entrances and exits to the hold," Kravis explained. "I am…her servant."

"You're her personal assassin," Ellie said.

"Yes, I am. I am also her companion, gardener, chef and bodyguard."

"Your wizard needs a bodyguard?" Jill asked.

Ellie grimaced. "She is not well loved."

Kravis snorted. "The Lord of Llysllyn is frightened of her power and influence."

Jill frowned. "Look, I don't really care about your politics. I just want to get to this door to Annwn and find Mae."

Kravis led them through a thicket and into a small clearing. There was a dwelling—Jill was not sure it could be called a house or cottage—growing from the trunk of a giant oak tree.

"That may be a problem," Ellie said. "Though the *swynwraig* is the only one who can open the door, the Lord of Llysllyn controls the door to Annwn itself. To reach it, we'll need to enter his hall."

"So, what's the good news?" Jill asked.

"The Lord will kill you quick and painless should he catch you," Kravis said with a smile.

"Oh, goody."

"I, on the other hand, will be tortured beyond endurance and tossed into the mortal world to die."

Ellie sighed. "Could you be any more pessimistic?"

"Yes. I am not one of his kinsmen." Kravis reached for the door and pulled it open. Sticking his head inside, he called out. "Lady Mirallyn! It is Kravis. I bear news and bring guests."

Jill followed him through the door.

The room might have been any sitting room, except the furniture grew from the same tree that shaped the house. Jewel-toned cushions and pillows adorned the many sitting and lounging surfaces. Tapestries of woodlands and other landscapes hung on the walls. Jill looked closely at one of a deep green forest. The leaves on the trees seemed to actually move, rustling in the breeze. She gasped when she saw a pair of silver eyes on a bark-brown face peer back at her before it vanished into the forest. Jill blinked and stepped away.

Ellie nudged her shoulder. "You shouldn't stare too long into the weave, lest you find yourself drawn in."

Jill looked up as a new voice spoke.

"Tell me you bring glad tidings, Kravis ap Thimp."

Jill felt herself go still inside. She had seen this woman before in a photograph. Less than five feet tall with silver hair to her knees, she was a vision of unearthly beauty in a long gown in the autumn colors of brown, orange and yellow.

Kravis removed his hat and gave her a small bow. "I fear, my lady, the news will but increase your sadness."

Jill watched as the woman's body stiffened, visibly preparing for the blow of Kravis's words.

"Say on, then," the woman whispered.

"The mortal magicians have broken the protection of Lowry's trains. There is no trace of one daughter, and the white hounds have taken the other to Annwn."

"Then we are doomed," the woman said softly.

"I'm sorry, my lady. I failed to protect her."

The woman shook her head. "I set you an impossible task. Our fate turns on Lord Murlannor, and he will neither deviate from his course nor listen to counsel."

Ellie nodded her head in agreement. Jill decided it was time to make her case.

"Excuse me," Jill said, moving forward. "But some of us aren't ready to give up yet."

The small woman turned, locking her silver-green eyes on Jill. "Are you a Champion, to storm the Great Hall of Murlannor, Lord of the Llysllyn Court, and walk into the frozen wastes of fallen Annwn? Tell me, human, what part do you play in this tragedy?"

Jill stepped closer to the faerie wizard, moving into the smaller woman's personal space and forcing her to take a step backward.

"I'm the woman who's going to bring Mae home. I'm the woman who's going to rescue your daughter. And you, lady, are going to help me."

"And how do you propose we gain access to the gate to Annwn?" the woman asked, the disdain in her voice clear.

Kravis cleared his throat. "We could use the confusion of the accident to slip into the Hall and to the door to Annwn by stealth," he said, echoing Ellie's plan.

Ellie nodded. "The warriors and healers will be exhausted after dealing with the accident. We should wait for them to retire."

Lady Mirallyn frowned. "The Lord and his Court will have long since abandoned the Great Hall for their beds and various clandestine gatherings. You would only need to avoid the night guard to gain access to the door. I can open it with a moment's work. I need only place a bit of my blood on the seal to unlock it. "

Jill nodded. The plan to sneak into the Great Hall had a simple eloquence. She was sufficiently versed in television sitcoms and dramas to know that the more complicated a plan, the more likely it was to explode in everyone's faces. That made for good comedy and pathos, which was the last thing Jill needed.

Ellie assured them she could manage the guards, and if all else failed, Kravis could provide a distraction. Jill and Lady Mirallyn needed to reach their goal; Ellie and Kravis could be left behind if necessary.

Mirallyn suggested they wait for at least another hour before they began their raid, which Kravis agreed to. He sat and allowed his lady and employer to heal what injuries she could with her magic. Jill watched, fascinated, a thousand questions on her tongue, as the faerie wizard chanted in her musical voice. Mirallyn's hands glowed blue and silver, and where she passed them over one of Kravis's injuries, that wound healed. A few of his other injuries, most notably where he had been bitten by the Cŵn Annwn, resisted her healing, and had to be treated with more mundane measures.

While Mirallyn worked, she explained to Jill how she, Mirallyn of the Lake, had encountered and fallen in love with the mortal man,

Thomas Wilson Malveaux, had born him twin daughters, and how one daughter was born with the power and magic of the fae, while the other was human and mundane. She spoke of the need to hide the magical child, named Fay by her father for her heritage, from the human mages who hunted her kind. A child with the blood of both races could be turned into a powerful weapon if controlled by those same mages.

And that, Mirallyn told her, was the cause of the parting between her and her human lover and human child. She needed to bring Fay to a place where she could hide and protect her, and that place was here at the lake, where Mirallyn was strongest. She knew Lord Murlannor would barely tolerate a half-blood child, and would never have allowed Mae, who was born a mundane human, to dwell in his kingdom. She had taken Fay into hiding while leaving Mae with her father and had never seen either again, too afraid to leave her refuge and risk exposing Fay to the growing threat of the human mages.

"But they captured her anyway," Jill said at the end of Mirallyn's tale. She noted Kravis, wearing clean bandages and looking much healthier, slipped out the door.

"Yes." Mirallyn sighed. "I told her of her heritage, explained to her about the world of her birth. Fay is, has always been, curious and prone to act impulsively. She became determined to see the human world. She slipped past her watchers and found a way to one of the doors. I suspect the magicians snatched her up almost immediately."

"Is it that easy to cross over to the other side?" Jill asked.

"Her blood," Ellie said. "It is the same blood that flows in Lady Mirallyn. The wards and locks responded to her magic because it was similar enough to her mother's, despite the protection we put in place."

"An occurrence I should have foreseen," Mirallyn said, cleaning her hands on a bright orange towel and putting away her medicines and supplies.

Jill chewed her lower lip for several seconds before she responded. "Why don't you—or someone else—go after her? For that matter, why are you all sitting around while the mages pick you off one by one? You've got magic and those guards I saw looked competent. Why don't you fight back?"

"Fear," Ellie said. "The mages have defeated our Champion. Without Gwynn ap Nudd to lead them, my people are too afraid to take to the field and confront the mages directly."

Mirallyn nodded. "And I must stay and protect the doorways. If I fall to the human magicians—and I would, despite my skill with the art—then all of Llysllyn would be left open to their attacks. The Court would be overrun by the mages and our magic stripped away in a matter of days."

"And my uncle will not risk any of his warriors or lesser wizards to rescue a half-blood child," Ellie added. "Kravis tried to get in several times, but they were too strong in magic and too diligent in their defenses for him to overcome their guards and wards."

"That is why we involved Maeve," Mirallyn said softly.

"What!" Jill cried, standing and looming over Mirallyn. "You abandoned Mae, haven't bothered to contact her to tell her you're alive and she has a sister, *but you knew how to contact her?*"

Mirallyn nodded, her face impassive. "I could not reach out to Maeve. I could not contact her for fear that our enemies might see and realize her importance, but I did set my agents to watch and guard her should she somehow manifest magic later in life."

"But when *you* needed help, you happily involved her in something dangerous that she didn't even understand!" Jill glared at Mirallyn. "Did you send those streetcars to Mae?"

"No," Ellie whispered. "Lowry's cars appeared to Mae for reasons we do not know. We—" the little winged woman paused, her eyes wide as Jill rounded on her.

"You were in on this too?" Jill asked quietly.

"We all were," Kravis said from the doorway. "I made sure Mae got those files for the magician's daughter. We wanted Mae to bring your mortal authorities and laws to bear on the mages. If they searched the Arneson home and found Fay, they would have removed her and then I could have snatched her away and back to safety."

"Well, all you managed to do was nearly get Mae killed a couple of times!"

Kravis grimaced. "I've been in your world too long. The hounds have my scent and I led them right to Mae. I'm terribly sorry, Jill Hall."

Jill shook her head, some of her ire deflating. "No. I think Hodgins and the Arnesons were afraid Mae was going to do just what you wanted her to. I think they set the hounds to stop her."

"Then we should act now." Mirallyn looked at Jill. "We can continue our discussion later. Now we need to find Mae and bring her from ruined Annwn."

Jill walked across the moonlit gardens with her escort, moving silently in the darkness until they reached the living oak palace of the Lord of Llysllyn. She leaned over Kravis's shoulder, studying the soldiers on nightwatch.

"There's only the three of them," Kravis said. "Maybe we should wait for them to move farther away."

"The longer we wait, the worse it could be for Mae." Jill was fed up with waiting. She wanted to move.

Lady Mirallyn touched Jill on the arm, feather light and lightning quick. "Patience. If we are discovered, it will not go well for any of us."

"Lady Rhyania of the Falls would give us shelter and sanctuary," Ellie said.

"You and Mirallyn, perhaps," Kravis said, watching the three guards as they went about their rounds. "For Jill and me, it would be a swift stroke of the sword and our heads in a basket."

"I'd rather not dwell on my own death," Jill replied.

Kravis smirked at her. "Me either, but there it is." He turned back to the guards. "They're moving. Be ready to run for the doors."

Jill placed a hand on the short faerie's back. She wanted to be moving as soon as he was. She trusted Ellie and Lady Mirallyn to keep up and find their way, but Jill was in a strange and potentially hostile environment. The last thing she wanted was to be separated from the other three.

The muscles under her hand bunched in anticipation, signaling Kravis's intent to charge. Her own muscles tightened in response. Kravis suddenly surged forward, faster than Jill could have imagined his squat frame could move. She hesitated for only an instant and set off after him, trying to run and be silent at the same time.

Jill and her three companions rushed up the wooden steps and into what Jill could only describe as a palace grown from the trunks of a series of birch, elm, maple and oak trees. Jill wished she had time to focus on the beauty around her. She wished she could climb these steps slowly under a bright sun and drink in the splendor and magic of this world.

Instead, she was skulking about like a thief. She reached the tall wooden doors three steps behind Kravis. Lady Mirallyn reached the doors next, Ellie bringing up the rear. Lady Mirallyn placed her hand on the door and began to chant in a quiet whisper.

Jill glanced nervously over her shoulder, looking for the guards to return. She reached into her coat and withdrew her baton. Jill was under no illusions about her ability to fight her way out of this place. The guards were well-armed and businesslike. They would cut her down if things became physical, but she would not let them stop her from reaching Mae without a fight, even if it was a doomed one.

There was a soft wooden groan and one of the large doors opened slightly, allowing them to slip inside. Mirallyn stepped through the door as if she had been announced by a herald, her head high and body language confident. Kravis shadowed the wizard. Jill followed, with Ellie right behind her.

They walked along the walls, moving through hallways of living wood: gold and brown decorated with green and yellow leaves and hung with tapestries. Small trees and live flowers dotted the pathways. There was subdued light, though Jill could not determine its source.

They reached a set of large oak doors bound in silver.

"I don't like this," Kravis said. "There should be guards posted at the Great Hall."

Ellie frowned. "Maybe they're helping with the survivors of the crash."

"Maybe they know we're coming and it's an ambush," Kravis replied.

Jill narrowed her eyes at the door, willing it to reveal its secrets. It did not. "Is that the only path to the door to Annwn?"

"Yes," Lady Mirallyn whispered, turning to look at Jill.

Jill realized the others were waiting for her to lead them. There was no point standing around. If it was an ambush, they were well and truly screwed, and if it was not, then they were wasting time. "Then that's the way we go."

Before the others could react, Jill walked forward and pushed the doors open.

She found herself looking down a long walkway to an oak throne, its wood polished dark from years of wear. Banners hung from the beams of the vaulted ceiling, bearing fantastical creatures and various types of trees. The emblems or coat of arms of faerie nobles, Jill supposed. Benches lined the walls, giving spectators a place to sit. Jill could imagine the room filled with creatures such as Kravis and Ellie and others she had observed on the streetcars.

"Where is the door?" Jill asked quietly.

Lady Mirallyn pointed to a spot just behind the throne. "There."

There was a round silver door set into the wall behind the throne. It was covered in softly glowing writings and symbols. A short, jeweled sword was set across the door, barring it closed.

The four conspirators were mere feet from their destination when bright lights flared in the Great Hall and the rattle of armor heralded the arrival of guards. Jill looked around, fighting down panic. They were surrounded.

A squad of four armed and armored fae appeared between them and the door to Annwn. Standing just forward of the guards was an almost mortal-looking male. He was dressed in a dark green robe, embroidered with red and yellow runes. He was heavy about the waist, his nut-brown face tired, his golden hair lank under the silver circlet he wore. Belted to his robes was a long dagger, emeralds and rubies winking from its guard and pommel. The feature that set him apart from a normal man was his ears. They poked up, pointed, from the sides of his head, their wrinkled tips beginning to droop and curl downward.

He glared at the group. "At last you show your true agenda, Mirallyn of the Lake."

Lady Mirallyn stepped forward and bowed her head. "My Lord Murlannor—"

"Silence." The Lord of the Llysllyn Court of the Tylwyth Teg looked from Mirallyn to Jill.

Jill shivered. He did not raise his voice, but the command held all the force of a shouted order. Her companions were instantly cowed, though Mirallyn at least looked squarely into his eyes.

He stepped toward Mirallyn. "I have been tolerant of you, Mirallyn. Tolerant of your indiscretion with a mortal lover. Tolerant of your subversive ideas to merge our people with Rhyania's Court. Tolerant of your half-blood child cavorting in my domain. I should have destroyed that abomination and banished you before your madness grew too great."

He stopped in front of Mirallyn. She stared into his eyes, unblinking, before frowning and speaking.

Jill could not understand Mirallyn's words. She had not thought anything of being able to talk with Kravis and Ellie and eventually the Lady Mirallyn, but suddenly she was cut off from the language, as if someone had flipped a switch. She watched Lady Mirallyn speak and saw the angry reaction of the Lord of Llysllyn. Next to her Ellie seemed to wilt and tears began to roll down her cheeks. Kravis paled. Jill might not have been able to understand the words any longer, but she could tell they were in deep trouble.

Jill looked at the door to Annwn. It was no more than five feet away. If she could reach it, and if she could drag Lady Mirallyn with her to open it, she doubted the guards would dare follow. Jill took a couple of deep breaths. She was larger than everyone in the room. She would have to attempt something—probably something stupid—if she were going to save Mae.

Lord Murlannor turned toward her, locking his dark green eyes on her, capturing her gaze, holding her frozen with the force of his presence. He favored her with a sneer.

"I do not know what you thought to accomplish, human, but I can smell the taint of magic and doom on your spirit, and I will not allow you to destroy my people."

"I just want to bring my friend home."

"You lie! We know the secrets of your kin. We know the same blood runs through your veins as that of a mortal mage. You cannot hide your nature from us. You would open the door to Annwn and bring your masters to our realms!"

Jill held herself still. There was no reasoning with him, this she could tell. It was obvious the faerie lord had made up his mind that, since she was related to one of the mages, she had come to destroy his people. Jill was horrified at this confirmation of Robert's involvement with the evil mages. She checked her allies.

Kravis and Ellie looked defeated, though they were still unbound and the guards had yet to draw a weapon. Only Lady Mirallyn kept her head up, her eyes fierce, but even she appeared either unable or unwilling to act. Jill knew nothing about magic, but she could tell the others were somehow being controlled by Lord Murlannor. From the moment the faerie lord had spoken, her companions had become helpless, but to whatever compulsion held them in place, Jill seemed immune.

Murlannor turned to his guards. "Kill the traitors. Remove the woman's eyes. Leave her blind and naked at the water's edge. She will be our message to her masters."

Jill tensed. She had no intention of being blinded, stripped and tossed into the snow to die. She could still act, and Mae was counting on her. Jill snapped her baton out to its full twenty-four inches and struck. The blow took the unsuspecting Lord of the Llysllyn Court across the back of the head.

Jill winced at the dull, wet thud. She reached out and grabbed Lady Mirallyn by the front of her gown, jerking the small faerie woman forward, over the crumpled body of Lord Murlannor and between the startled guards. She heard the hiss of swords being drawn. The loud roar of Kravis's battle cry and Ellie's high scream of fear provided counterpoint to the shocked cries of the guards and fae in the Great Hall.

Jill pushed the wizard against the door and turned to face the first of the guards. "Open it!" she screamed, trying to deflect the stroke of a silver sword.

The guard's blade slid along her baton. Jill managed to turn her body just enough to avoid losing her left arm. Her heavy winter coat cushioned most of the slice, though she felt a trickle of warm blood running toward her wrist.

"The door!" Jill screamed, pushing back against two guards who were pressing her, trying to force her against the wall and disarm her. An arrow struck the wall next to Jill's head, digging into the wood, quivering.

There was a sudden blast of cold air, as if winter's fury had battered down the walls and was trying to crush them in a blizzard's grip of freezing wind and icy rain. The screams of outrage from the assemblage in the Great Hall turned to cries of panic.

Jill had only an instant to register the opening of the door to Annwn before the guards overbore her and knocked her to the ground. She lay stunned, waiting for the final blow to fall, the bright flash of the blade that would end her life.

One of the guards fell on her, his surprised face inches from her own. Jill heard his death-rattle as breath and life left him. She jerked violently, throwing off the dead body. She was lifted from the floor and she screamed, both in fear and as a challenge, as she raised her baton to strike.

The blood-splattered face of Kravis peered at her, and Jill held her blow. Another explosion of cold air, terrible and fierce, tore through the Hall, blasting many of the fae from their feet, sweeping them along the floor, away from the open portal.

"This way," Kravis shouted, dragging her toward the open door.

Before the door to Annwn, her back to the battle raging mere feet away, stood Lady Mirallyn. Her arms were opened wide as she faced the gale. She held the sword that had barred the door in one hand. Snow and ice tore at her cloak and gown. Her silver hair whipped like a ragged banner around her head. Jill could see Mirallyn's lips moving, though she could not hear the words.

"Hurry!" Kravis yelled. "She cannot hold back the storm for long!"

Jill slipped under the arms of the wizard, struggling into the blizzard, Kravis pushing her, urging her forward.

Jill crossed the threshold into a land of winter and white. She turned to Lady Mirallyn, her hand outstretched. Behind Mirallyn, Kravis wheeled, sword in hand, defending his lady from the attacks of the grim-faced faerie-guards. Mirallyn tossed the sword that had barred the door into Annwn. It landed at Jill's feet.

One of the guards managed to slip past Kravis and strike Mirallyn with his shield. She stumbled and turned toward her attacker. The door closed and vanished. Where Mirallyn had stood before, there was only flat, frozen ground for as far as the eye could see. With the closing of the door between Annwn and Llysllyn, the blizzard winds abated, leaving only a gentle breeze and softly falling snow.

"No!" Jill cried out to the uncaring expanse before her, her voice swallowed by the sound-deadening snow. She wiped the tears from her face. She was tired, frightened and sick from all the death and violence, but there was nothing else to do except go forward.

She collapsed her baton and placed it back into her coat. Picking up the sword, Jill surveyed her surroundings. A frozen forest of snow-covered trees stood some distance away.

Jill started toward the far-off woods, certain it was where she would find Mae.

Dear Wall,

Elise brought breakfast to me this morning. She was very distracted, and I managed to steal the silverware. Now I can hear all the silver in the house. It is only a matter of time now before I bend it to my will, then I will be ready to make my escape.

My arm still hurts. I looked at where they cut me. It's all red and angry looking, not healing at all like it should. It may just be because my body and magic are tired, but

I fear it might be an effect of the magic they performed when they took my blood.

Ilona brought Chrysandra to my room. She stayed until lunch, but didn't say anything. I'm worried that her brain might be lost. When Elise and Ilona came and took her away, Elise said it was time to freshen her up. I heard the two women arguing about the amount of magic they were expending on Chrysandra. Ilona apparently doesn't like it, but Elise reminded her that the decision has been made. For a moment I thought Ilona was going to blurt out Mr. Hodgins's first name, which would have put me that much closer to his full name, but she stopped herself.

It was after lunch that the real action started. I could hear the hounds, baying and howling, come into the mansion. There was a surge of magic. I could feel it, even past the wards they're using to hold me in place.

A little later Mr. Hodgins came in to check on me. He stood and stared at me for a long time, frowning, not saying anything. He looked tired and pale, but he's alive, and he's still strong.

I could smell my blood on him, in him. They used my blood to heal him. That's a mistake. I just need to break past the defenses on this house, and he's mine.

JILL STRUGGLED THROUGH THE deep snow, using the faerie sword like a walking stick. Every few steps she drove it through the icy crust and into the ground for stability, a function for which it was ill-suited. Stumbling on something unseen under the thick white blanket, she used the sword to pull herself back to her feet.

Her feet were numb, the unrelenting cold having pierced her boots and double pair of wool socks. Her legs ached with the cold, shaking, making her unsteady. The white glare caused her eyes to water. Jill found herself constantly blinking to clear her vision.

"Come on, Jill. Keep moving." She was only about fifty yards from the tree line. She looked skyward, peering into the bright but sunless sky. The snow had stopped falling. She chuckled at how happy that made her feel.

She wondered if she could start a fire once she was in the forest. Jill's experience in the wilderness was slim—a few camping trips as a child where every detail was so well-planned the outing might as well have been catered, and one bug-infested day of hiking in college. She doubted her ability to produce flame by rubbing two sticks together or using the blade of the sword to strike a spark off a rock, never mind finding tinder or wood dry enough to catch fire.

Jill paused at the first tree, leaning against it as she tried to catch her breath. Her lungs burned with every intake of frigid air, and her nostrils were frozen shut. She wiped her watery eyes with her coat sleeve. The snow was not as deep in the trees. Further into the forest she saw green trees, possibly firs and pines. Jill moved toward them, hoping for more cover, less snow, warmth and a clue as to Mae's whereabouts.

Jill found the first footprints only a few feet into the forest. She squinted down at the imprints in the snow. They were smaller than her own. They could be Mae's. There was a faint impression of paws as well. Jill gave the deep woods before her a wary look. The hounds had been here.

With no real choice and no real plan, Jill moved forward. Once she found Mae, she did not know how they would escape Annwn. She had assumed that Mirallyn, or Kravis, or even Ellie would be with her. One thing at a time, she decided. One thing at a time. She stopped for a minute, sitting on an ice-covered boulder for a few moments before she stood and bent at the waist, gloved hands on her numb knees.

"Let's go, Jill. Can't sit too long. Sitting can kill. The cold can kill. Keep moving," she whispered to herself.

The tracks were easier to follow as she traveled deeper into the forest. She peered at one of the long icicles hanging from the limbs of a leafless oak. Jill reached out and touched it. She gasped at the sight of a small creature frozen in the ice and stepped backward, coming up against another boulder. She put a hand down to steady herself and discovered what she thought was a boulder was actually a frozen white cow.

"Mae!" she gasped, fearful that her friend had suffered a similar fate.

Jill dove into the forest, panic giving her strength. She followed the tracks deeper in, past an ever-increasing number of faerie creatures frozen in grotesque poses on the ground or hung from the trees.

Jill stopped, drawing ragged breaths. Her side hurt, and her legs were numb below the knees. Her toes and feet did not seem to exist anymore. She heard baying and sharp howls behind her.

The Cŵn Annwn were coming.

She lifted the sword and turned back to the tracks, determined to reach Mae before the red-eared fiends pulled her down.

She entered a small clearing. In front of her was a frozen man sitting on a throne that grew from a giant tree. Behind her, the sounds of barking and baying increased. Jill turned and lifted the sword, prepared to meet the threat.

The first of the white hounds burst into the clearing and pulled up short, seemingly surprised to encounter a living creature.

Jill screamed and charged. The lead hound rushed her, growling. She attacked, slashing down with the sword. Her arms and shoulders registered the shock of the blade digging into her opponent and striking the bones. There was a sickening thunk, and black blood flew through the air, covering Jill and the other hounds.

Jerking the blade loose, she stumbled, going to one knee in the snow as two of the hounds recovered from their surprise and attacked. The first one impaled himself on her blade, wrenching the weapon from her hand. The second struck at her face with its yellow teeth.

Jill jammed her arm into its mouth. She felt its teeth punch through her coat, reopening the blade wound from the battle in the faerie court. Jill fumbled in her coat for her baton as the hound's momentum knocked her onto her back. She rolled the hound over and drove her knee into its soft belly. The creature howled in pain, letting go of her arm. Jill sprang backward, stumbling to her feet, her baton drawn and extended. She shook the hair out of her eyes and turned quickly, looking for more opponents.

Two of the Cŵn Annwn lay dead in the snow. A third hound was crawling away, giving a low whine. The others were nowhere to be seen.

Collapsing her baton and placing it in her back pocket, she stepped to the hound she had stabbed. Placing a booted foot on the corpse, she jerked the sword free. Jill turned back toward the trail of what she hoped were Mae's footsteps. The tracks stopped suddenly near the back of the frozen throne, at the beginning of what appeared to be a path deeper into the forest.

Jill shivered. The cold was working through her coat, while post-battle cool down and blood loss were sapping her body heat. She turned in a circle, seeking some sign of Mae or any living creature.

In the crook of the limbs of a dormant birch tree, neatly folded and stacked, lay a complete set of clothes. Jill reached up and pulled the stack of clothing down to examine it. Blue jeans, wool socks, a blue sweater, bra, panties, a heavy coat and boots. Jill recognized the sweater and coat Mae had worn when she had visited Jill's office.

Panic settled on Jill, driving all concerns of death, all the pain from her injuries, all the worries about how to escape Annwn, from her mind. She spun in a frantic circle.

Jill almost missed the sight of Mae, camouflaged by the snow and ice.

"No. Oh please, no," Jill whispered, horrified. Her whisper turned to a raw scream. "No!"

Mae's limp, naked body hung from the giant oak tree that was the frozen man's throne. She was impaled through the chest by one of the tree's sharp, icy branches. There was a dark, ugly puncture wound in her stomach and a long gash along one of her pale arms. There was no bleeding, though Mae's torso and injured arm were covered in dry, dark blood.

Jill collapsed, falling to her knees in the snow. She hung her head and let the tears fall. It was over. She had failed. Mae was dead. Soon she would be dead as well, frozen in the wastes of Annwn.

She rubbed the tears away and looked up at Mae. "I'm sorry. I'm so sorry."

Then she turned away from the sight of Mae's body and placed her head in her hands. She took two deep breaths as her shoulders began to shake. A third deep breath. She looked up at the sunless sky and screamed, a raw, primal explosion of fury and grief. Jill shouted out her anger and pain to the uncaring world around her. She screamed until her throat failed and her cries became nothing more than a series of hoarse gasps. Snow started to fall, and the wind began to increase, strong freezing gusts driving heavy, wet flakes at Jill.

"No," she rasped out. "It doesn't end like this. I said I'd bring Mae home, and you are not going to stop me. You can't have her. You're not keeping her."

Her body was numb from grief and cold, but she made herself move. Jill walked up to the tree from which Mae's naked body was suspended. Jill could only reach to Mae's knees, could not get enough leverage to pull Mae off the limb holding her. Jill lifted the sword.

She was not going to leave Mae hanging from a tree like some rotting piece of meat in an abandoned butcher shop. Jill swung the sword over-handed. It hit the branch, and chips of ice flew. Jill swung again, more frozen shards scattering. With a snarl of rage, Jill began chopping at the wood as fast as she could swing the weapon, ignoring the burning in her arms, the exhaustion in her shoulders. She hacked at the tree limb mercilessly, oblivious to the ice chips cutting into her face, neck, and hands with every stroke. The skin on her palms and fingers began to blister and tear under the unfamiliar strain.

Jill squeezed the blood-slick hilt and continued her attack. A shard of ice struck her left eye. Jill cried out in pain and defiance and swung again, the blade biting into the frozen wood of the tree.

"Give her back to me!" Jill screamed, hitting the tree again and again. "Give her back to me, damn you!"

She heard the crack of wood and stopped her work. Another crack. Jill saw the limb start to bend downward, breaking under the strain of Jill's furious chopping and Mae's limp weight. She dropped the sword and reached for Mae, grabbing her around the waist as the limb snapped. The point of the limb jabbed Jill in the back as Mae's body slumped over Jill's shoulder.

Jill struggled, if not to keep her feet, then to at least not collapse completely. She let Mae's weight drive her down to her knees. Jill settled and shifted Mae off of her shoulder, moving Mae's still form into her lap.

"I've got you. I've got you," Jill said, pushing Mae's thin blond hair from her face and leaving a red streak along Mae's cold cheek. "I've got you. We're going home."

Jill reached down, her hand sticky with her own blood, and gripped the limb protruding from Mae's chest. She pulled. It slipped from Mae with little resistance. Jill threw it to the side and hugged

Mae's limp body close, rocking Mae back and forth, rubbing her ruined, bloody left hand and arm across the open wound on Mae's exposed back.

"We're going home. I'll carry you back. I just need to rest for a moment."

"Cold," a tiny voice said against her breast.

Jill looked down, looked directly into Mae's dark brown eyes. "Mae?"

"Cold."

Jill watched, amazed and confused, as Mae's wounds closed, leaving her pale skin whole, though scarred and smeared with blood.

"You came for me," Mae said, shivering.

"Damn straight I came for you." Jill smiled through her tears as Mae sat up and looked around at her surroundings. "I've got your clothes." Jill nodded toward the pile of clothing sticking out of the snow.

They both crawled to the pile, where Jill helped Mae dress. Once she was clothed and no longer shivering as violently, Jill saw Mae give her a serious head-to-toe once over.

Mae frowned at her. "Jesus, Jill, you're bleeding all over the place."

"Yeah, I know." Hearing Mae speak the words made it real for Jill. She tipped over, blood loss and exhaustion finally taking their toll now that her adrenaline was no longer pumping. Being prone felt good. She thought she might just curl up and nap, only for a moment. She could rest now, Mae was alive.

Someone shook her. She looked at Mae out of her right eye. Her left one was swollen shut and not working right for some reason.

"Come on. Sit up," Mae said to her. "Let's get your coat on."

Jill tried to rise to a sitting position, but decided it was too much work. "I'm good right here," she rasped out.

She felt Mae yank her arm, dragging her to a sitting position. "No, you're not. Come on, Jill. You can't die now, not here, not in this place."

Jill shook her head as she felt Mae work the sleeves of her coat over her arms and button it up. "Tired. Cold."

"I know. I am too, but you've got to stay with me. I need you to stay awake."

"Too hard," Jill whispered. She felt someone tug at her arms, trying to make her stand.

"Come on, Jill. We're not home yet. I need you to show me where you came in."

She climbed wearily to her feet. She had said she would bring Mae home. They were not home yet. She had to keep moving. She leaned gently on Mae's shoulder, trying to minimize the amount of weight she was putting on the smaller woman. She peered through one blurry eye at the woods around her. "This way."

Jill led Mae past the dead Cŵn Annwn and out of the forest. She walked in what she hoped was the direction she had come from, swaying and weaving despite Mae's help. They reached the beginning of Jill's track.

"I came in here. There was a door." She slid off Mae's shoulder and collapsed to the ground. Jill tried to remain sitting up as Mae looked around at the arctic expanse. It was a losing battle. She closed her eye and fell with a dull thump into the snow.

"Jill! Jill, get up!"

"Can't."

She felt her head being lifted. It settled on something soft.

"Jill, you can't die. You have to sit up. Come on, stay with me."

"Can't. Too tired." Jill tried to snuggle closer to the soft thing she was lying on. She thought she heard a bell in the distance.

The voice above her turned fierce. "Don't you dare die on me, Jill Hall! Not now, not after you've come this far. You can't just walk into the Underworld, rescue me and then die. That won't do, it won't do at all, do you understand me?"

The sound of the bell was getting closer. Jill cracked open her good eye. Mae's face was inches from her own. A tear rolled down Mae's nose. Jill felt it land on her cheek.

"Mae—"

Mae gazed down at her. "I can't very well take you for a lover if you die on me, now can I?"

"Mae, listen to me—"

"You're not dying! I need you, you silly thing."

Jill smiled. "Need you too. Now be quiet and listen. I think our ride's coming. There's change in the left-hand pocket of my jeans."

Mae's face looked confused for a minute, and then she must have heard the bell as well. Jill turned her head in time to see the big yellow streetcar roll up and open its bright red door. The sign on the front read: "Malveaux Express. Eastbound."

Jill felt Mae reach into her pocket. She closed her eyes as her smile widened. *I finally convinced Mae to get into my pants,* a tired part of her brain thought.

Jill felt herself being lifted up. She opened her eye and tried to laugh. She had done it. She had charged into the wastes of Annwn. She had found Mae and brought her out alive. They were going home. *I did it!*

She passed out.

Mae would have been more amused by Jill's nearly incoherent mumblings of "Clang, clang, clang went the trolley," if Jill didn't look like she had just been sucked into a jet engine and spit out the other side.

Mae was not sure how she managed to lift Jill into the streetcar on her own. *It's amazing what sheer panic can do for you.* Once they were both safely in the warm car and the car started moving, Mae turned all her attention to her injured friend.

Jill was covered in blood, most of it her own, Mae guessed. Her black hair was a tangled mess of sticky, dried strands. Her face and neck were riddled with tiny cuts and scrapes, like she had been standing in front of a window that exploded.

Mae was afraid to even try to assess the damage to Jill's left eye. The lid was closed, bruised black and red and swollen shut. An unpleasant-looking greenish-yellow substance was seeping out under the eyelid. Mae feared Jill's eye would be matted shut, but perhaps that was a mercy.

She managed to work Jill out of her coat, trying to inspect her friend for any possible life-threatening injuries, though Mae was damned if she knew what she would do if she found any.

Jill's left arm was her first concern. There was a long slash down her forearm, with puncture wounds around that injury. The whole mess was oozing blood. There was a shallow, superficial cut on Jill's right hip, just enough to break the jeans and draw a thin line across the skin. Jill's jeans were done for, but the cut itself had stopped bleeding on its own. The small puncture wound on Jill's back did not look serious, though Mae could not be sure because of all the crusted blood.

Jill's hands were ruined. There was no other word for it. The skin on the palms was a flayed and tattered mess. The backs of her hands were covered in cuts and abrasions. Mae wished she had something clean and soft to wrap the wreckage in. Infection was too real a danger at this point.

Mae had never felt so helpless. She stroked Jill's bloody forehead.

"Oh, Jill. What happened to you?"

Mae knew Jill needed immediate medical attention—serious, trauma unit medical attention. She had no idea what she would tell the doctors—or the police when they inevitably showed up—but that did not matter.

"Keep doing that," Jill muttered, keeping her eyes closed. "Feels good."

Mae continued her ministrations. "Hang on. I'm going to get you to the emergency room. We're going to get you fixed up."

"'Kay." Jill mumbled. "How are you?"

"Don't worry about me. I'm fine." Mae paused, unsure how to put into words what she was feeling. "You came for me."

"'Course I did. Water?"

Mae picked up the water bottle she had found in Jill's coat in the same pocket as her baton, and opened the cap. She held Jill's head steady against the sway of the streetcar as she touched the mouth of the bottle to Jill's lips and slowly poured. Jill swallowed and licked her lips.

"More, please."

Mae repeated the process. Jill swallowed and took a handful of deep, ragged breaths and gave a small plaintive moan, her face scrunched up in pain. Mae reached out and stroked Jill's head again, trying to soothe her while fighting down the panic rising in her. She had no idea what type of internal injuries Jill might have suffered. Mae felt the streetcar begin to accelerate, as if it were responding to her sense of fear and urgency.

"We're almost there. Just hang on a little longer." Mae had no idea how far they were from anything, or how quickly she would be able to summon help once they got there.

"Hurts," Jill whispered.

"I know. I know it hurts. Just a few more minutes, and we'll have some help. I'll take care of you. I promise."

Jill nodded and swallowed. "I know."

"You should try to sleep until we get to the hospital."

"Too scared I might not wake up."

The thumping of the brakes made Mae look up and grab the baton from where she had left it on the seat. She could not see anything outside of her window. The streetcar stopped. Mae tried to figure out how to get Jill off the vehicle without hurting her more. She was turning to ask the conductor and motorman for aid, when the door opened, and help rushed aboard.

Kravis, a bloody bandage on his head and another on his left arm, strode onto the car. "How in the name of the Seven Guardians did you escape Annwn?"

"I need help. Jill's been injured."

Without hesitation he dropped the sword and rucksack he carried and walked directly to Mae and Jill. "Don't worry. There's someone here who can take care of her," Kravis said. He turned back toward the front of the streetcar. "Lady Mirallyn! We need you here now. Jill is injured."

"Where is she?" a soft female voice asked.

Mae looked up. Standing in the aisle in front of the smaller Ellie, wearing a blood-covered gown and a pensive look, was a woman who Mae only knew through a faded photograph.

Mae stood to face her mother.

"You?" Mae asked.

The woman nodded, pushing past Mae to kneel next to Jill. "Yes."

Mae stood, shaking for several seconds. She looked from her mother to Jill and back again. "I—I can't do this right now. We need to get Jill to a hospital."

The car began to move again, rolling and picking up speed.

Ellie reached out and touched Mae's arm. "Your friend will be tended by someone who can help her more than any of your doctors could."

"But—"

"Mae, I need you to please trust me."

Mae looked closely at Ellie. Her gown was covered in green blood, her face bruised. She was leaning on a wooden cane as the car swayed and rattled along.

"What happened to you?" Mae asked.

"Later," Ellie said. She nodded toward Jill and Mae's mother. "For now, we need to assist Mirallyn and seek safe haven."

Mae turned back to Jill. The woman—her mother, Mirallyn—held her hand over Jill's eyes chanting softly. Kravis was binding Jill's injuries with strips torn from Mirallyn's gown. He looked up at Mae and nodded to the makeshift bandage on Jill's arm.

"Hold this tightly," he said. "Do not disturb the *swynwraig*."

"The what?"

"The wizard. Mirallyn. Now hold this."

Mae collapsed the baton and slipped it into her pocket. She pressed on the bandage Kravis had indicated. "Jill's eye, it's—"

"I believe I can save it, daughter," Mirallyn said.

Mae gave her mother a sharp look. "Then save it and help her, but once Jill's out of danger, you and I are going to talk."

"Yes, we will," Mirallyn said. "There is much to explain."

Mae frowned. There were a million things she wanted to say to her mother. She wanted to yell, wanted to cry, wanted to demand the woman explain herself. But the most important thing at the moment was Jill, who was mumbling and whimpering.

"Ma'am."

Mae turned toward the voice. The conductor, Lowry, was standing next to her.

"Yes?"

"We need a destination."

"Home," Mae said without a second thought. She could get Jill to the townhouse and call for real help, and damn whatever voodoo her mother thought she was working. Jill needed a real doctor.

"No!" Kravis said. "Your home will be watched by the hounds. The magicians will swoop down on us in an instant."

Mae rounded on the short faerie. "Jill needs to be in an emergency room!"

"I can heal her injuries," Mirallyn said.

"I don't even know you! You left me! Why should I trust anything you say?"

"Mae—" Ellie said softly.

"We need to hide," Kravis growled.

"Lake house," Jill whispered. "I have the keys in my coat."

"Jill—" Mae said, leaning over her mother. "Jill, you need a hospital. And the Arnesons live on the lake. I don't think we should be that close to them."

"Trust me. Your mother can heal me, I've seen her heal Kravis, but we need someplace where no one will find us," Jill gasped. "No one is at the lake house. It's a good mile from the Arneson place and tucked off the road." Jill took a raspy breath. "Please, Mae. Trust me."

Mae swallowed and took a deep breath. She could see Jill pleading with her one good eye. Mae nodded and turned back to Lowry. "Conductor, please take us to Jill's house on Lake Minnetonka."

"Yes, ma'am." The car accelerated.

Mae knelt in the aisle, holding the torn cloth over the wound on Jill's arm while Mirallyn worked on Jill's other injuries. Ellie pawed through Jill's coat, producing a set of keys just as the brakes on the streetcar began to thump.

The car stopped, and the red door opened. Ellie zipped out the door in a blur, keys in hand. Mirallyn wordlessly followed, as Kravis lifted the now-unconscious Jill, leaving Mae scrambling to catch up. As she reached the door, the conductor called out to her.

"Miss! Your bag!"

Mae turned. The conductor was holding her battered messenger bag. "Where did you find it?"

"You left it behind after the accident. We've been holding it for you."

Mae took the bag, slinging it over her shoulder. "Thank you."

The conductor touched the bill of his cap. "My pleasure. Good evening to you, ma'am."

Mae stepped out of the car and it rolled away. She turned and looked at the two-story cottage down a short snow-covered lane.

"We have a problem," Kravis said, shifting Jill's limp form in his arms.

He nodded toward the pack, a dozen hounds between them and the hoped-for safety of the lake house Mae and her companions needed to reach. The white hounds howled and growled, their red ears slicked back on their heads. Their eyes glowed red, their teeth gleamed in the early dawn light.

Mae drew the baton from her pocket. There was no point in running. The pack would pull them down before they could ever reach any safe place, and the streetcar was already gone.

Kravis was holding Jill, Ellie was hurt and limping, and Mae didn't trust her newly found mother. Overcome by a horrible urge to hit something, Mae set her sights on the hound she thought was the pack leader. Mae snapped the baton to full extension, screamed and rushed the Cŵn Annwn.

The pack scattered before her like dead leaves in the wind, their barks and howls of triumph suddenly turning to yowls of fear and confusion. Mae bore down on the pack leader, weapon raised, holding eye contact with him as she charged. The hound tried to turn and slink away, but was too slow. He rolled over as Mae loomed over him, staring at her with frightened eyes, showing his belly in submission.

Mae checked her downward swing, and the hound cringed and whined. She looked up at the rest of the pack. They milled about among the snowy trees and shrubs, whining, barking in short yips.

The darkness rolled away as the first light of true dawn shone in the east. Mae pressed the end of the baton on the pack leader's throat. The hound looked at her with wide eyes. It whimpered. Mae withdrew the baton from its throat, holding it at the ready.

"Go on then. Get. All of you, get out of here!" Mae yelled.

The pack leader scrambled to all fours and ran for his mates. The entire pack formed up and, with a last look at Mae over their shoulders, turned and raced away, howling and barking.

Mae turned back to the others.

"What the hell happened?" Kravis asked. "One second they were about to rip us apart, and suddenly they're scared of you?"

"I—I'm not entirely sure why they acted that way."

"There is no time to wonder. We need to tend our injured," Mirallyn commanded.

Ellie, Mirallyn and Kravis—the latter still carrying Jill—raced toward the cottage. There was a flash of light as a door opened, and Mae saw Kravis carry Jill into the house. She followed them up the path as quickly as her tired legs would carry her. By the time she reached the door, Ellie was there to meet her.

"Mae?" Ellie said softly, embracing her. "Let's get you inside."

"Jill—"

"Don't worry. She's going to be okay."

Mae started to shiver. Now that she was someplace relatively safe, she let her fears free. She went to pieces.

Mae wrapped her arms around Ellie and burst into wracking sobs, her entire body shaking from the force of her emotions. Mae did not know how long she stood there, sobbing out her sorrow while the small faerie woman held her tightly and spoke soothing words.

A strong hand took her arm, and Mae felt herself being led into the cottage. Ellie and Kravis helped her out of her bloody, torn coat. Mae allowed herself to be settled in the middle of a low couch. Kravis placed her bag on the floor near her feet and draped a blanket over her shoulders as Ellie pressed a hot drink into her hands.

Mae looked around. She was in a room that was warm, not just because of its rustic woodlands decor, but also because of the cheerful-looking fire in the fireplace. Ellie sat to her right, perched on the edge of the couch to avoid crushing her wings. Mae took a sip from the cup in her hand. It was hot chocolate. She wondered idly how Ellie had found and made it so quickly but decided she didn't care right now. She closed her eyes and exhaled as a little shiver ran down her spine. "Promise me Jill's going to be okay."

Ellie started cleaning Mae's face and neck with a kitchen washcloth. "I can promise you that Mirallyn will do everything she can for Jill."

Mae nodded and opened her eyes, glancing around the house. She noticed wooden stairs going up along the wall to her left. She glanced up and saw a loft. "Is she upstairs?"

"Yes," Ellie said, starting on Mae's hands. "Kravis took her up to one of the bedrooms. Mirallyn is tending to her, and Kravis is out making sure nothing lurks outside. What happened to you?"

"I think I died."

"In Annwn?"

Mae paused and frowned. "How did you know I was in Annwn?"

"The sign on the streetcar said it was coming from Annwn." Ellie fidgeted, dropping the blood-stained towel on the table in front of them. "I saw the hounds take you from the wreckage. I—we were all surprised to find you on the streetcar. You should not have been able to escape Annwn without Mirallyn's aid."

"I wish those cars had never revealed themselves to me."

Mae could not keep the bitterness out of her voice. She took another sip of her chocolate and looked down at the rug. Visions of Jill permanently maimed and scarred filled her mind. She felt Ellie place a hand on her knee. She glanced up as a new thought passed through her brain.

"How did you know Jill's name?"

"She, ah, she arrived at the scene of the wreck on another car."

"Don't tell me you sent Jill to rescue me?"

"Once she found out where you were, she was determined to find you. Someone had to travel to Annwn to retrieve you. We did try to impress on her how dangerous the journey would be. That it was an undertaking which could well lead to her death. She went of her own free will."

Mae glared at Ellie, who was now fingering her blue hair nervously. "She could have died! She still might! What the hell were you thinking?"

"She wouldn't leave you in the Underworld!" Ellie snapped, a stray tear rolling down her cheek. "Jill would have struck out on her own searching for you eventually. This way we were able to provide her some small amount of aid." Ellie gave her a tired sigh. "Would you have stayed home if it had been Jill taken by the hounds?"

Mae was quiet for several seconds. "No," she finally said. "No. I would have done the same as Jill. I would have been scared shitless, and I probably would have died of fright without doing anyone any good, but I would have tried."

"Of course, you would have, so please don't be mad."

Mae sighed and leaned back, resting her head on the couch cushions. "How did it all come to this?"

Ellie patted her knee. "You tell me."

Mae spoke calmly about her fight for life on the light rail train and the subsequent accident on the streetcar. She told Ellie everything Death had explained to her.

"And then—and then he touched me and the world exploded for a time."

"Death touched you?"

Mae looked up at the question. At some point during her story, Kravis had returned, sitting across from the couch in one of the large, overstuffed chairs.

Mae nodded. "Yes. It was just a featherlight brush on the cheek."

Kravis frowned.

"What?" Mae asked. She turned to Ellie. "What aren't you telling me?"

Ellie's eyes widened. "You're sure?"

"Yes," Mae said, confused. "It was—it was nice. I felt—I can't exactly explain it," she finished with a slight blush and a shrug.

Ellie turned toward her and took a deep breath, obviously steeling herself to tell Mae something terrible.

"Mae. You should be dead. Death *touched* you. Do you understand what that means? He came for you."

Mae looked at her companions. Kravis had a crazed grin on his face. Ellie looked horrified.

Mae looked at the floor and frowned in thought. There was something in her memory, something she had not had a chance to examine since Jill had rescued her. Mae looked closely at the memory. Death *had* touched her. She remembered the feel of his fingers on her skin, the sudden burst of sensations that blazed through her body. She had tasted sound and felt the scent of hounds and heard the trees and seen...

She had a vague recollection of undressing, of a voice telling her she would not need her clothes where she was going.

And then he had lifted her up and slammed her body into a tree, impaling her.

Mae looked at her chest, reached up and placed a hand on the spot where the limb had burst through her body. She took a pair of shallow, ragged breaths.

"I died," she whispered. She looked up at the others. "I died."

Ellie put her hands on her mouth. "Oh, Mae..."

Mae sniffed. "I died and I—I need to use the bathroom. And I need to see Jill."

"I think I saw a bathroom this way," Ellie said.

Mae let Ellie lead her upstairs. She showed Mae the door to a bedroom.

"I'm afraid right now it's a mess, but we'll have it ready by the time you finish in the bathroom. Jill should be cleaned up and ready to see you by then. Just go in and be with her."

"Thank you—"

"It's my pleasure. I'll root around and find you something to sleep in tonight and some clothes for tomorrow," Ellie said. She paused for a minute, and threw Mae a sly smile. "You don't mind sharing with Jill, do you? Kravis could make up the couch for you—"

"I don't think that will be necessary," Mae replied, blushing. "I'm sure Jill and I will be fine."

Mae finished in the bathroom as quickly as possible. She desperately wanted a shower, but the urge to make sure Jill was safe and alive overrode any desire to stop and shower first. She opened the door to the bedroom and peered inside, trying to be quiet in case Jill was sleeping.

Mae looked around the room. There was a pile of crimson-stained sheets on the floor, next to Jill's bloody clothes.

"Hey, you," Jill whispered from the bed.

Jill was propped up by a pair of large pillows behind her back. Her hair and face were washed, the blood and mess cleaned away. She wore a flannel bathrobe so large it threatened to swallow her. Mae could see a flannel shirt peeking out from underneath the robe. She had a piece of white cloth covering her left eye, though Mae could not see how it was held in place. Jill's face was covered in small, angry looking nicks and cuts. Her left arm was wrapped in a gauzy bandage, as were her hands. Her skin was pale, and there was an unpleasant, metallic smell clinging to her. Mae thought she was the loveliest sight in all existence.

Mae sat on the bed and reached out, placing her right hand on Jill's face. She ran her thumb over Jill's cheek. "You look a lot better."

Jill smiled at her, wide and cocky. "You should have seen the other guys."

"You're quite ferocious."

Jill gave her a serious look. "They were between me and what I wanted."

Mae looked into Jill's pale blue eye. "Jill—Jill, I—"

Mae licked her dry lips and pulled Jill closer. She reached up and placed her left hand on Jill's cheek, then glanced down at Jill's lips, inches from her own. They were too far away. She brought them to her own lips; tentative, shy, unsure of what the other woman's reaction would be.

Mae need not have worried. Jill kissed her in return, at first softly and then harder, bringing her bandaged hands up and around Mae's head and shoulders. Mae held the kiss for a moment longer before breaking it off and placing her forehead against Jill's.

"You came for me," Mae whispered. "You brought me back."

"Actually, you're the one who got us out of there."

"No, Jill Hall," a female voice said. "You brought her back from the land of the dead. Your blood, hot and mortal, poured into Mae's wounds and awoke her stilled heart."

Mae turned to look at her mother. The room seemed too quiet, too still to her senses, as if the cottage itself were holding its breath. "Jill, this is my mother."

"We've met," Jill said. "She opened the door into Annwn for me."

Mae turned back to her mother. "I don't know if I should yell at you or thank you."

"Why don't you thank her for patching me up?" Jill said softly.

Mirallyn looked past Mae to Jill. "Truly, Jill Hall, it was my duty and an honor to heal the one who saved my daughter." Mirallyn turned her eyes to Mae. "I know you and your love have some catching up to do. We can discuss anything you desire, after you both have rested."

Mae nodded. "I think—yes. I think—" Mae frowned at her mother. "You *will* be here in the morning?" she asked, her voice tense.

"I swear to you, daughter, upon my magic, that I shall be here and prepared to explain my actions to you when you are ready."

Mae nodded. "In the morning. Right now, I just want to crawl into bed and rest."

She watched her mother, the woman she had a million questions for, step out of the room with a slight nod.

Jill wrinkled her nose and laughed. "In that case, you should go take a shower because you, my dear, stink."

"I've been dead, what can you expect?"

"Death does not preclude proper hygiene," Jill said with a straight face.

Mae laughed. "I'd ask you to wash my back, but...."

"These bandages will be off in the morning."

Ellie cleared her throat, reminding Mae and Jill of her presence. "I'll leave whatever clothes I find for you on the bed."

"There's another robe hanging from the back of the bathroom door," Jill added.

Mae slipped into the guest bathroom. She looked at herself in the mirror. Ellie had done an admirable job of cleaning her face and neck, but there was still dried blood in her hair. Her sweater was ruined, torn on the sleeves, with a bullet hole at her stomach and dried black blood caking the garment stiff.

Mae undressed, dropping her soiled clothes on the floor. She would pick them up later. For now, she wanted a shower. Mae turned the water on, making it as hot as she could stand.

She let the hot water clean her body, sweeping away the blood, grime, sweat and death of the last two days. Mae watched the dark mess swirl down the drain as she lathered on soap and shampoo from the bottles resting in the shower caddy.

She had seen her family while hanging from that frozen oak tree. Her grandma and grandpa Malveaux had been there first, telling her how proud they were of their little girl. Then her father had come to her. She remembered crying on him, just as she had after nightmares when she was a child. He told her that her mother loved them both, but she had to go away to protect them all. He said she would be waiting when Mae returned, to explain why things had to be the way they were. Mae wiped her eyes. He had loved her mother so much. It was the only reason she had not exploded in a ball of fury when her mother had appeared at the bedroom door. And then he had told her to forgive herself for things that were not her fault, but merely unfortunate and tragic. She sighed as the water rushed over her.

She had spoken to other dead people as well—people like Minneapolis Police Sergeant Mary Alice Dean, wife and mother of two small sons—who had lost their lives because of Hodgins and others like him.

Mae leaned forward, letting the hot jets of water caress the back of her neck and shoulders. She watched the last of the blood and dirt vanish, leaving soapy water in its wake as she rinsed her body.

Hodgins and his ilk believed their wealth and magic made them above normal mortals. Their greed and indifference to life allowed them to destroy fae and mortal alike with no regard to the pain they caused. In their minds, as long as their own desires were met, their actions were justified.

Mae ran a firm hand over her breasts and stomach. The wounds had healed, but there were pale scars where she had been bitten by faerie hounds, accidentally shot by a police officer, and impaled on a tree by Death. She gave her body a rueful smile. Scars were good.

They were tangible reminders. She would carry them for the rest of her life and she would *never* forget what Hodgins and his cronies had done to her, had done to countless others.

The trail of death they had left in their wake stopped here and now.

Mae turned the water off and reached for the towel. She dried off and slipped into the white terry-cloth bathrobe, tying it around her waist. She continued to work at her hair with the towel as she left the steamy bathroom and walked back into the bedroom.

"Clean?"

Mae looked at the bed. The covers were kicked to one side and Jill was lying on the sheet, wearing a large black-and-red flannel shirt Mae suspected belonged to Jill's brother or father. The shirt covered Jill to midthigh, leaving the rest of her legs bare. Jill was smiling madly.

Mae returned the smile. "Yeah. I feel about a thousand percent better about life."

"You smell about a thousand percent better too."

"That was the plan." Mae sat on the edge of the bed and finished drying her hair with the towel. "Ellie was supposed to leave me some clothes."

"She must have forgotten."

Mae glared playfully at Jill, her wet hair falling onto her face. "Whatever shall I do?"

"I guess you'll have to go without."

Mae slipped into bed, still wearing the bathrobe, and turned off the lamp. She grabbed the covers and brought them up over her and Jill. "I thought you were supposed to be resting?"

Jill rolled over to face her. "I'm not as damaged as all that."

Mae shifted closer to Jill and draped an arm over her, pulling her closer. "Let's wait until you get those bandages off your hands."

"Got plans for these hands, do you?"

Mae grinned. "Maybe."

"Well then, how about instead of—"

Mae stopped whatever it was Jill was about to suggest by placing her lips firmly on Jill's. They kissed gently, and when Mae felt Jill's tongue, her lips parted without a thought. Mae ran a hand down Jill's side, over the swell of her hip, past the hem of the shirt and along her bare leg.

Jill broke the kiss. "I wouldn't have gotten so banged-up rescuing you, if I'd known things were going to go down like this."

"It's okay. I'm just being friendly, not looking for a full-blown tumble. That can come later."

Jill gave her a mock pout.

Mae laughed and kissed her again. "Later, after the bandages are off. You should be resting, Miss Hall."

Jill laughed. "Fine, I'll get some rest. We'll take this up another night. It'll give me a chance to shave my legs."

Mae drew Jill closer to her. She did not think she would need to sleep after being dead for who knew how long. She sighed as Jill started to snore softly. It was the most soothing sound she had ever heard.

She thought she'd close her eyes, just for a minute.

Sunday, 29th of October

MAE AWOKE. HER BATHROBE was twisted, the knot around her waist was still tight, but the rest of the heavy garment was in disarray, so much so that Mae might as well have not been wearing it.

She sat up and looked around the room, blinking away sleep, before turning on the lamp.

Jill was not in the bed, but the clothes Ellie had promised her had magically appeared on Jill's side of the mattress. Mae slipped from under the covers, untied the knot on the robe and let it fall. She dressed in the faded black long-sleeved T-shirt and a pair of jeans that had seen the inside of a washing machine a few too many times. Heavy gray wool socks went over her feet. It was all several sizes too big for her, making her roll back the cuffs of both the shirt and jeans. She brushed her hair, located a safety pin in a drawer, heavy enough to help hold the jeans on her body, and went in search of everyone else.

She found Jill and her mother at the kitchen table, a steaming mug in front of each woman. Jill still wore the flannel shirt. Mae saw she was also wearing a pair of black sweatpants. Her mother was in clean clothing as well, a heavy dress of green, trimmed in white with a high collar. Jill's bandages were piled on the table, stiff with blood and some kind of green substance. The sharp metallic smell Mae had noted on Jill last night was thick in the air. Her mother was examining Jill's hands.

Jill looked up at her. "Good morning, sleepy-head. Or actually, good afternoon."

"There is tea on the stove," her mother added, never taking her eyes from Jill's hands.

Mae found the cups and filled one with the dark brown liquid. She took a sip. It was slightly bitter, but Mae had no idea where to find the sugar. Jill noticed the face she made and nodded toward the counter. Mae followed Jill's single-eyed gaze, finding a canister with a spoon lying next to it. Mae sweetened the tea to her taste and settled at the table.

"How are they?" Mae asked, pointing at Jill's hands.

Jill flexed her fingers. "They'll be fine."

Mae reached out and took one of Jill's hands in her own, turning it palm up. The skin was healed, though it was still red and angry looking.

"I'm so sorry," Mae said, tracing a line of scars on Jill's palm with one finger. Mae glanced at the vivid red wound on Jill's arm. The bite and cut were healed as well, though they too would leave a disfiguring mark.

"They still work. That's the important thing." Jill gave her a serious look. "I know I'm not the only one who ended up permanently scarred."

Mae sighed. "I just wish..." she shrugged, unable to voice what she was feeling.

"If wishes were horses—" Jill said.

"—then beggars would ride," Mae finished. "What about your eye?"

"We were just discussing that," Mae's mother said. "I am unsure what is going to happen."

"You still *have* your eye, right?"

"Yes. It's just that Mirallyn's concerned about…well, about magical side effects."

Mae looked to her mother for an explanation.

"When a Champion receives a wound such as Jill's while in magical lands, especially in service to their charge or their love, they are usually changed somehow."

Jill leaned into Mae. "Apparently, I'm a Champion."

Mae frowned at Jill. She turned back toward her mother. "Changed how?"

"There is no way to know until I remove the covering."

Jill picked up her cup, took a sip, set the cup down. "Mirallyn and I both think it's a good idea to wait until everyone gets back."

Mae nodded in agreement. "Where are Ellie and Kravis?

"Ellie went to check with our cousins about sanctuary. Kravis has gone to retrieve some things of importance."

Mae considered this. She decided it was a good time for a private conversation between herself and her mother. "Why did you have to leave us?" There was no accusation in Mae's voice. She had spoken with her father. She knew there *was* a reason.

Jill cleared her throat nervously. "If you two need—"

"No," Mae said resting a gentle hand on Jill's knee under the table. "I want you to stay. I need you to stay."

"In that case, I'll pour more tea," Jill said, standing.

Mae turned back to her mother. "I know you had a reason."

"I had to hide your sister."

Mae frowned at this revelation. "My what?"

Her mother reached across the table and placed one of her small hands on one of Mae's. "Sister. You are twins, born on the same night, but you and Fay are in no way identical."

"I have a sister?" Mae was dazed at this news. "What's she like, my sister?"

"You would not know she is your twin. She is but a third of your age."

Mae's eyebrows rose. "She's twelve?"

"Yes. Time flows oddly for the Tylwyth Teg of Llysllyn, and her strong fae blood adds to the effect."

Mae nodded, her face set in a neutral mask. She glanced at Jill, who poured tea in all three cups and placed the canister of sugar and a spoon in the middle of the table. Jill sat back down, touching her knee to Mae's under the table in silent support.

"What else?" Mae asked, a slight edge on her voice.

Mirallyn's face reflected pride and concern. "Fay is her name, and fae she is indeed. She is as bright as sunlight on snow, beautiful as spring in the Shining Realms, quick as a hummingbird on the wing, as powerful as the druids of old and curious to the point of recklessness."

"She sounds special."

"She was born to be a Champion, to lead her people to a new dawning."

"But not me?" Mae asked softly.

She watched her mother's pained reaction.

"No," Mae's mother said. "Not you. So, you did not need hiding."

"You know what, I think that's okay," Mae said. "After the last few days, I'm glad I'm just plain old Mae Malveaux."

She watched her mother lean back in her chair and frown in thought. "And yet you and your companion have done more in the last few days to bring the conflict between the circle of mortal mages and the Tylwyth Teg into the open than any before you."

For several moments the three women sat together, each lost in their own thoughts.

"You needed to hide her from the Cŵn Annwn?" Mae asked to fill the sudden silence.

Mirallyn looked up at her. "To a point. I might have been able to hide Fay from the white hounds, at least for a time. The more pressing matter was the circle of mortal mages. They would have sensed the flame of Fay's magic and come for her, eager to make it their own. That, I could not protect her from."

"And you took her—?"

"I took her to my home. To the Llysllyn Court of the Tylwyth Teg."

Jill cleared her throat. "Kravis said she was lost. I'm guessing these mages have her?"

Mirallyn nodded.

Mae gasped. "How did they capture her?"

"Her curiosity. She wanted to walk in the human world, to see the place she was born. She slipped away while her watchers and I were distracted. I suspect the hounds or mages surprised her, snapping her up almost as soon as she set foot in your world."

"And you left her?" Mae ground out.

"What would you have me do, daughter? I cannot go to her myself. That is what her captors desire, and though my powers are formidable for my kind, I would fall against the combined might of their entire circle."

Mae stood up, knocking her chair backward as she leaned on the table.

"Surely, someone could help you," she snarled.

"I sent Kravis, but he was unable to penetrate the mages' stronghold. Their magic is simply too strong."

Mae felt Jill place a hand on her arm, stopping her angry reply.

"You don't have any other allies in your Court, do you?" Jill asked.

"I do not. The late Lord Murlannor barely tolerated Fay. My people hold half-bloods in general disdain. They would have driven us both out, except I am the only one with the strength to hold the door to Annwn and your world closed. That is the only reason they did not kill me after you slipped into Annwn. Those are my charms and guards on the door. As long as I live, the door will stay locked."

Jill frowned. "I was able to get into your lands."

"Because you were brought in by someone the portal recognized. Lady Elliefandi ferch Myfleria, as a member of the Lord's family, could bring in visitors if she chose."

"Wait. *Late* Lord Murlannor?" Jill asked softly, going pale.

Mirallyn nodded.

Mae looked at her companion. "Jill?"

Jill had gone white, her mouth opened slightly, forming a silent *oh* and trembling. After a moment, Jill narrowed her eyes and closed her mouth. Her face took on a hard look. "He was between me and Mae."

Mirallyn nodded. "And he would have blinded you and left you to die. Your actions were both necessary and justifiable."

Mae reached out to Jill, touching her face. "Jill, I don't know what to say."

Jill turned toward her. "I'd do it again." Jill looked to Mirallyn. "How did you escape?"

Mirallyn frowned. "Kravis lifted me to his shoulders and fought his way out of the Hall. I'm afraid he slew a few too many guards while escaping Llysllyn. Even Lady Rhyania of the Falls will not offer him shelter now. Lady Elliefandi slipped out in the confusion. Technically, she is the ruler of Llysllyn with the death of Murlannor, though I suspect the nobles would arrest and banish her for her part in our little adventure." Mirallyn swallowed and continued her tale. "We stopped at my abode long enough to secure a few supplies and necessities before we fled into the human realm.

We found one of Lowry's trains waiting and climbed aboard, hoping to reach some kind of sanctuary. We discovered you both and now we are here." Mirallyn frowned again. "What I would like to know is how you escaped Annwn. Unless a gatekeeper or the Lord of Annwn opened a portal, you should have been trapped and yet we found you on a streetcar."

Before Mae could respond, they heard the front door open and the sounds of heavy breathing. Mae, her mother and Jill walked into the living room. Kravis stood there, looking as if he'd lost a fight with a locomotive and carrying two of Mae's bags.

"There's been a complication," Kravis gasped out.

"What kind of complication?"

Kravis sighed. "Why don't we all settle so I only have to tell the tale once?"

"I shall prepare another pot of tea," Mirallyn said.

By the time they were all seated on various couches and chairs, Mae's anxiety had risen to the point of nervous shakes. She smiled gratefully as Jill reached out and took her hand.

"Is this one of those 'good news and bad news' situations?" Mae asked.

"Mostly just bad news. The nobles of the Llysllyn Court have declared Mirallyn, Ellie and me traitors and enemies. They have impressed upon the Lady Rhyania of the Falls that we are a danger to all our kin and have secured their aid in hunting us."

Mae felt a cold chill. "Shit. Is that what happened to you?"

Kravis nodded gratefully at Mirallyn as she set a steaming cup of tea in front of him. "Yes. I was ambushed by a squad of warriors of Rhyania's Court as I went to the meeting place Ellie and I had agreed upon. I beat the information out of one of the survivors."

"And Lady Elliefandi? She went to speak to Lady Rhyania, what is her fate?" Mirallyn asked in a whisper.

"I don't know," Kravis said, reaching out carefully for his tea. "They might have taken her to the Court for justice. They might have killed her on the spot." He took a long drink of his hot tea and swallowed. "We should stay hidden."

Jill frowned. "Mae might be on a forced vacation, but I have to be at work tomorrow morning."

"And how shall you explain your injuries?" Mirallyn asked.

Mae shook her head. "We need more information." She turned to Jill. "I think hiding here is a great idea, but won't someone notice a group of people suddenly showed up at your family's second home? I'd think the neighbors will come to check it out, or call your family."

Jill shook her head. "No. It's private enough that no one will notice for a few days."

"Jill shouldn't go out in public anyway," Kravis added. "You're not the most popular mortal on the various planes of existence right now, especially with the fae."

Mirallyn agreed. "You slew the Lord of the Llysllyn Court, Jill Hall. My people will be keen to extract revenge for such an act, and they will call upon Lady Rhyania of the Falls to help them. I suspect your death has been ordered by the nobles of the Tylwyth Teg. The Lady of the Falls will honor that order of execution, and members of her Court will seek you out. She might even leverage an agreement with the nobles. If she can bring them your head, they will bend to her will." Lady Mirallyn smiled without humor. "It would be in their best interest for the nobles of Llysllyn to find an honorable way to merge our peoples. With no lord to lead them, the barrier between our lands and mortal shall begin to fade."

"Murlannor has no other heir?" Mae asked.

"Lady Elliefandi is the last member of the royal line not bound to Annwn," Mirallyn explained. "I fear my friend may be dead now," she said in a small, sad voice.

Mae set her cup of tea back on the coffee table and stood from the couch. "I can't sit around, not while they have my sister. Not after they attacked Jill and me." Mae glared at the others. "I won't let them get away with kidnapping and murder."

Mae knew her outburst had caught them all by surprise. She glanced around the room. Her mother's face also held a stubborn set. Kravis frowned. Jill simply looked up at her, waiting to hear what Mae had to say.

Kravis and Mirallyn started talking at once.

"Mae, maybe you—"

"Daughter, I think—"

"Quiet!" Jill snapped. "Let her finish what she's saying."

Mae smiled down at Jill. "Thank you."

Mae sat on the couch and picked up her messenger bag, which had lain forgotten after the events of early morning. She snapped it open. Giving the wreckage of her makeup case and a small bottle of lotion a rueful grimace, she withdrew the manila folder containing Chrysandra Arneson's illegally copied file. She opened it and placed it on the table.

"This file is a person, a little girl. This little girl's family is in on this, and now *she is dead*. This little girl is dead, and her body has been reanimated by Hodgins and these mages. I can't help but think she might not be the only child this has happened to. Now you tell me they have *my sister,* and it doesn't seem to me that any of you are in any position or hurry to do anything about it."

Mirallyn's voice was cool and controlled. "What makes you think *you* are in a position to do anything?"

"I never said I thought I was, but someone has to try. Who else is going to help Fay? The police? The courts?"

"You do not understand," Mirallyn snapped. "We *have* tried. I sent my best weapon to retrieve her, and he was unable to secure

Fay's safety. If I were to attempt to rescue her, they would overwhelm me and destroy Llysllyn through me. They are too powerful."

"You're all thinking about this the wrong way," Mae said. "You are all thinking about making some kind of direct assault on their home."

"And what are you thinking, Mae?" Kravis asked, giving her a shrewd look.

"I'm thinking we break their connection to Annwn."

Mirallyn frowned. "Their connection is through Gwynn ap Nudd. You would have to sever the connection."

"I know," Mae said. "I don't suppose any of you know how they hold power over him?"

Mirallyn closed her eyes in thought. "They must have access to Annwn. A door of their own. If one could find the door and seal it, that might break the connection."

"And if it doesn't?" Kravis asked.

Mae looked to Jill as the black-haired woman cleared her throat.

"Then Gwynn ap Nudd must die," Jill said.

Mae's mother opened her eyes and looked at Jill. "I asked you once, Jill Hall, if you were a Champion, to walk into Annwn and rescue Mae, and you proved your worth in that cause. But what you propose—to slay the greatest Champion of the Tylwyth Teg—that is utter folly."

Jill narrowed her eyes and leaned toward Mirallyn. "The greatest Champion of the Tylwyth Teg is sitting frozen on his throne. I'm pretty sure I could walk up to him and whack him with a heavy stick. I happen to have a heavy stick."

"Let's see if we can find a way to close that door before we go whacking demigods," Mae said.

"I told you," Mirallyn said. "I cannot enter their sphere of influence. If I cannot stand before the door, I cannot close it."

"But the door will respond to your blood?" Mae asked. "Or even someone who carries your blood?"

"Yes. But you have no magic."

"No, I don't. I'm about as magical as a dead gopher."

Mae let the statement hang in the air. After several moments Jill started to laugh, drawing a frown from Mirallyn. Kravis nodded his head, the barest smile on his broad face.

Mae grinned at Jill. "Figured it out?"

"Yeah. All we have to do is break into a mansion full of mages bent on killing both of us, rescue your sister, find the door to Annwn, then hold off the combined might of the hounds and mages while a preteen works a complicated bit of magic to cut off their power. Then we have to escape the mansion and avoid said angry mages."

Mae shook her head, trying to contain the manic laughter threatening to bubble up from her chest. "When you lay it out like that, it does sound kind of stupid, doesn't it?"

"It sounds like *all kinds* of stupid. When do we start?"

"I was thinking we'd continue hiding out here. It puts us closer to them, and gives us a chance to check out the Arneson home, see what shakes down."

"You're both mad," Mirallyn said.

Mae grinned at her mother. "Think about it. You keep saying how they'll have these magical protections to detect and stop you or someone like you, but Jill and I, we're as mundane as mud."

"How do you plan on entering the mansion? They will have normal, mortal means of defense as well," Mirallyn said.

"Alarms and guards for sure," Kravis said, "and the Cŵn Annwn can detect both of you. Neither of you are invisible to the Fair Realms anymore."

Mae held up a hand to stop their protests. "I'm going to do this. It's really just a matter of are you with me or not?"

She turned to Kravis with a questioning look. The nasty smile on the creature's face was answer enough. He would follow her to the end.

"I am afraid for you. I am afraid that I shall lose both of my daughters." Mirallyn sighed. "Yet I hoped you and your Champion would be willing to see this through."

Jill nudged Mae with her shoulder. "I'm a Champion," she whispered again, giggling.

Mae raised an eyebrow at her. "You do realize what typically happens to Champions in these kinds of tales?"

"They get the girl and live happily ever something?"

Mae took both of Jill's hands in hers. "That's what happens in cartoons for children. In the old tales, the Champions would complete their mission, making the world safer, or saving the day, or some other great deed, but they usually died in the process."

"Well, then, we'll have to make sure neither of us dies," Jill said, turning serious. She gave Mae a thoughtful look. "Again, in your case."

Mae nodded. "Yes, I'm in no hurry to die again." She released Jill's hands and sat back with a sigh. Mae looked around at the others and decided to change the subject. "Now, what about Jill's eye?"

"Yes, what about Jill's eye, because this patch is getting itchy," Jill added.

"I think we should go carefully," Lady Mirallyn said. "Perhaps even allow it to remain covered for another night. There is no way of knowing what changes her violent contact with the ice of Annwn might have caused."

"Or I could just take the damned thing off," Jill said, ripping the white padding off her face.

Mae bit her lower lip. The area around the eye was an angry red and the lid was bruised and still slightly swollen. Jill looked down at the floor and opened her eye carefully.

"No heat rays or death beams," Jill said in a shaky voice.

"Let's have a look then." Mae touched Jill's chin and directed Jill to look at her. Jill blinked a few times, trying to let her eye grow accustomed to the light. "Well, that's not so bad," Mae said, examining it carefully.

"Either tell me what you see or get me a mirror."

"It's—well, it's—"

"Yes?" Jill asked. "It's what? Deformed? Enlarged? Growing hair?"

Mae gave her a sympathetic smile. "It's—"

"The iris, it is silver!" Mirallyn said, peering over Mae's shoulder.

Mae tried not to laugh at Jill's surprised expression.

"Shit!" Jill said, looking over her shoulder at Mirallyn.

Mae raised an eyebrow. "What?"

Jill swallowed and frowned. "How am I going to explain this to everyone, and why the hell is Mirallyn glowing blue and silver?"

"Oh," Mae whispered. She looked over her shoulder to Mirallyn for an explanation.

Mirallyn glanced down at Mae, and then leaned forward, looking more closely at Jill's silver eye. "That is the color of my magic when it manifests. Look to Kravis, and tell me what you see."

Jill turned her eyes to the squat faerie creature. "Purple and red. He's glowing purple and red."

"That explains everything," Mirallyn said.

"Well, please explain it to me," Mae said.

"I told you that the injury might alter her somehow."

Jill blew out a long breath. "Yeah, and how was I altered?"

Mirallyn gave both Mae and Jill an amused smile. "Congratulations are in order, Jill Hall, you have picked up a quite useful skill. You can see magic."

Dear Wall,

I am sick. My stomach has felt wrong all day. When they took me down for dinner, I couldn't even work up the energy to be defiant. I think that confused Mr. Hodgins and Elise. I think it made some of the others a little worried.

My stomach was cramping all through dinner. I threw up the pasta and bread almost immediately. "Mother" was very concerned, checking my head for a temperature, asking me questions about my stomach. She wanted to take me to something called "urgent care," but "Grandfather" and Mr. Hodgins told her no. She got a little hysterical and all the plates on the table broke, then she went glassy-eyed and still, staring at me the whole time. Elise led her away.

"Mother" kept looking over her shoulder at me, worried, her tiny little pupils staring at me, like she was seeing something she couldn't describe. I must have worried Mr. Hodgins and "Grandfather" as well. They called the whole group of mages together.

Ilona was there, in her black clothes and heavy makeup. She seemed amused by something after they were done chanting over me and waving their arms and doing all the ridiculous stuff they do. Mr. Hodgins seemed relieved and "Grandfather" looked…uncomfortable.

At bedtime, Elise brought me hot tea. She had Chrysandra in tow. They've freshened her up again. She looks almost like a real girl, except for some missing clumps of hair, black fingernails, and a little red-mottled discoloration on her nose and cheeks. She still smells pretty awful.

The hot liquid soothed the hurt.

Chrysandra asked me in her raspy, dry voice what was wrong with me. I told her what was happening with the cramps, stomach upset, bloated feeling and, since dinner, the blood. Chrysandra laughed. Then she explained what was happening. She promised to bring me the things I would need, told me not to worry—it had happened to her before she died and she would help me.

Do you know how very odd it is to talk about having your first menstruation with a corpse? It was strange and uncomfortable. Still, Chrys might smell funny, but she kept my hair out of my face while I got sick in the toilet. She's become a good friend.

JILL DRIED THE LAST of the dishes and replaced them in the cabinet. She dropped the dishrag across the sink divider and turned to the living room. Mae and her mother were sitting together on the couch, talking quietly. Kravis was perched on the fireplace hearth, the slow rasp of his whetstone along his curved sword eerie and unnerving.

They had spent the afternoon discussing different plans to gain entrance to the Arneson mansion, weighing various pros and cons of each idea while Mirallyn worked to heal Kravis's injuries. The problem was that their most experienced breaking and entering artist was Kravis, and he had tried and failed to enter the mansion three times. By the time dinner rolled around, they were rehashing earlier ideas and everyone needed a break.

Kravis had not lied about being a chef. He and Jill had found several walleye fillets in the freezer. They added rice, opened up a can of corn and made biscuits from a boxed mix, the two working together in the little kitchen to produce a hot and hearty meal.

Jill sighed to herself. She would have to tell Mae about Robert, both his connection to the mages and the invitation to the Halloween party he had extended to Jill. Tonight, Jill decided. She would tell Mae in private.

"I'm thinking about heading to bed," Jill said, joining the others in the living room.

Mirallyn nodded agreement. "I think an early night would do us all good."

"Then we should decide where everyone is sleeping." Mae stood.

Pausing to admire Mae as she stretched, Jill raised an eyebrow and smiled. "You're with me." She had enjoyed having Mae in her bed, even if all they had done was kissing and cuddling before falling asleep.

Mae grinned back at her. "I didn't want to presume."

"The bandages are off." Jill raised her hands.

"Yes. Well," Kravis said, resting his whetstone and sword on the hearth. "I shall sleep down here then. If someone tries to gain entry in the night, I shall hold them here until you three escape."

"I doubt we'll be attacked," Jill said. "Mirallyn can take the second bedroom. It's—"

"I saw where it is," Mirallyn said, rising from the couch. "In the morning Kravis and I shall venture out. We need more information, and I want to know Elliefandi's fate."

"I'm still not sure that's a good idea," Mae said.

Jill took Mae's hand and steered her toward the stairs. "How about we argue more over breakfast?" Now that she had made up her mind, Jill was anxious to get Mae alone and explain about Robert.

Mae smiled widely, probably thinking Jill had something in mind for bed that wasn't talking.

The three women climbed the stairs. Mirallyn wished them a pleasant night and turned the opposite way at the landing, disappearing into the smaller bedroom.

Jill closed the door to the room and turned, finding Mae sitting on her knees in the middle of the bed. The smile on Mae's face faded as she watched Jill.

"You've got a look on your face," Mae said. "A look that means something is wrong."

Jill sat down on the bed next to Mae. "There's something I've been meaning to tell you for the last few days. Really, ever since you took me for that streetcar ride."

"Oh?"

"Yes. I…I haven't told you yet because things got weird and dangerous, but now you have to know. It's important that you know."

Mae frowned. "Maybe you should just say it. Do it quick and clean, like ripping off a Band-Aid."

Jill took a deep breath. "You remember me talking about my brother?"

"Robert Coleman Hall the Stinking Third?"

"He's one of the mages."

Jill watched as Mae opened her mouth as if to say something then stopped, closing it and frowning. Mae looked down at the bed, her frown deepening.

"I just recently figured it out," Jill said. "Some things fell into place and…well, now I know the truth."

Mae shifted, untucking her legs from under her body, resting them on the edge of the bed as she moved closer to Jill. Her frown never wavered. "Start at the beginning, please."

Jill swallowed and looked down, fidgeting with her hands. "In the last couple of years, he's occasionally asked me things. He'll ask me if I've ever made something happen, something impossible, or seen things that shouldn't exist. I always told him no, because that was the truth." She looked up at Mae. "I saw him conjure a flame in the palm of his hand once. I told myself then that I was mistaken, that I'd had too much to drink or it was some kind of trick. But then you took me for that streetcar ride and I started thinking more about those questions he asked me."

"Because now you know magic is real." Mae's expression was grave. "Have you seen him do anything else?"

"I think so, looking back on it. About the time he started asking me if I'd ever made something unexplainable happen, he started wearing this ring. A big, gold thing with an emerald. He fiddles with it a lot. I've noticed when he does…" Jill paused. "When we were out for dinner last time, I saw him play with it while he talked to the waitress. I didn't think anything of it, but the girl suddenly became much more attentive of him, to the point of ignoring her other tables. It was like no one else but Robert existed. I've seen that happen before."

"That's disturbing," Mae said.

"He brags about his sexual conquests all the time. To think he might be using magic to make women sleep with him…" Jill shuddered.

"Sick," Mae muttered.

"Yeah. When I was in Mirallyn and Kravis's realm, before I went into Annwn, their Lord Murlannor said he knew the blood of one of the mages in me. He knew. He knew my brother was one of those hunting his people." Jill swallowed, her body shaking. "And now you know."

"Crap," Mae muttered. She reached over and took Jill's hand. "I'm sorry. If you can't help me rescue Fay because of your brother—"

"Oh no. I'm coming with you. In fact, I'm your in to that mansion."

"You are?"

"Yes. Remember when I said Robert had invited me to a party on Halloween?"

Mae's mouth opened in surprise. "You are not serious."

"I am. It's at the Arneson mansion. I can walk right through the front door as an invited guest."

"Jill, honey, they know we're living together. If you go into that house, you might never come out."

"Or I might be able to get you in. We know your sister is in that mansion. I want to do this. I want to do this for you. And for Fay. I want to do this for us."

"Even if it means going against your brother?"

Jill grinned. "That's just a bonus." She gave Mae's hand a squeeze. "I was worried how you might react, finding out my brother is one of the bad guys."

"You can't control the family you're born into." Mae turned and gave Jill a hug. "You stormed the Underworld for me. I don't doubt you, if that's what you're worried about."

They sat holding each other for several minutes, Jill letting relief wash over her as she continued to hold Mae close.

"We should tell the others," Mae finally whispered. "This does change things."

Jill swallowed. "Yeah. Let's go tell them."

Twenty minutes later everyone sat in the living room again, warm green tea at hand, taking in Jill's story. There was a long silence.

"This would not be the first time that siblings strove against each other," Kravis said with a shrug. "Myth and folklore are rife with such tales."

"This changes our plans," Mae said. "Jill can get us inside the Arneson home."

"The danger is great," Mirallyn pointed out.

Jill rolled her eyes. "The danger is going to be great no matter how we get inside. Hell, we're in danger right now sitting here."

Mirallyn frowned. "Yes. In truth, now that the immediate threats have passed, I am beginning to fear that Kravis and I are too close to the mage's stronghold. They might sense our magic."

"But not Jill and I," Mae said. "I think we should stay here. It's so close that they may not think to look for trouble."

"And it would allow you and Jill to scout out their home," Kravis said, "but Lady Mirallyn is right about her and me."

Mirallyn leaned forward, thoughtful. "Yes. Though as Kravis said, you could scout. Jill's ability to see magic is passive. It should not trigger any of their defenses, and she will be able to spot any magical protections on the grounds."

"I still don't like the idea of splitting up," Mae said. She turned to Jill. "What are the odds that your brother might show up? Would he come by here on his way to the Arneson party?"

Jill thought about it for a minute. "I think we're safe. I doubt he'd bring a woman out here in the winter, not when he has a condo in downtown. I can't see any other reason for him to stop by."

"I'm glad he wasn't here when we arrived," Mae said.

Kravis nodded. "Yes. That would have made things…interesting."

"Do you think the hounds have told Hodgins or the Arnesons we're here?" Jill asked.

Mirallyn shook her head. "No. I think they don't have full control over the hounds anymore."

Kravis gave her a long, questioning look.

"Mae commanded them to leave and they followed her orders," Mirallyn said. "That means something, though I do not understand what or why."

Mae yawned and blinked. "Maybe understanding will come after a decent night's sleep. We haven't been attacked yet. I'm inclined to sit tight until we get into that mansion."

"Agreed," Jill said, yawning back at Mae. "I think I'm really ready to go to bed."

She and Mae bid the others good night, leaving Mirallyn and Kravis in the living room. They climbed the stairs again, going back into the bedroom. Jill hesitated at the door.

"What?" Mae asked.

"I—my family is the enemy. Are you sure—" she was cut off by Mae placing a finger on her lips.

"I'm sure. Now come to bed, Miss Hall."

Jill followed Mae to bed, settling next to her. "So…" Mae kissed her, gentle and soft kisses on her lips, chin, cheeks, over her eyes and back to her lips. "Mae…"

Mae pulled her closer, bringing Jill's head to her shoulder and wrapping Jill in her arms. "Hush. Let's just sleep tonight."

"Mae. Thank you."

"For?"

She closed her eyes as Mae ran fingers through her hair. "For not wigging out about Robert."

Mae chuckled. "Jill, honey, there are so many things I *could* be freaking out about that I've decided to just go with it, no matter how weird things become."

"That seems like good advice," Jill murmured. She sighed and let the feel of Mae's fingers in her hair and the rhythm of Mae's heartbeat lull her to sleep.

Monday, 30th of October

Dear Wall,

Hot tea, oatmeal and pads with little wings were the highlight of my morning. I couldn't decide if I wanted to cry from frustration and embarrassment, or laugh at how incredibly absurd my life had become.

Chrysandra was sweet, patiently explaining to me what's happening to my body and what to do. We talked for a long time this morning, Chrysandra and I.

They're going to try to switch us, her spirit into my body, mine into hers. She overheard Ilona and Robert talking about it. They think Chrysandra is mostly unaware of her surroundings so they talk in front of her.

They're really stupid sometimes.

I told her it seemed like an awful lot of magic would be burned up trying that. She nodded. I asked her if she remembered what happened to her, what it was that killed her body. She still doesn't know. I think she may never remember. It must have been something awful. Mr.

Hodgins must want Chrysandra alive for some reason, and it can't just be to keep "Mother" sane.

Then it hit me. You see, if Chrysandra's spirit and personality is in my body, they can control her and use my blood to get to my mother, and through Mother, the rest of the Court.

I looked at Chrysandra for a long time, trying to decide if I still trusted her. I finally asked her a question that had been bothering me for a couple of days.

She doesn't know who her father is, but I do. It only makes sense, and now that he carries my blood, I can sense him in Chrysandra as well. I know she's been dead longer than I've been a captive. He must really love her, to convince his peers to burn enough power to keep Chrysandra going, not knowing how he was going to save her in the end.

And then I stumbled into the human world, giving Hodgins the perfect opportunity to both save his daughter and finish destroying my people.

I'm so stupid. I have to escape before he makes the transfer, though that means Chrys will—well—die.

I've set the last trigger phrase. Thank you, words, for your help.

Mae held her mother at arm's length. "I want you to promise me you'll be careful. We know Rhyania's people are all looking for you, and the hounds are still out there prowling."

Mirallyn nodded. "We will be quick. In and out of faerie before anyone can detect us. I know a place we can hide."

"We'll stay at the lake house until Halloween."

Kravis joined them then after taking the opportunity to scout out the location and make sure no one was watching the property. "It seems safe enough here, though I dislike your proximity to the mage's stronghold."

Mae nodded in agreement. After listening to Jill's explanation last night, she was more than a little worried that Robert Hall might drop in on them unannounced, but the lake house still seemed the strongest position from which to stage their raid and rescue mission. Behind Mae, the bell on the streetcar rang. She turned to her mother. "Stay safe," Mae said. "Stay hidden from the hounds."

"I shall, and I have my own Champion to guard me," she said, nodding toward Kravis, who was standing by the streetcar's red door. Her mother paused, giving Mae a pensive look. "Daughter, *promise* me you will not do anything foolish. I desire Fay's rescue as much as you, but if you find yourself overmatched, swear you will retreat."

"Promise." The bell rang again. She pulled her mother close and kissed her on the cheek. "I'll bring her home."

She turned to Jill with a frown as Mirallyn and Kravis stepped through the red door into the yellow machine, off on their search for Ellie or information about her fate. The car pulled away, swaying and clacking along on its tracks. "Have we figured out how these streetcars work? 'Cause I'm pretty sure I never saw any rail tracks anywhere near this place before that car showed up."

"I thought it had to do with where the cars had traveled before, back when they worked in our reality. Sort of a case of phantom tracks for phantom streetcars, but that doesn't seem to be how it works, at least not with this one."

"It's the fact that the sign reads Malveaux Express that freaks me out."

Jill gave her a surprised look. "You're just now getting freaked out?"

She shivered in the worn, fur-trimmed robe she had borrowed from her mother. "Well, for relative values of freaked out."

Jill held out a hand to her. "Ready?"

"You look dashing," Mae said, nodding toward the black eye patch and leather jacket Kravis had procured for her friend. It added to the overall "I am a badass, and you had best stay out of my way" effect Jill seemed to be projecting. Mae supposed battling faerie warriors and walking into the Underworld might put a little swagger in your step. She just hoped Jill was not getting overconfident.

Jill flipped her long hair and smiled brilliantly. "I have that pirate queen thing going on, don't I?"

"More so with all the nicks and cuts all over your face," Mae said.

"I earned them fair and square." Jill laughed.

Mae nodded. "I know." She paused and bit her lower lip as Jill opened the door and led the way into the kitchen. "Are you sure you want to keep hanging around with me?"

"Mae—"

"I'm just asking because, well, I nearly got you killed, and I couldn't and wouldn't blame you one bit if you changed your mind."

They settled into the wooden chairs at the kitchen table. Mae looked directly into Jill's face, hoping she would find understanding, afraid she would find something else entirely. She started to tremble as Jill regarded her with one pale blue eye.

Jill sighed dramatically. "You are the silliest girl in the world."

Mae frowned. "I wouldn't go that far. And who was worried about me changing my mind last night?"

"Yes, well, that is true. I'm not giving you up after all the work I've put into this relationship."

Mae grinned, her good humor restored by Jill's answer. "You realize the relationship's only a few days old?"

"Beside the point. I tramped into and through the frozen wastes of the Underworld, battling hell hounds the whole way, for your skinny butt." Jill leaned forward and gave Mae a mock leer, made all the more sinister looking by Jill's eye patch. "And you promised me a tumble, girly. I'm holding you to that."

"Need to get your piece of flesh?"

"Yes. But right now, I need to get breakfast."

"Let's see what we can find." Mae stood, but Jill waved her away.

"I know where everything is. I'll take care of food."

"Okay. You still need to call your boss too."

Jill made a dismissive noise. "I'll call Millard later. He'll wonder what happened and start to worry. When I do call him, he'll be so relieved I'm all right and didn't quit that he'll accept any old line I feed him."

"That's cruel," Mae said.

"Yeah, but it will work."

Mae watched as Jill bent down, nearly disappearing behind the counter. She heard a door open and the sounds of Jill searching the cabinet for something. Jill came back into view, holding a toaster.

Mae nodded toward the toaster. "How long will that take, because I'm starving."

Jill set down the toaster and opened the freezer. "We're having toaster waffles. It will be a handful of minutes at best, greedy." She pulled out a frost-covered package of waffles and placed four in the toaster.

Mae smiled at her. But her smile vanished as she remembered their circumstances "Do you think you'll be up for a little scouting after breakfast?"

"What about the Cŵn Annwn?"

Jill took a bottle of syrup from the pantry and placed it on the table. The toaster popped out crispy, golden-brown waffles. She placed them on a serving plate and started four more.

"I stand in awe of your mad waffle toasting skills," Mae said with a straight face.

"Then you can set the table. Plates are in that cabinet, silverware in this drawer." Jill pointed Mae to the appropriate places. "Now, back to my original point. What are we going to do about those hounds?"

"I don't think there's anything we can do," Mae said, pulling plates from the cabinet and placing them on the breakfast table. "We'll just have to hope we can avoid them."

Jill frowned. "There's butter in the fridge. We're going to need it. And when the hounds do show up?"

"We ad lib."

Jill joined Mae at the table, waffles in hand. "That's the worst plan ever."

"The floor is open to ideas," Mae said, grabbing a waffle with her fingers and moving it to her plate, dressing it with butter and syrup.

"I didn't say I had a better idea."

Mae took a bite and chewed, letting the butter, maple syrup and crisp fried dough melt in her mouth. She watched Jill, who was not attacking her food with her usual reckless gusto, but instead was being very precise in her cuts and chewing slowly, apparently savoring every bite.

Mae considered how they were planning to get into the Arneson house, free her sister and close the door to Annwn. Jill would be walking through the front door as a guest. Right into a potential trap. Mae did not like the plan, but it was all they had.

She watched Jill set her fork on her plate and dab at her face with a paper napkin. Jill stood and grabbed her cell phone. "I'm going to call Millard."

Mae took the two sticky plates to the sink and started to rinse them off, still lost in thought. She had been sure of herself earlier, and though she was wavering now, it did not change the need to rescue her sister. Cutting off the door to Annwn was secondary to saving Fay.

Mae left the plates in the sink and poured herself a cup of coffee. She heard Jill's phone ring in one of the other rooms. Jill's voice drifted into the kitchen. Mae was unable to understand anything Jill was saying, but the tone in Jill's voice sounded surprised.

Mae sat back down at the table and looked out the window. A white winter world of snow-covered landscape greeted the morning light. They would have to take as close a look at the Arneson place as possible and hope an opening presented itself.

Jill walked into the kitchen holding her cell phone, a bemused look on her face.

"Did you reach your boss?" Mae asked.

"Yeah. No worries there."

Mae nodded, waiting for Jill to continue. "You're not going to believe who called," Jill finally said.

"Santa Claus?" Mae deadpanned.

"Not even close." Jill walked to the coffee pot and poured the last of the dark liquid in her cup before settling at the table across from Mae.

Mae decided she could not take the suspense anymore. "Okay. Who called?"

"My brother. Reminding me that I'm invited to attend a private event some family friends are throwing tomorrow night. He said he thought it would be good for me to meet some people who could 'help me reach my true potential.'" Jill raised her cup to her lips and paused. "So...trap?"

"Trap."

Jill grinned. "We're going to walk right into it anyway, aren't we?"

"Yes," Mae said. "We are."

Dear Wall,

Chrysandra told me that "Mother" and Mr. Hodgins had a big fight last night about something called Halloween. "Mother" wants to take me, as "Chrysandra," out trick-or-treating. Chrysandra explained to me what this is.

I should have known that was why I could feel something coming. In two nights, the veil will be thin. Death in all Its forms will walk near the surface of the world.

They're going to try to switch us, Chrysandra and me, on that night. That will be the perfect night to perform their ritual, in their minds. I suspect that is also the night they plan on trying to attack the Court. They're doing something to Annwn. I know because the hounds have been responding to Mr. Hodgins, and he most certainly is not Gwynn ap Nudd.

The silver answers when I call. It will do as I bid.

MAE TURNED TO JILL and whispered into her ear. "Do you get the feeling we're being watched?" She glared out into the gathering darkness. The two women were slowly moving away from the Arneson mansion, the object of their scrutiny for the entire day, and back to the Hall lake house.

"Just from the moment we stepped onto the Arneson property," Jill replied with a shiver that had little to do with the freezing cold. "That place is damned creepy."

Mae silently agreed that the huge old Victorian mansion was an imposing structure, made the more so because they both knew what was going on inside the doors. "No. This is more like someone stalking us."

Jill paused and lifted her eye patch. Jill's new ability to see magic had probably saved them more than once during their little scouting foray, guiding them around the many magically enchanted and charged items they could have stumbled upon during their investigation. Mae had no idea what any of those magics could do. For all she and Jill knew, they had tripped some kind of security alarms or surveillance spells, but the fact they were still alive and had not been attacked was enough to make Mae thankful.

"I can't see anything," Jill finally said. "Come on, let's get back to the house before it gets *really* dark. I don't feel like stumbling around in the snow-covered underbrush, especially with my complete lack of depth perception."

Mae started to reply, but the words in her throat turned to a startled shriek as *shapes* seemed to detach themselves from the trees and step into the gray light of evening. Jill stepped in front of her, blocking her view, and drew the baton from her pocket, snapping it open in one swift motion.

She's taking this Champion thing far too seriously.

"Who's there?" Jill yelled into the gloom, making her words a snarled challenge.

Mae stepped around Jill, standing to the taller woman's right. The forms took on distinct shape as they moved closer.

They were each of them as tall as Mae, some a few inches taller perhaps. They were golden of hair and armed with curved swords and ornate bows covered in symbols. Their armor was polished and reflected the moonlight, their faces angelic and pale. Splashes of colorful ribbons and other decorations contrasted against the gold and silver of their beings. They moved forward, silent and grim, their weapons at the ready.

Mae realized they were the fae her mother had warned them about, and they had come to kill Jill.

"Jill—"

"I know."

"We have to run."

"There are too many of them. You need to get out of here while I handle this."

"You really think you can fight all of them?"

"And win? No, of course not. But it's not you they're after."

"Your paramour speaks the truth," a voice, high and refined, called from the gloom. "We have no wish to harm you. Our quarrel is with the mortal woman who slew the Lord of the Llysllyn Court. You may go in peace, Maeve Malveaux."

"I don't think I'm going anywhere."

One of the shapes stepped forward. As blond and golden as the rest, he was slightly taller than his fellows, with more in the way of ribbons and decorations adorning his armor. "We do not *wish* to harm you. We *will* if you interfere."

"We don't have time for this," Mae said, stepping around Jill. She looked at the leader of the warriors. "I'm going to rescue my sister from her captors. I'm hoping to bring down the circle of mages that have almost destroyed your cousins in the Llysllyn Court. To do that, I need Jill by my side." Mae held her hands in front of her, open and pleading. "Please. Give us until the dawn, two days from now to finish this. After that you can start trying to kill us all you want."

The tallest faerie frowned. He glanced over his shoulder at his dozen warriors and turned to the two women. "I have my orders. The murderess dies tonight."

"A challenge."

All eyes turned toward Jill, who had shrugged out of her leather jacket.

"What do you propose?" the warrior asked.

Jill gave him a grim smile. "You and I fight it out, right here, right now. Champion versus captain. It's a time-honored way to settle differences. If I win, you give us the two days we need."

"And if I win?" he asked.

Mae felt a chill in her stomach. "Jill, don't."

"If you win then I'm already dead, and you've done what you came here for. You let Mae go about her business."

"Rules? Conditions?" the captain asked, suspicion in his voice.

Jill smiled sweetly at him. "None. Anything goes."

"I accept."

Mae watched horrified as Jill sprang forward before the last syllable of the captain's acceptance died in the air. She slashed down, her baton whistling.

The captain twisted, catlike, out of the way of Jill's attack. He drew his weapon as he turned. The long, curved blade glowed blue in the darkness. He slashed at her unprotected back, his blade cutting a thin line through her sweater.

Jill made a hissing noise and turned to face her opponent. She batted aside his second cut with her baton, the metals screeching against each other, and stepped into him. He spun away.

Mae cried out as the faerie captain turned and threw what looked like a transparent glowing dart at Jill. There was a burst of sickly green light on Jill's right thigh, and the black-haired woman stumbled.

The captain charged at Jill, his face demonic in the blue-glow of his blade, sure of his kill.

Jill threw a handful of snow and debris into his face, and surged forward, driving her shoulder into the faerie captain. Jill was taller and possibly heavier than her opponent. The two tumbled into the snow, both their weapons lost from their hands as they rolled.

Mae ran forward, trying to follow the struggling pair.

Jill landed on top of her opponent, striking downward with her forehead. Mae heard a terrible crunching noise and Jill's scream of pain. She watched Jill, now sitting astride the captain, bashing him with her right fist.

As Mae reached the two, the captain, his face covered in blood from his ruined nose, drew a small dagger from inside his armor. He stabbed at Jill, but she caught his hand in hers. For a moment they were still, locked in place, then Jill flung herself off him and to her right.

The captain flowed to his knees, but stopped when Jill brought his own sword to his throat. She gave the edge just enough pressure to draw a thin line of blood.

"Yield." Jill's voice was cool and steady as she held the blade to his throat.

The captain glanced down at his glowing sword. He looked at Jill and favored her with a small smile. "I yield."

The tension in the dark underbrush seemed to melt at his words. Jill lowered the weapon and sagged. Mae scrambled to her side.

"Are you all right?"

Jill handed the glowing sword back to her opponent, who nodded to her and stood, stepping away. "I'll be okay. It's not that bad a cut, though I guess this sweater is ruined."

"Damn it, Jill!" Mae cried, letting her tears fall free. "What were you thinking?"

"I was thinking that we couldn't both die in some stupid fight over a dead faerie lord and misplaced notions of vengeance, not when we're this close to rescuing your sister."

Mae bit her lower lip. "I hate this," she finally whispered.

Jill's face softened and she reached out and gathered Mae into a hug. "I hate this too. Unfortunately, unless you think the police are going to go into that house and rescue your sister, it's pretty much up to us."

"That doesn't mean I have to like it," Mae muttered into Jill's shoulder.

"We should get back to the lake house," Jill said, breaking the moment.

Mae released her grip on Jill and stepped back. "Yeah. I think we both need to clean up and have something hot to eat and drink." She turned to the faerie hunting party, looking directly into the eyes of their bloodied leader. "Do we have a truce?"

The blood-covered faerie nodded. "Neither I, nor any of my brethren shall attack your Champion until the third dawn." The captain gave Jill a cold glare. "At which point we will exact revenge for Lord Murlannor's death." He nodded to the women and turned away.

Mae watched as the silent shapes retreated and dissolved into the darkness.

She and Jill walked in silence back to the lake house, moving slowly. Jill kept limping on the leg that had been struck by the magic dart. Mae unlocked the door and locked it behind them once they were inside.

She turned to Jill. She was still angry at her reckless behavior, but she understood why Jill issued the challenge. It was an argument that could wait for later. Right now, Jill had injuries that needed tending.

The cut on Jill's back was shallow and had already stopped bleeding. Jill's hair was in disarray, tangled and matted with melting snow and mud. There was blood on her face, though Mae saw no signs of actual bleeding. She helped Jill limp to the kitchen table, settling her in one of the wooden chairs.

"Coffee, tea or cocoa?" Mae asked.

"Tea, preferably with honey and whiskey," came the muffled reply.

Mae looked up to find Jill resting her head on her arms. She was watching Mae work on the tea.

"Are you hungry?"

Jill closed her eyes and frowned. "Maybe later. I think I'd throw up anything I ate right now, though a shower would be nice."

Mae waited impatiently for the water to boil, then made them both a cup of strong, sweet tea liberally laced with whiskey. She placed two mugs on the table. Mae pulled a chair around and slowly rubbed Jill's back with one hand. "Drink your tea," Mae commanded.

Jill sat up weakly and gripped the mug in both hands. She took a sip and then a deeper drink of the warm liquid and sighed.

"What I want to know is where in the world did you learn to fight like that?" Mae asked. "I mean, I've seen you in class tossing around our instructors and whacking the hell out of everyone else with bamboo sticks, but damn!"

Jill gave her a lopsided smile. "College."

"College? Did you take fencing or something?"

"I took every self-defense and martial arts class I could afford, and I had this friend who was a stick-jock in the SCA. He taught me a lot about fighting with a long weapon."

"And you challenged a fully trained warrior to a duel? Are you completely mad?"

Jill gave her a hard, blazing look. "You're about to go charging into a mansion of powerful mages who have control of the pack of the Wild Hunt. You don't have any magic of your own, and you're not even as well trained a fighter as me, poor excuse for a Champion that I am. Don't talk to me about mad."

Mae realized that no matter how calm and matter-of-fact Jill had been on the surface about the duel, it was all bravado. The look on Jill's face and her shaky body language told Mae that Jill had been terrified.

Mae took a long gulp of her own tea, scalding her tongue in the process. She was feeling more than a little shaky herself. She needed to get Jill cleaned up before the shock of it all overwhelmed them both. She stood and touched Jill's shoulder. "Come on, let's shower and go to bed."

Jill gave a weak nod and, finishing her tea in one gulp, stood from her chair. She swayed on her feet.

Reaching out to steady her, Mae placed Jill's arm around her shoulder. They walked slowly up the stairs to the master bathroom, Jill leaning on Mae as much as needed, despite Jill's protests that she was fine.

Mae settled Jill on the closed toilet lid, letting her place her head in her hands, while Mae started the shower water running. Once the water was hot enough, Mae turned to Jill, who was trembling violently.

"It's okay," Mae said. "You're fine. I've got you."

Jill looked up at her, locking her good eye on Mae. "He could have killed me."

"But he didn't."

Jill stood and started to slowly undress. "Mae, he let me win. There's no other explanation. He was faster than me, he had magic to use. He's probably been fighting with a sword for centuries. He let me win."

Mae reached out to help Jill, whose hands were shaking so badly at this point that she could not unbuckle her own belt. "Well, I'm glad he did. I much prefer you alive and well." *And maybe that will keep you from taking unnecessary chances.*

It seemed reasonable to Mae that the faerie captain had indeed thrown the battle. He had stated that his fight was not with Mae. Perhaps he had wanted to accept their offer, but had to find a way, even if it was a token way, to make it look like he had tried to kill Jill and accomplish his mission. She wondered if other faerie creatures could sense the fae blood in her.

Mae helped Jill undress, taking a moment to check her injuries. The shallow wound on her back would need cleaning. Mae looked at where she had seen the glowing dart strike Jill. The leg was bruised but not punctured. The dart had been some kind of magical energy, Mae realized. She hoped there would be no lingering magical effects.

Once Jill was safely in the shower, Mae gathered up all the dirty clothes and took them into the master bedroom, dropping them into a corner. Silently thanking Kravis and possibly Ellie, Mae opened up their luggage and withdrew clean clothes for both of them.

"I brought you a change of clothes," she called out through the steam in the bathroom.

"Thanks," Jill's voice spoke over the sound of running water. The water switched off. "Can I have a towel?"

Mae handed a towel over the shower curtain to Jill. It vanished, and a moment later Jill appeared wrapped in it as the curtain was swept aside. "Your turn."

"How are you feeling?"

"Better. Being clean helps." Jill leaned forward and kissed her. "Thank you."

Mae smiled at Jill, happy warmth spreading through her body. "It was my pleasure."

Mae waited until Jill was finished drying herself. Jill picked up her clean clothes and slipped into the bedroom, leaving Mae to shower.

She went about the business of getting clean in an efficient manner, washing herself quickly under the steaming water. Mae did not want to leave Jill alone any longer than necessary. Ten minutes later Mae was dressed in flannel pajamas and drying her hair with the towel. A moment of searching in the linen closet produced peroxide, sterile gauze and white medical tape. She added cotton pads to the pile and went in search of Jill.

It was a short search. Jill was stretched out crosswise on the large bed, lying on her stomach. On the floor was a tray with two steaming cups of tea, a carafe and a plate piled high with toast. Peanut butter and two different kinds of jam rounded out the impromptu dinner.

"You've been busy," Mae said, nodding toward the food and drink.

"I thought we'd both want something, so I decided on quick and easy food. There was a loaf of bread in the freezer."

Mae settled on the bed next to Jill. "I'm going to clean your cut. The last thing we need would be for you to get an infection."

Jill made a grunt of assent and shifted around, lifting her shirt to give Mae access to her small injury.

It was only a moment's work for Mae to clean the cut and cover it with gauze. As she worked, Mae noticed the thin red reminder of an earlier wound, the cut across Jill's hip, peeking up from the waist band of Jill's pants. She taped the gauze over the new cut securely and let Jill's shirt drop. She gave her friend a soft pat on the rear.

"Done," Mae said.

Jill looked over her shoulder and grinned at Mae. "What? You're not going to kiss it better?"

Mae dropped the remains of the improvised medical kit on the floor. "Flirt."

"Shameless," Jill acknowledged, sitting up and lifting the tray onto the bed.

Mae scooted around to face Jill over the food. For the next several minutes both women concerned themselves with the contents of the tray. Mae noticed that Jill seemed to be returning to normal, attacking her toast and tea.

She also noted the dark bruise on Jill's forehead. A large part of their plan tomorrow concerned Jill going to the party. They would need to hide that bruising under her hair or cover it.

Jill gave her a thoughtful look and started nervously playing with the sheet. "Can I ask you a question?"

"Of course."

Jill exhaled nervously and licked her lips. "It's just—this may not be the ideal time to ask about this, is all."

"Go ahead."

Jill lifted her head and locked her mismatched eyes on Mae. She reached out and took both of Mae's hands in her own. "You remember the night I told you about my suicide attempt?"

"Of course."

Jill's voice was little more than a whisper. "You told me I needed to forgive myself, and that someday I'd take what I'd learned and help someone else. I said you sounded like the voice of experience and you told me that was a story for another night. I was just wondering…"

Mae took a deep breath. "You're not the only one who made mistakes as a young woman."

"If you don't want to talk about it, that's okay."

"No." Mae gave Jill's hands a squeeze and took a deep breath. "It's fine. I—I had a child when I was in college. A son. His name—his name was Liam."

"Was?" Jill asked.

"He died. When he was still a baby."

"Oh, Mae, I'm so sorry."

Mae gave Jill a weak smile. "I loved him like I've never loved anyone. It's just that, for a long time after he died, I blamed myself. I couldn't help but think if I'd done something differently, he might have lived. It's not true, of course. There was *nothing* I could have done. He was doomed from the moment he was born, and sometimes—sometimes that makes it worse, you know? Because if I'd been using any sense, he would never have been *born*. He would never have had to *die*."

"I take it he was not a planned child?"

Mae shook her head. "No, he actually was planned. Would you like some more tea before I tell you about the truly awful thing I did?"

Jill gave her a surprised look. "Okay."

Mae poured the last of the tea into the two cups. "It was when I was going to the U. My father had died. He was my only family."

Jill's face took on an expression of understanding. "You didn't want to be alone."

"I was *desperately afraid* to be alone. I was a freshman, living away from home. I had no family and no friends. What I did have was Jerry, my more-or-less boyfriend."

"Oh, Mae. You didn't."

"I did, but not because I expected him to marry me. In fact, I was pretty sure he would bolt when he found out I was pregnant." Mae gave a humorless snort. "He did not disappoint."

"What happened?"

"Jerry was the only boyfriend I ever had. We'd been a couple since middle school, but it was more a relationship of convenience than anything else. He was one of the boys I played hockey with. We lived near each other. We'd ride on the bus out to the little frozen lakes in South Minneapolis together. I'd never had another male show any interest in me, flat-chested, plain little thing that I am, and I didn't have the self-confidence to pursue another boy."

Jill grinned. "It sounds like maybe your subconscious already knew which way you swung."

"Looking back on it, I had little enough interest in the boy I was with and none in the other young men around me. Still, boy-and-girl relationships were all I knew at the time because it was all I saw in school."

Jill nodded in understanding.

Mae took a deep breath. "So, I never went after another boy, and Jerry was too lazy to pursue other girls. In truth, he was just someone to take me out once in awhile, or go to school functions with. I stayed with him because I was afraid I'd never find anyone else. He stayed with me for the occasional sex. Simple as that. We probably would have married eventually, just because there was nothing better to do."

"And then your father died," Jill said.

Mae nodded. "And then my father died. I don't know what I was really thinking. I just—I didn't want to be alone."

"How did you manage?"

Mae shrugged. "You find ways. I got pregnant and Jerry ran. I dropped out of college for a year and took a job waiting tables."

Mae paused and gathered herself. She did not want to cry, but there was no stopping it. She looked down at her lap and let the tears come. "Liam was born with a heart defect, a condition called tricuspid atresia. His heart didn't have a tricuspid valve."

"Oh," was Jill's only reply.

"The doctors did everything possible for him. They kept him alive for almost six months, but in the end it wasn't enough." She looked up at Jill and sniffled. "When he died, for the longest time I hated myself."

"Why?" Jill asked, her voice very small and quiet.

"I brought him into the world. I brought him into the world for purely selfish reasons. I couldn't help but think that his death was my punishment for being such a terrible person."

Mae looked back down at her lap. She felt Jill reach out and gather her close. Mae leaned into Jill.

"Did you love him?"

Mae nodded against Jill's shoulder. "Yes. More than anything."

"That's all that really matters," Jill whispered.

Mae felt Jill begin to stroke her hair. She closed her eyes. "I know. And I know his death wasn't my fault. It was—it was just stupid bad luck for both of us." She felt Jill's head gently rest on her own.

"We're quite the pair, aren't we?" Jill said.

Mae sniffed. "I'm glad you asked, truth be told."

"Yeah, well, now we know each other's pasts."

Jill kissed the top of her head, hugged her tight, and then released her. Mae looked up as Jill set the half-empty box of tissues on the bed.

"Thanks," Mae mumbled, pulling several tissues from the box. She wiped her eyes and blew her nose. "Thanks."

Jill set the tray of dirty dishes on the floor. Mae sighed as Jill gathered her close, holding her in her arms, drawing her down to the bed. It made her feel safe. It made her feel loved.

Mae closed her eyes and snuggled closer to Jill. She was exactly where she wanted to be. Mae raised her face toward Jill's, stopping with her lips less than an inch from the other woman's. Jill gazed down at her, her eyes filled with hunger.

Mae felt herself being pushed backward as Jill's lips met her own. She let Jill take the lead, enjoying the feeling of Jill kissing her.

Mae ran a hand through Jill's hair, guided Jill to the base of her neck, moaned when Jill's lips started toward her shoulder. She pulled Jill closer, twined her legs in Jill's and gave a gentle thrust of her hips upward. Jill growled, started back up Mae's neck with her lips. Emboldened, Mae dared to reach under Jill's shirt, gently stroked along the curve of Jill's left breast. Jill broke off her kisses and pushed up on her arms, looking down at Mae with a wide smile. Mae withdrew her hand from Jill's breast and ran a finger over Jill's cheek. She leaned up to kiss the skin next to Jill's silver eye and then rained a soft series of kisses along Jill's jaw and neck. Jill turned her head, her lips reaching for Mae's. Mae happily obliged her when Jill's tongue touched her lips, seeking entry into Mae's mouth.

She was not sure when or how Jill had unbuttoned her top, but Jill's clever hands were caressing her breasts, stroking the flat of her stomach, slowly working down, reaching under the elastic of Mae's pajama pants.

"Yes," Mae murmured. "Just like that..."

Dear Wall,

It was a rat. He got into the walls and chewed most of the way through the paneling. I dug the rest of the way to him with the butter knife I stole. I have my herald.

Of course, that involved giving him something he wanted, which meant stealing meat from the dinner table. I've always refused meat, so Mr. Hodgins was more than a little suspicious when I asked for my serving of the bacon-wrapped steak they had for dinner tonight. I had to eat almost half of the meat to convince him. I really thought I was going to vomit, especially since my stomach is still rolling unpleasantly.

I managed to secret the rest of the meat away. I snuck it into my room, gave the rat his bribe and sent him on his way with my message to Mother. Hopefully she gets it.

I'm willing to sit tight tomorrow. I'll take a wait and see approach until the veil starts to thin, then it's everyone for themselves.

These pads are really uncomfortable.

I wish Chrysandra was here. At least I've got you and the silver.

I need to shove something over the hole the rat came in before Elise notices.

Good night, words. Good night, wall.

Tuesday, 31ˢᵗ of October

MAE OPENED HER EYES. She felt a moment of panic as she took in her unfamiliar surroundings, but settled at the sound of Jill's soft snoring.

She stretched, languid and lazy. The sheets were cool and crisp against her naked body.

Last night had been something beyond wonderful. Mae had forgotten what it was like to make love with someone you cared deeply for. It had been far too long.

Mae rolled over on her side to face Jill. She had convinced Jill to leave the eye patch off during the night. Jill had hesitated, but gave in to Mae's wish. The eye had looked unchanged, silver instead of the pale blue of Jill's other eye. Mae wanted to assure Jill that, at least when they were alone, Jill could leave her changed eye uncovered. She could also, Mae pointed out, get a colored contact lens to cover the silver eye.

Mae reached out and caressed Jill's cheek. Jill looked softer, almost vulnerable in her sleep. All the worry from her face was erased, and her black hair lay in a wild tangle around her. Mae thought she could stay and gaze at this woman forever.

Unfortunately, her body was letting her know there were certain pressing needs it wanted addressed. Mae sighed and slipped from the bed, grabbing her clothes from the floor as she made her way to the bathroom.

Once Mae made her bladder happy, she brushed her teeth and dressed. She looked in on Jill, who had rolled over onto her back and sprawled out, taking up three-quarters of the bed. One pale leg was uncovered, dangling over the side of the mattress, and the sheets had pulled down, leaving her exposed to the waist.

Mae resisted the urge to crawl back into bed and reprise last night's lovemaking. It would be enjoyable, but they had a rescue to undertake. She slipped out of the room on silent feet, leaving Jill to whatever pleasant dream she was having.

Coffee was the first thing on the agenda. Mae found the canister of grounds and the filters on the counter where they had left it yesterday. She set the pot to drip and went about finding breakfast.

Her search yielded a package of freezer-burned cinnamon rolls. Mae thought she might be able to make them palatable by smothering them in butter and letting them microwave for a bit. Mae took a can of peaches from the pantry, placing it on the counter, ready to be opened when the rolls were done. She set the timer on the machine and snuck back into the bedroom to retrieve the carafe and serving tray she had seen last night.

Jill had flipped over onto her stomach, tangled up in the sheet and comforter. Her hair made a dark halo around her head.

She's so pretty.

Jill stretched and rolled over, opening one sleepy eye. "You're awake," she mumbled, almost in accusation.

"Yes."

"And you're dressed." Jill reached up and pulled Mae over to her by the bottom of her pajama top.

Mae sat down and leaned into Jill. She liked the way Jill felt first thing in the morning: warm and soft.

"I didn't want you dressed," Jill murmured. She began to unbutton Mae's top with one hand while running the other lightly over Mae's leg.

Mae leaned over and kissed Jill, hard and deep, bringing the sleepy woman fully awake.

They broke the kiss and pulled apart. Jill sat up and looked up at her, a playful smile on her face, mirth in her mismatched eyes.

"Jill—" said Mae, intending to head off whatever Jill had in mind.

The word had barely left her mouth before Jill began nuzzling at her throat, kissing along her collarbone and into the little area where her neck and shoulder met. Mae gave a tiny whimper of pleasure. It had not taken Jill long to discover that spot. Mae felt her top being pushed off her shoulder and suffered a moment of panic.

Last night had happened so quickly, Mae had not been able to worry. But now in the light of morning, old insecurities and fears reared their heads.

She knew she was not just petite, but in truth rather boyish in build, with small breasts, no butt to speak of, little in the way of curves. Mae could not even tell herself she was cute. Her lank blond hair and the angular face that greeted her in the mirror every day saw to that. At her best, Mae felt plain. It was difficult for her to imagine that someone like Jill, a woman who was as gorgeous as they came, would find her desirable.

Jill must have sensed her change in mood, because the urgent kisses on her skin stopped. Mae opened her eyes and looked at her partner, an apology on her lips. She had unconsciously raised her arms to cover her breasts. "I'm sorry, I'm—"

"Beautiful," Jill whispered. "You're beautiful." She took Mae's face in her hands and leaned into her.

The kiss was soft and urgent. It told Mae everything she needed to know. She let her arms fall to her side; allowed Jill to slip her top the rest of the way off. Mae pushed Jill onto her back, all thoughts of poor body image and breakfast forgotten.

Dear Wall,

Chrysandra told me the Cŵn Annwn did not come back from wherever it was Mr. Hodgins sent them yesterday.

They sent her to my room early this morning. Ilona and Robert keep checking on us. When they open the door, Chrysandra winks at me and goes all blank-eyed and limp at the same time I pull the covers over my head and pretend to sleep. It's a fun game.

Every time they open the door, they weaken the magical seal. If they don't remember to recharge it soon, I'll be able to let Chrysandra open the iron studded entrance for me.

Something must have gone seriously wrong. I can hear raised voices, some of them voices I've never heard before. Chrysandra said "Grandfather" mentioned something about "calling together the full covenant," whatever that means.

I told Chrysandra about my rat-herald. I have to trust her. I can't escape on my own. I hope she doesn't turn on me. You never know what's happening in that decomposing brain of hers.

I should try to get some rest. I need to be alert in case they give me an opening.

MAE WATCHED JILL FROWN at the second bite of her cinnamon roll. "Man, these are stale."

"Sorry," Mae replied. "I got distracted and left them in the microwave."

"Well, I'll forgive you, just this once."

Mae kept a blank look on her face as she held Jill's gaze. They were silent for a moment, and then both women burst into laughter.

They were seated across from each other at the table in the eat-in kitchen, each with a warm-though-stale cinnamon roll and a hot cup of coffee before them. They had decided to shower and dress after their morning exertions. When they reached the kitchen, Mae remembered the pastries in the microwave. They managed to salvage them, but it was not the finest breakfast either woman had ever eaten.

"At least the peaches and coffee are good," Mae said. She noted that while Jill was complaining about the lack of freshness of the rolls, she was still wolfing them down.

"The coffee is perfect," Jill agreed, raising her cup. "But we're going to have to figure out a way to get some real food if we're going to stay here much longer. "

They finished breakfast in silence, both of them occasionally looking out the window at the grounds outside and the slowly freezing lake beyond. It was snowing again, large fat flakes drifting slowly from the sky to the ground.

Mae rose and brought the coffee pot back to the table, refilling both of their cups. She watched Jill spoon sugar into her drink. She gave Jill a bemused look.

Jill smiled at her. "I thought I might need a little boost."

Mae replaced the pot in the coffeemaker and settled across from Jill. She pushed the sleeves of her sweatshirt up to her elbows and rested them on the table.

"Happy Halloween," she told her new lover.

Jill snorted. "I'd rather be handing out sweets to screaming munchkins than going to that party tonight."

"Speaking of which, do you have something to wear?"

"I'm sure I can find a dress in one of the closets. The family used to throw parties here all the time. I'll bet Mother left something I can wear."

Mae raised an eyebrow. "I'd think everything would be summer wear."

"A little black dress works no matter the season."

"I look forward to seeing you in that."

Jill smirked and raised her cup. "You mean you look forward to getting me out of it." She took a sip around her growing smile.

"That too," Mae agreed. She returned Jill's smile for a moment, then licked her lips. "When this is over, then what?"

"Assuming we survive? We go about our lives."

Mae frowned and leaned back in her chair. "I'm not sure it's going to be that easy. I doubt I'll be able to continue working for CPS." Mae leaned forward again, placing her elbows on the table and fidgeting with her cup. "Even if we rescue Fay and cut Hodgins and his friends off from Annwn, they're still going to be rich, influential people. Rich, influential people who are going to be angry with you and me."

"We'll deal with them when the time comes."

Mae swallowed and looked down at the table. "It feels like everything will change, no matter what tonight's outcome. Either we're going to end up dead or spend the rest of our lives running and looking over our shoulders."

Mae heard the scrape of Jill's chair as the woman rose and moved to the chair next to her. Jill reached out and took her hands, but Mae was unable to look into her eyes.

"I'm sorry I got you mixed up in this," Mae whispered.

Jill took her by the chin. Mae let the other woman turn her face so that they were looking at each other. She was surprised to find Jill smiling at her.

"Okay, first of all, I'm not sorry I got mixed up in this. No matter what goes down tonight, I got what I wanted. That would be you. Second, my *goodness* but your moods *are* up and down, aren't they?"

"I blame it on the faerie blood," Mae said, the tiniest bit of humor back in her voice.

"Blame it on whatever you want, but stop it. All we can do is take this one step at a time. The first thing we do is rescue your sister. If we have to spend the rest of our lives hiding from angry mages and murderous faeries, well, so be it." Jill leaned back in the wooden kitchen chair and crossed her arms. She paused in thought. "I wonder what my brother and his friends are planning. For me, that is."

"Something awful," Mae answered. "I want you to be extra careful."

"I will. I think I can handle myself, as long as what they're planning doesn't involve elder gods and a lot of tentacles. If that's the case, expect me to run screaming from that mansion."

Mae snorted. "I doubt that's what you'll encounter. I would remind you about what Hodgins nearly did to me. He was by himself and almost took control of my body. Tonight, you'll be walking into a houseful of people like him."

"Regular ray o' sunshine, that's what you are. Is there any significance to tonight, besides it being Halloween and the spookiest night of the year?"

"According to mythology, tonight is the night the veil between the realms is the thinnest. It's supposed to be a good night to communicate with the dead."

Jill nodded. "Great, so I should expect zombies? Vampires? Ghouls?"

"Yes. What time is your brother coming to pick you up?"

"Sixish." Jill finished her coffee. "We're going with the original plan?"

Mae nodded. "I'll head across country to the house immediately after you leave. You get inside, find a bathroom with an exterior window and unlock it."

"I'll need something to signal you. I can leave a piece of cloth in the window or something."

"Sounds good," Mae said. "I'll need to make sure I have a way to cut through a window screen."

"There are tools in the garage. We'll find something," Jill said. "Once I've unlocked the window, I'll give you twenty minutes, then I'll try to slip away and look for you, all the while keeping my eyes open for any clue to Fay's location or the place where they access Annwn."

"And if one of us finds Fay before we've found each other?"

"Grab Fay. If she knows how to find the gate, then go to it. If she doesn't, then run. Call the other one when possible."

Mae nodded. Of course, it was all well and good for them to talk about abandoning the other, at least in practice. In reality, Mae suspected they would both fail to follow that part of the plan. "We should set our cell phones to vibrate."

Jill shook her head, making her black hair dance around her face. "We sound like a bad spy movie."

Mae kept her expression carefully neutral. "Should we set up recognition words, just in case?"

"You're kidding, right?"

"Only half."

"Well, at least it *is* only half. What do you think Fay looks like, anyway? It occurred to me that neither of us have ever seen her."

Mae smiled without humor. "I'd suspect she resembles Mirallyn."

"True," Jill said.

"I wish Kravis and Mother were here."

"Should we go over the plan again?" Jill asked after swallowing her last sip of coffee.

Mae shook her head. "No. Let's rest and not worry now."

"Rest?" Jill asked, her eye filled with mirth.

Mae stood and took Jill by the hands. She pulled the taller woman from her seat and started dragging her down the hallway back toward the bedroom.

"Well, maybe *relax* instead of rest." Mae laughed.

Dear Wall,

My rat-herald came back, which would be good news if Ilona and Elise hadn't been in the room when he showed up.

He managed to tell me help was coming before they killed him. Ilona touched the onyx on her choker and whispered a word I don't know. My poor rat squealed and died. Elise was furious with me, of course. Ilona just gave me this cold look. Then she laughed at me.

I probably shouldn't have tried to claw her eyes out. I'm going to have the ugliest bruise on my face, and my lip still hurts.

Elise tied me to the chair Chrysandra usually sits in. Mr. Hodgins and "Grandfather" watched as Robert nailed a board over the hole in the wall. Ilona smirked at me while they worked. I kept glancing at the marks I left on her face and grinned back at her. I saw something, a symbol I think, carved into the wood on the side they nailed to the wall.

I'm glad I hadn't written anything on that wall yet. I don't know exactly what they did, but the whole wall has an unpleasant hum and I get a bad taste in my mouth, all coppery and sharp, anytime I stand too close.

According to Elise, I'm supposed to be at the "family" dinner tonight. I wonder how they're going to explain my black eye to "Mother"?

I wonder who's coming for me. Mother? Mae Malveaux? Someone else?

I need to take my cold shower and change for dinner.

Jill pulled the hem of the dress down with both hands, not that it did any good. "I know I'm not the *exact* same size as my mother, but either I miscalculated how different we are, or there are whole aspects to my mother's personality that do not bear closer examination." Jill shook her head at her reflection in the full-length mirror. "I think this might be a little too—"

"Short?" Mae supplied helpfully, a broad grin on her face. "Snug?"

"Slutty."

Mae looked her up and down. Jill began to blush from the attention Mae was giving her.

"Well, you *are* showing a lot of leg," Mae said.

"And cleavage."

Mae's face lit up. "Slinky. That's the word you're looking for. Slinky."

"This is my mother's dress, you know."

"Try not to think too hard about it."

"Now to accessorize," Jill said, moving away from the mirror. She picked up the small clutch purse and black pumps they had discovered in the same closet as the dress and walked out of the bedroom, Mae following in her wake. Jill stopped in the living room long enough to transfer various necessary items from her regular purse to the small clutch. She dropped the pumps on the floor and picked up her keys. Jill turned and started down a short hallway, into a part of the house she had yet to show to Mae.

"What about your eye and—well—the scars on your arm?" Mae asked as they walked along. They had managed to cover the bruise on her head by styling her hair over it and then covering the rest with makeup. The bruise on her leg from the magic dart had faded away overnight. Jill had looked at it with her silver eye and reported no magical residue.

"I'm going to wear the eye patch. I want to hide the eye from them, since they're mages. I'll lift up the patch and have a look when I can. I'm going to leave my arms bare. I thought about wearing a shawl or something to cover them, but decided against it."

"And this decision is based on?"

Jill paused in front of a heavy wooden door. She shuffled through her keys until she found the one she wanted. "I decided there's a certain intimidation factor involved. They have to know that I know it's a trap. I'm going to walk in with all my 'battle scars' in plain sight. Maybe it will make them hesitate when things go sour." The lock clicked and Jill opened the door.

The room was male to the point of reeking of testosterone. The heads of various dead animals dominated the walls. There was a large mahogany desk with a leather executive chair. Two large additional leather chairs flanked by low tables that matched the desk rounded out the furniture. A full gun rack stood in one corner, and stacks of outdoor magazines lay on the tables. Framed pictures of hunts past hung on the walls. The faint smell of cigar smoke hung in the air.

Mae followed her into the room. "You're assuming things are going to get ugly?"

"Yes. Aren't you?"

"A part of me hopes we can do this and no one gets hurt. I realize I'm being a bit of a Pollyanna, but there it is," Mae said with a shrug.

Jill sat down in the chair behind the big desk. "I hope you're right, but I'm gearing up for the worst." Jill opened the top drawer of the desk and pulled out a small revolver.

"Are you sure that's a good idea?" Mae asked.

Jill opened the revolver's cylinder and checked the rounds. She snapped the cylinder shut and checked that the safety was on. She dropped the weapon into her clutch and stood. "I hope I don't need it."

"I'm worried that we're already going to be in enough trouble. If you shoot someone on top of everything else..."

Jill shooed Mae out the door. She turned and checked that the room was locked. "Would it make you feel better if I told you I have a carry permit?"

"No."

Settling on the couch, Jill slipped into the pumps. "Would it make you feel better if I told you I only plan on using this in an emergency?"

"I'd much rather you ran away."

"In these shoes?" Jill asked, wiggling her feet.

"True," Mae allowed. "Still, how likely are bullets to stop anything non-human?"

"Not very, but I'd be stupid not to use every advantage I can." Jill stood. "How do I look?"

"Edible," Mae said, nodding her approval.

"I'm not sure that's a good thing, everything considered."

"Every male in the place is going to act stupid around you, even with the 'battle scars.'"

Jill slipped the eye patch on. "That's the plan."

The doorbell rang, startling both women and making them jump.

"That would be Big Brother." Jill had called Robert a bare half hour earlier and informed him she was at the lake house and could she get a ride? Jill had purposely kept their location from Robert until the last minute, hoping the tight timeframe would stop the mages from swooping down on them. Jill slipped into her leather jacket and picked up the clutch. She turned to Mae. "Walk me out."

Mae followed Jill to the front door. Jill grabbed the doorknob and took a deep breath. "Here we go," she muttered, opening the door. "Robert! It's good to see you, big brother!"

Mae took the opportunity to give Jill's older brother a quick once over.

Robert Coleman Hall III was dressed impeccably. A black tailored suit, white shirt, black necktie, leather shoes. The watch on his wrist was probably worth more than everything Mae owned combined. His dark brown hair was short, stylish and styled. It was obvious he spent time in the gym. Robert Hall's entire countenance and demeanor screamed "wealthy and powerful." Mae had to admit he was a handsome man.

He had a momentary look of surprise on his face as he took in Jill's scars, but covered it quickly. He gave Mae a quick once over with his dark blue eyes before flashing her a boyish smile.

He turned back to Jill. "Ready to go?" he asked.

"Yeah," Jill said. She turned to Mae, who was standing slightly behind her. "I might be late."

"Don't stay out too long." Mae gave her a look full of promises of things to come, trying to add to Jill's game of tweaking her brother. Out of the corner of her eye, she could see Robert's expression turn sour.

"I'll be home eventually." Jill leaned down and kissed Mae, hard and deep. "Maybe I'll call it an evening early," she said, pulling away from Mae and walking out the door.

"Have fun!" Mae called out, waving goodbye at the door.

Dear Wall,

I don't know exactly what they did to me. There were eight of them, all of them in their special robes and wearing enough in the way of low powered talismans and charms to set my teeth on edge. "Mother" was even in attendance tonight. She chanted the chants with the rest, but it looked like she did not know where she was.

They brought Chrysandra into their circle at the end. They laid her failing body in the middle, and poured salt water and some of my blood all over her. Her eyes were completely white. I hope she's still in there.

Tonight's the big night. I heard Robert tell "Grandfather" and a couple of the others that he had arranged the perfect sacrifice. They talk too much when I'm around.

I think, but I'm not sure, that this sacrifice is going to help power the transfer between me and Chrysandra.

This should be enough words. I need to get the silver ready to play its part. I need to make sure it understands what it should do if I die or vanish from this plane of existence. I was hoping to get some time with Chrysandra, but I guess that's not going to happen.

Tonight, I will either escape or die trying.

Goodbye, wall.

Jill walked out to the black Mercedes parked near the front door. She turned and waited for her brother to unlock the car, then climbed in and sat in the leather seat. The car smelled new. Robert settled behind the steering wheel and started the big German-made vehicle. He gave her a sour look.

"This isn't a costume party," he said with a frown, exiting the circular driveway and pulling onto the street.

"This isn't a costume. I pulled the dress out of Mother's closet." Jill replied, keeping a calculated coolness in her voice. She was both relieved and distressed at how quickly she could fall back on old mannerisms and survival traits from her youth.

"Then why the getup?"

Jill took a deep breath. The superior tone of voice he always used with her grated on her nerves. "There was an...incident. I lost my vision in one eye." She gave him a nasty smile and reached for the eye patch. "It looks quite horrific. Would you like to see?"

He shot her a wary glance. "No, that's all right." He gave the scars on her arm a quick look before turning to stare out the windshield, suddenly very interested in the dark road before them.

Jill kept her expression neutral. Her brother was nervous in her presence, a situation that was foreign to her. She thought about pressing him, but decided to change directions.

"How are Mother and Father?" she asked.

"If you'd come home occasionally, you'd know."

Jill relaxed. This was familiar territory. "So Father is still destroying people's lives while playing captain of industry, and Mother is still a beloved high-society belle and drunkard?"

Robert's frown deepened. "Why do you hate them so much?"

Jill sighed and looked out the darkness on the other side of the window. "If you don't already know the answer to that question, I could never possibly explain it to you."

"Look, Jill, I know you feel like your childhood sucked, though I don't understand how. We both grew up with everything we could ever want, but if you *feel* that way, okay. Still, don't you think it's time to stop playing at being an average working girl?"

"I like what I do."

"You need to come home. You need to come back to the life you were born to."

She glared at him. "I'm not interested in being anyone's little trophy wife." The words came out as a rough snarl.

Robert twisted the ring on his finger around once before he turned the car up the long driveway toward the cheerfully lit Arneson mansion. "Then don't be. Look, Jill, there are people here who can give you a boost up. There's no reason for you to be working for the *county* when you can be one of the people who really makes things happen."

Jill glanced at him as he parked at the end of a long line of expensive luxury vehicles. "Why are you doing this?"

He gave her his winning smile. "Because you're my favorite sister."

She raised an eyebrow. "I'm your only sister."

Robert sighed and turned off the engine. "Mother asked me to invite you and make introductions if you came."

Jill stepped out of the car at the same time as Robert. "Are Mother and Father here?" The last thing she wanted was for her parents to be involved in whatever games the Arnesons and William Hodgins were playing. It was bad enough she was going to have to take on her brother. To have to engage her parents as well would be too much to bear.

"No. They had another commitment."

Jill followed him up to the mansion's front door, which was held open for them by a man in a tuxedo. Inside, they passed their coats to a bored-looking gray-haired woman. The woman offered to take Jill's clutch purse, but she held onto it.

Robert leaned toward Jill. "Promise not to embarrass me tonight," he said into her ear.

She gave him a wicked smile. "Where's the fun in that?"

"Jill..." he said as a distinguished-looking older man stepped forward to great them. Robert introduced him as James Arneson.

For the next twenty minutes, Jill found herself being introduced to everyone in a lavishly decorated parlor and ornate ballroom. She noted that it was a small gathering, less than a dozen people. Jill knew none of them personally, though she knew them all by reputation.

She made polite small talk with the iron-haired lady of the house while sipping red wine. Maureen Arneson kept looking at her as if she expected Jill to grow horns and attack at any moment. At last, the woman made her excuses and drifted away.

Jill checked her watch. She needed to unlock a window.

She looked around the room and spotted her brother standing under the crystal chandelier, talking to a short, busty woman with too much eyeliner and hair so black it could only be dyed.

"Sorry to interrupt," Jill said, bulling her way into the conversation.

Robert pressed his lips together. "Jill."

Jill smirked. "Brother mine. Who's your friend?"

Robert took a deep breath. "This is Ilona. Ilona, this is my sister, Jill."

Jill turned to the short woman, offering her best smile and her hand to shake. The woman gave Jill a curious look and took her hand.

"I am pleased to meet you," Ilona said.

"I'm sure Robert's told you all kinds of terrible things about me." Jill held onto the woman just a moment longer than necessary, lowering her eyelid and changing her smile from friendly to flirtatious. She leaned down to the woman. "I'm the bisexual, black-sheep troublemaker in the family," she said in a conspiratorial faux-whisper as she released the woman's hand.

Ilona gave a small laugh and turned to Robert. "She comes as advertised."

Jill gave Robert a mock glare. She looked back down at Ilona. "Sadly, most of the tales are probably true. But the reason I so rudely interrupted whatever you two are plotting is that I need a bathroom."

Ilona pointed at a side door. "If you go out that door and follow the hallway, it is the second door on your left."

Jill nodded. "Thanks."

Ilona offered a hand. "I can hold your drink while you're gone."

Jill passed the short woman the glass of wine and strolled from the room, conscious of the eyes following her as she left the gathering behind. She walked down a short hallway, paneled in dark wood. There were portraits along the walls, and the soft string music followed her from the ballroom. She looked at the ceiling and noticed speakers cleverly disguised in the mural of happy people by the lake. A pair of tall tables, each adorned with flowers and candles, stood opposite each other near the bathroom door.

Jill hesitated. There was something about the placement of the tables that bothered her, but she would have to walk between them to reach the restroom. She lifted the eye patch. The candles glowed with a faint yellow light. They were magical, but she had no idea what the magic was. Steeling herself for an unpleasant surprise, Jill walked cautiously past the tables. Nothing happened—at least nothing she could detect. There was no point in waiting. With a last look down both sides of the long hallway, she slipped into the bathroom.

It was every bit as opulent as the rest of the mansion, the vanity sporting a black marble top, the faucet a brightly polished gold. Jill suspected the gold might be real.

No Dixie cup dispensers here, Jill thought.

She looked at the window. It was shuttered from the inside, but that was easy enough to take care of. She opened the shutter latch and found the window lock. She lifted the window slowly, trying to avoid any loud noise. She supposed there could be a silent alarm, but there was nothing for it.

Jill opened her clutch purse and withdrew a metal nail file. She jabbed it into the screen and ripped across the soft wire mesh, opening a gash Mae would be able to exploit. She pulled out a red piece of fabric and pushed it partway out of the cut screen. She shut the window and closed the shutter, careful to make sure the latch did not catch.

She washed her hands, just to make them damp and slightly chilled, and pulled her eye patch back down before opening the door of the bathroom.

Ilona was waiting for her in the hallway.

The short woman gave her a humorless smile. "Your brother sent me to make sure you were all right. I think he was concerned that you would wander off."

"I do have a history of getting into trouble." Jill laughed.

Ilona gave her a measuring look. "Perhaps we should return to the party."

"Lead on," Jill said, following the short woman back to the ballroom.

"What took you so long?" Robert asked, his face anxious as he handed Jill her wine glass.

She favored him with a cool look. "Why so nosy?" She started to take a sip of her wine and paused. There was no way she was drinking it after leaving it alone with her brother.

"I just didn't want you to go poking about in our host's home and get into places you shouldn't be."

"Why? Do they have something to hide?"

"No, but it would be rude."

A woman carrying a tray of drinks came around. Ilona and Robert drained their glasses and took another serving of the wine. They each gave Jill a curious look. She would need to find some way to discreetly pour the drink out into a potted plant.

"So how do you know my brother?"

Ilona smiled up at her. "We are associates in an exclusive club."

"Oh, what kind of club?"

"Ilona..." Robert started, a warning in his voice.

"It is a thaumaturgical, spiritual and esoteric research club."

Jill felt a shiver go down her body. That the woman was being this open about what they were, practically admitting they were mages, did not bode well for Jill. She put on a mask of feigned interest.

"Like the Golden Dawn?"

Ilona snorted. "Those charlatans were nothing. This place is a place of power. All of us in this room, we are power. Those attending tonight are the most powerful of our order."

"I'm not a member of your order," Jill said.

Ilona laughed aloud. It caught the attention of the entire room. Jill took a step backwards as the other revelers turned and started walking toward her.

"No, Miss Hall," a new voice, a male voice, said. "You are not here tonight as a member, even as a prospective one. We have another use for you."

Jill turned to look at the source of the words. She found herself staring into the smiling face of William Hodgins. His was not a warm or friendly smile.

"Sorry, Jill," her brother said. "It's nothing personal."

She tried to pull away as Robert grabbed her. There was a sharp prick on her arm and she turned to find the gray-haired woman who had taken her coat holding a small syringe. Jill wobbled on her feet as a low buzzing started in her ears. She made an unsteady lunge at her brother, reaching for his throat.

"You sold me out, you fu—"

Jill fell to the cool, polished wood floor, landing on her knees. She looked up at her brother. He frowned down at her. Next to him Ilona's face held unconcealed glee. Hodgins simply seemed bored.

Jill tipped over, her vision clouding and the buzzing in her ears becoming a high-pitched whine. The delicate sound of her wine glass shattering on the floor was the last thing she heard.

MAE WATCHED AS THE big black Mercedes carrying Jill and her brother turned onto the street at the end of the long driveway. When the taillights vanished from sight, Mae made a short dash into the kitchen. She dressed for the night and cold, grabbing a few items, including Jill's baton. She peered out the window, just in case Jill and her brother had returned for some strange reason. Detecting no signs of them, she stepped outside.

The familiar ringing of a streetcar bell reached her ears.

Mae swore and jogged down the driveway. One of the big yellow streetcars was parked in the street, its red door opened wide.

Mae paused in front of the streetcar and glanced up at the destination sign: Malveaux Express. She climbed aboard.

"Ten cents, please."

Mae smiled at the conductor and fished in her bag for a dime. She dropped the coin into the fare box.

"Welcome aboard, Miss Malveaux," the conductor said, handing her a transfer. "We'll reach your destination in plenty of time."

"Thank you, Mr. Lowry."

The bell rang twice and the door closed. Mae turned to look at the other riders as the streetcar rolled away with a click-clack. She grinned at the two occupants of the car and walked toward where they sat on the back bench.

"Kravis. Death. How are you both this evening?"

Kravis wore a heavy coat over his red shirt. A sword with a short, curved blade lay across his knees. "Ready to take on a few mages."

Mae frowned. "You shouldn't go into that mansion."

"Probably not. Is the plan for gaining access to the mansion in motion?" Kravis asked.

"Jill is already inside. She has a piece of red cloth she's supposed to put in a window as a sign it's open. Once in, we find Fay and close the door to Annwn if we can, run if we can't." She glanced at Death. He looked somber in his black business suit. There was an expensive-looking leather briefcase next to him on the seat. He regarded her with his star-filled eyes.

"My business is your business this night."

Mae gave him a stiff nod of her head. For all she knew, his business was with her tonight. She hoped not, but if it was her time, she hoped he had plenty of business with others first.

"I hope you're not planning to stake me to another tree."

Death cocked his head to one side. "Why should I desire to do such a thing?"

"I'm just remembering the last time we met."

"Those were different circumstances, Maeve."

"Good," Mae said, taking a seat on the bench next to Kravis. She gave Death a smile. "I thought I told you to call me Mae."

"That was before I impaled you on the Great Oak in the frozen wastes of Annwn."

"Mae's not one to hold a grudge, are you?" Kravis said.

Mae turned toward the misshapen creature and raised an eyebrow. "Depends on exactly what you've done to cross me. Hang me from a tree in a mythical Underworld, that I can forgive. Kidnap my sister and use her for God only knows what purpose, that will get you killed."

"You've become a fierce little thing," Kravis replied.

"She has always been such," Death said in a soft voice.

Mae turned her gaze back to the dark faerie. "Where is my mother?"

"She has gone into hiding, away from the long reach of those you would confront tonight, and is protected from Rhyania's hunters."

Mae nodded, reassured that her mother would be safe even if the mission went poorly.

"And Ellie?" she asked.

"She arrived at Rhyania's Court seeking sanctuary, but was taken prisoner. Because she is nobility, she was given rooms in the palace, but a prisoner she is. I have heard from a trusted friend that Rhyania refuses to turn her over to the Llysllyn nobles until Mirallyn is captured as well."

"Why would she do that?"

Kravis gave her a hard, grim look. "I suspect that she needs Ellie and Mirallyn alive in order to transfer titles and power over to her before she can merge the two Courts. It might be for the best. If Ellie and Mirallyn cooperate, the Lady of the Falls will likely give them asylum and protection from the Llysllyn nobles."

"Arneson Manor," the conductor called out. "Last stop on the line."

"Here we go." Kravis stood and offered Mae a hand up.

She took his hand and rose. The three riders, mortal woman, dark faerie and Death himself, stepped off the streetcar and into the night. The streetcar bell rang twice. Mae glanced over her shoulder, but the big machine was nowhere to be found.

Mae took a deep breath and jogged away from the long drive, into the trees surrounding the estate. She paused by the trunk of a particularly large snow-covered maple. She squinted into the darkness, searching for the trees, structures, odd stone cairns and statues she had marked in her head during the scouting foray she and Jill had undertaken. Jill had pointed out every magical object she could find and Mae had made a point to commit each to memory, but faced with them in the dark, Mae was unsure. The estate grounds and buildings looked wildly different at night.

Mae turned to her two companions. "I know they have all sorts of magical—I guess—things scattered all over the yard. I don't know what any of them do."

"They do not concern me," Death said mildly.

Mae frowned at him as she drew the baton from the messenger bag. "Well, they concern me. Are you going to follow me around all night?"

Mae thought she detected the slightest bit of a smile. "Yes."

"Because having you following me around is going to get on my nerves after a while. I don't want to be distracted at the wrong moment."

Death faded from her vision. "Is this better?"

Mae swallowed. "Yeah. That will work." She looked at Kravis. "What about you?"

He gave her a tight frown. "Sorry, I don't bend light."

"I mean, what's your part in all this?" Mae leaned close to him. "If you go inside that mansion, you'll set off all kinds of alarms. What are you really planning?"

"I'm here, Mae, in case you fail. If you don't emerge after a reasonable amount of time, I'm to assume both you and Fay are dead and act accordingly."

"More likely you shall fail and die, my faithful servant," a female voice said from the trees.

Mae and Kravis turned to face the newcomer. Kravis lifted his sword. Mae snapped Jill's baton to full extension.

Mae's mother stepped from behind an old oak tree, wrapped in heavy winter robes trimmed in dark fur. "Would the two of you strike me down?"

Mae lowered the baton. "Mother?" she whispered.

Kravis sheathed his sword. "Lady Mirallyn, you should not be here."

"I have more right to involve myself in these events than you, my faithful servant. These are *my* daughters who are threatened."

Mae stepped in front of the smaller woman. "You can't go into that mansion. You said it yourself. You'll trip every magical alarm in the place."

"Yes. And while those inside concern themselves with my presence, you shall be able to seek your sister unimpeded."

"No," Kravis said. "I'll go in with Mae and provide the distraction."

Mirallyn gave him a haughty look. "The circle would overwhelm your small magics in moments, after which they would slay you and capture my daughter. My magic is far stronger. I will keep them occupied for a time, and then make my escape."

"We don't have time for this!" Mae said through gritted teeth. She pointed to the mansion. "Jill's in there right now, all alone." Mae glared at her mother. "Are you determined to do this?"

"I must try."

Mae turned toward the mansion and shifted her weight forward. "Good. Keep up."

She ran toward a stand of elms and maples on the side of the house, near the four-vehicle garage. She reached the trees and gave the grounds a close look. Her next step would be to make a dash between the garage and a shed while trying to slip past the security camera. She sprinted across the strip of open ground, keeping low and to the shadows. Panic and adrenaline gave her feet wings, though her bulky coat and heavy boots slowed her pace. She reached the shed and flattened herself along its side. Taking two quick breaths and trying not to think about how positively silly she must look, Mae dived around the corner of the shed. She paused to catch her breath. She looked at her two shadows. Kravis's face was troubled. Her mother seemed serene. Mae assumed Death still traveled with them and had no concerns about his ability to keep up.

Mae peered into the darkness. There was no one patrolling the grounds. She saw the mansion was mostly dark. There was supposed to be a party inside, but the building gave no indication of activity. A creeping fear that something had gone wrong traveled up her spine. She slipped around to the back of the garage and started moving toward the large Victorian structure.

"There," Kravis said, pointing.

Mae followed his finger. She spotted the signal cloth hanging from the dark window. Giving the grounds another look, Mae started forward.

"Wait!" Kravis said behind her.

Mae stopped in her tracks. "What?"

He pointed to the corner of the mansion nearest the marked window. Perched on the edge of the roof was a stone gargoyle. It turned to watch the yard with glittering jeweled eyes.

"Is there any way to slip under or past it?" Mae asked.

Kravis shook his head. "No."

"Then we shall need to destroy it," Mirallyn said.

Kravis scowled at the faerie sorceress. "And that won't draw unwanted attention in any way. No, they'd never notice a big explosion of magical energy on the bleeding roof!"

"I'd rather stay hidden a bit longer," Mae agreed.

"If you both would be silent for a moment." Mirallyn said.

Mae turned back to her mother. The diminutive faerie's eyes were closed, her lips set in a hard line. She seemed to be concentrating on something. Mirallyn clapped her hands together once, the echo sharp in the silence of the winter night.

The sound of tiny feet scrabbling on wood and stone above their heads made the three intruders look up. Four raccoons swarmed over the stone gargoyle, their clever little digits and teeth working loose the crystals in the eyes of the stone guardian. The furred bandits accomplished their task and vanished into the snowy dark with the scrabbling of clawed feet, taking their trophies with them.

"I can't believe you used cute fuzzy animals to save the day," Mae said.

Her mother shrugged. "They answered my call. One works with the tools that present themselves."

Kravis leaned in between them. "We should get you two through the window before those crystals explode."

Mae asked. "Explode?"

Kravis nodded. "In about a minute."

"Great. I've helped kill a bunch of defenseless furry animals."

Mae turned back to the designated window. She ran as quickly as her short legs would carry her through the shin-deep snow. She came up hard against the wooden siding of the mansion, under the window. Mae looked up. There was a piece of red cloth dangling from a cut in the upper left corner of the window screen. It was too high for Mae to reach while standing flat-footed. She collapsed the baton and handed it to her mother before grabbing Kravis by the shoulders.

"I'll need you to give me a boost. Make a stirrup with your hands and lift me."

Kravis gave her a sour look but did as she asked. Mae placed one booted foot in his hands. She reached up and tore the screen away. She managed to perch precariously on the outer sill of the window. She felt Kravis put his hands on her legs to help stabilize her.

Mae peered through the cracks of the closed shutter at a dark room. It looked and sounded empty. She slowly lifted the window up, listening for the sounds of habitation on the other side of the window. The wooden shutter cracked open a few inches when she bumped it. Mae pushed it open and peered inside.

Mae realized it was what the builders would have called a water closet. There were no bathing facilities, only a toilet and two-sink vanity. The room was dark and empty, but Mae noticed faint light under the door.

She looked down at Kravis and her mother. "I'm going in."

Mae tried to swing one leg over the sill. She missed. Her foot caught, making her tumble through the window and hit the tiled floor with a dull thud. She bit down on her tongue to keep from cursing and crying out.

"Mae?" Kravis called quietly from outside. "Are you okay?"

Mae stood. She had landed on her left arm and hip. Both hurt from the impact, but nothing seemed damaged except her pride. She leaned out the window.

"I'm fine. Toss me the baton." She caught it easily when Mirallyn pitched it upward.

Her mother turned to Kravis. "Lift me."

The dark faerie rolled his eyes, then knelt in the snow and made a stirrup with his hands for the second time.

Mae saved her mother an undignified landing by reaching up and helping the woman off the window sill.

Mae leaned back out the window and looked at Kravis. "Good luck," she said.

Kravis nodded solemnly to her. "And to you, Mae."

Mae closed the window and shutters. She took a deep breath and walked to the door, her mother trailing in her wake. Mae pressed an ear to the wood. She could hear nothing.

"How long before they realize you're in the house?" she asked her mother.

"They may be aware of my presence at this time. I will not know if I am detected until they move to eliminate me."

Mae exhaled a long, nervous breath. She opened the door a crack and peered out. There was a well-lit hallway outside the door. Dark paneling stretched out for ten feet, ending at a door of dark wood. There was no indication of people. She opened the door and peered around it. More hallway, a couple of tables facing each other, and a series of portraits hanging from the wall greeted her. There was a bright light shining through an open door at the end of the hall. She stepped into the hallway, her mother behind her.

Mae started to walk toward the open door, moving to flatten herself along the wall. Her mother grabbed her arm.

"Those candles are set to detect anyone who passes them. If we walk between them, it will alert our foes." Mirallyn turned to her with a raised eyebrow. "We can, however, crawl beneath their gaze."

Mae walked as close to the tables as she dared, then crawled on her hands and knees past them. She made sure she was well clear of the detection devices and stood. She checked over her shoulder, making sure her mother was still with her, and continued toward the light.

She reached the open door and stood next to it for several minutes, listening for any sounds that might alert her to danger. Hearing nothing, Mae peered around the doorframe.

She found herself looking into what was either a hall or a ballroom, with a polished floor and a vaulted ceiling dominated by an ornate crystal chandelier. At the other end of the room, she could see through an open set of double doors into the parlor where she had first encountered the animated corpse of Chrysandra Arneson.

On the polished, honey-colored wood floor lay a black clutch purse next to a shattered glass and the sticky remnants of dark red wine. Mae dashed to the purse, ignoring her mother's hissed warning to be careful. She knelt and picked up the purse with trembling hands, opening it. Jill's revolver was still inside. Mae snapped the purse shut and stood. She walked back to the hallway and regarded the two tables near the bathroom door.

Somewhere in this house her lover and her sister were being held prisoner. Mae shrugged out of her heavy coat, letting it fall to the floor: it would only impede her movements. She opened Jill's purse and withdrew the snub-nosed pistol. She stuffed the pistol into her pocket and drew the baton, snapping it open. She placed Jill's purse in her bag and slung the bag over her shoulder.

Mae walked purposefully toward the two tables, stopping long enough to crawl under them.

"What are you doing?" her mother cried, grabbing Mae by the arm.

Mae gave her mother a hard look and pulled her arm free. "They've got Jill. They've got Fay. This house is too big for me to search quickly, and it's probably trapped to a fair-thee-well. It would take me too long to find them skulking around, and I'm not even sure anyone is even here. There was supposed to be a party, and instead the place is quiet and dark. So I'm changing the plan. I'm going to charge in and hope for the best."

Mae turned away from her mother, stepping steadily toward the door at the end of the hallway. Mae reached out and grabbed the doorknob. A sharp tingle struck her hand. She pulled it back and clutched it to her chest. It could have been static electricity, but somehow Mae doubted this.

"What have you discovered?" her mother asked.

Mae looked at her and bit her upper lip. "I think the door is a trap. I got shocked when I touched the knob."

"Perhaps we should—"

Mae gritted her teeth and grabbed the doorknob. The shock traveled up her arm and shoulder, making her teeth hurt. She turned the knob and pushed the door open.

Another hallway greeted them. Doors—some opened and some closed—lined either side. Mae caught the smell of food and alcohol. She moved to the first door and peered into the room. It was a dining room with a large cherry table and seating for a dozen. Mae pressed on, past the formal dining room toward the next door. The lack of resistance was making Mae's mind imagine any number of horrible scenarios, all of which ended with Jill dead.

The opening of the door took Mae and her mother by surprise. For an instant the two women locked gazes with an older, larger woman with gray hair and a severe look on her face. Mae recognized her as the woman who greeted her on the night of her ill-advised visit to the Arneson home. The woman gasped and raised her hand. A gray-silver light began to discharge from a ring she wore. Behind Mae, Mirallyn hissed in pain.

Mae reacted on instinct. Raising the baton to chest level, Mae ran into her opponent, aiming her shoulder at a point beyond the woman's back. The woman made a satisfying shriek as Mae overbore her and knocked her flat. Mae pressed the baton into the woman's throat.

She sneered down at the gasping woman. "Hi, I'm Mae Malveaux. We met a few days ago." She frowned. "You and your employers have some people that are important to me. I'm here to take them back."

"Make her take off the ring," Mirallyn said.

"You heard her," Mae pressed the baton harder on the woman's throat. "Do it!"

The woman took the dull gray ring from her finger and dropped it on the floor with a sharp metallic clatter.

Mae leaned toward the woman's face, shifting her weight slightly forward. "Tell me what you've done with Jill Hall and where you're hiding Fay."

The woman's face became set in the look of someone who was content to stonewall until help arrived, and knew help would be showing up at any moment. Mae had not exactly been silent during her attack. Any element of surprise, any chance of being sneaky and subtle about the rescue, was blown. It would have to be brute force after all. She steeled herself, ready to bash the information out of the woman and leave her unconscious on the floor.

Mirallyn knelt next to the woman, placing a hand on her face and catching the woman's eyes. "You know what I am. I could tell by your reaction upon seeing me. What you do not know is *who* I am." Mirallyn caressed the woman's cheek, stroking it as if she were touching a lover. The woman's eyes glazed over. "Tell me where my daughter is," Mirallyn said in a gentle voice. "Tell me how to find Fay."

"You're too late. The ritual has begun."

Mae saw her mother's expression change from calm to fierce. Mirallyn's face darkened, her silver eyes turning black and her small pointed ears growing longer. She grabbed the woman under the chin, above Mae's baton, and began to squeeze her throat with fingers that had elongated and grown sharp nails.

"Where is she?"

The woman's eyes widened in fear. She made a gasping sound. "Down the stairs! The door on the left is the library. There is a door behind the tapestry on the wall." The woman's demeanor changed from fear to a nasty sneer. "It's warded against your kind."

"Yeah, but not against me, I'll bet." Mae stood. "We need to hurry."

"Yes," her mother replied. Mirallyn's hand squeezed and twisted in a sudden motion. There was a snapping sound and the woman's mouth opened in surprise.

Mae took a step backward, shocked at the sudden, casual way her mother had killed. She bumped into something solid. With a shriek, Mae turned and raised the baton.

Death smiled sadly at her. "Harden yourself, Maeve Kathleen Malveaux." He knelt next to the dead woman and opened his brief-case. "This one's death is but the first of many this night shall see." He vanished from her sight, leaving Mae to stare at the dead body on the kitchen floor.

Mae swallowed back the acid-tasting bile in her throat and stepped over the corpse. She adjusted the bag on her shoulder and followed her mother down the stairs in the corner of the kitchen. They paused at the bottom of the stairs. There were two doors, one on each side of the landing. Mae looked at her mother.

"Now what?" Mae asked.

"The woman told me true. That I could read from her eyes. This is the door to the library and beyond that, their sanctum. They must know we are here. I suspect there will be someone behind the door waiting for us."

Mae collapsed the baton and placed it in the back pocket of her jeans. She adjusted the bag on her shoulder. She drew the pistol from her front pocket, turned off the safety and looked at her mother.

"I've never killed another person. I don't want to."

"Even if that means the death of your love?"

Mae gave her mother a grim look. "I didn't say I *wouldn't* kill. I said I don't *want* to."

"That is the difference between you and those we hunt."

Mae looked away from her mother, still troubled by the violence upstairs. She raised the pistol and took two quick breaths, blowing both out completely. She inhaled deeply, twisted the knob and pushed open the door.

Mae stepped into the library. Scanning the room, she found no sign of opposition. No one jumped out from behind the desk or emerged from a shadowed corner to challenge them.

Mae walked carefully toward the tapestry on the wall, moving as silently as possible. She pulled the tapestry away to reveal a door stained dark brown, so brown it was nearly black. She could hear voices on the other side, though she could not make out the words. There was a cloying smell of incense. She glanced over her shoulder at her mother.

"I believe the door is all that is warded against me," Mirallyn said. "Once you have opened it, I should be able to enter the room."

"I hope so," Mae mumbled, grabbing the small knob. "Otherwise this is all going to end badly."

"I suspect it will end badly no matter what we do, daughter." Mirallyn paused. "Should I fall, you will need to move quickly to save Fay, Jill and yourself. Kravis will destroy this entire manor shortly after my death."

Mae looked at Mirallyn. She had only just found the woman and now her mother talked as if her death in the imminent confrontation was foretold. "Mother..."

"It is a possibility. A strong one, in fact, and there is nothing to be done about it except that I shall strive to survive the night. Now, Mae, open the door, please."

Mae licked her dry lips and took one deep breath. She blew it out in a loud sigh, her shoulders rising and falling with its force. She lifted the revolver and twisted the knob. Then she pushed the door open and took two steps into the room. She stepped sideways to her left, allowing her mother entrance.

Mae had an instant to take in the scene before her. A group of men and women, dressed in formal wear, stood in a semicircle around the room. Mae recognized several of them instantly: William Hodgins, surprised and angry. The three Arnesons, the two elders in shock at her appearance, Marie in tears. County Attorney Backstrom turned to look at Mae, horror on his face. Jill's brother, Robert, stared like a rabbit caught in the headlights. The dark-haired woman Hodgins had called Ilona. The two others—a young red-haired woman in a green dress and a large blond man—seemed familiar, but she did not know their names.

Sitting in wooden chairs were two little girls. One was small and fair, with slightly pointed ears. She resembled Mirallyn and was slumped back, her eyes closed and mouth open. The other child was Chrysandra Arneson. Chrysandra's skin was the pallor of the dead and mottled red, her hair mostly fallen out, her lips black and cracked.

Behind them was the frame of a mirror and in the place the glass should be was the frozen landscape of Annwn. Mae felt cold air rushing into the room through the portal.

Jill lay on a table with grooves carved into it. Her eyes were open, but unfocused. A slight trickle of blood ran from her nose. Her arms were out-flung. The hem of her dress was pulled up to her waist, exposing her underwear. Someone had drawn dotted lines on the inside of her thighs and arms. Her brother stood over her, holding a scalpel. There was a glint of red on the polished blade. A slow drip of blood ran down Jill's left arm where Robert had begun to cut her.

Mae felt a surge of anger. A feral thing welled up inside of her, hammering at her chest, begging for release. Mae lifted the revolver and stepped deeper into the room.

The first bullet took Robert Hall in the head. He fell backward, the scalpel flying from his hand toward Ilona, who was reaching for the choker around her neck.

Her next shot missed William Hodgins by a good foot. It smashed a hole in the dark wooden wall, sending small splinters flying. Mae tried to track on Hodgins as he ducked for cover, ignoring the screams of the room's other occupants.

The third bullet struck James Arneson in the shoulder. He cried out in pain and fear, dropping to his knees. His wife knelt beside him, trying to cover his wound with her hands.

The blond man Mae did not know, but whom she now recognized from a recent cover of a local business magazine, rushed her. She fired point-blank, shattering his face. Mae took a step sideways to avoid his plunging body as it crashed at her feet.

Her fifth shot grazed Hodgins's back as he dived for the portal. It traveled on, smashing a glass bottle filled with clear liquid on a low table. The room filled with the smell of alcohol.

Mae caught a quick glimpse of her mother, changed into her more horrific aspect, standing before the portal.

Mae saw movement to her left and turned. Ilona was charging her, a small curved blade held high.

The final shot passed harmlessly over Ilona's shoulder, striking the wall next to the red-headed woman, who screamed and dived to the floor.

Mae threw the empty pistol at her opponent, forcing Ilona to break her stride as she ducked the impromptu projectile.

Mae took a step backward and reached into her back pocket. She withdrew Jill's baton. As she snapped it to full extension, Ilona cut her with the curved knife, slicing down the front of Mae's shoulder.

Mae took another step back and lashed out with the metal rod. There was the sharp snap of impact. The mage screamed and dropped the knife.

Mae turned at movement to her right. Her mother was standing in front of the portal, back to it. She was surrounded in a yellow glow. On the floor at her feet lay the girls, Fay still bound to the tipped-over chair; the undead child lying on her stomach, working on the fabric binding Fay.

Hodgins, Backstrom and Marie Arneson stood in front of her mother. Hodgins and the Arneson woman were holding hands, Hodgins chanting fast and furious while Marie wobbled on her feet. Backstrom had produced a crystal sphere, similar to the one Hodgins was using. They held their crystals at eye level and advanced on the small faerie woman, chanting loudly in a language Mae did not recognize.

It was up to her mother to close the connection to Annwn.

Ilona and the redhead slammed into Mae. She collapsed under their combined weight, losing her grip on the baton, which slid across the floor. Mae tried to roll away, but the women held her fast, pinning her to the ground.

Mae lashed out with her fingernails, ripping one of her attackers across her eyes. The redhead screamed and grabbed at her wounded face. Ilona slapped Mae. She felt her head roll with the blow as darkness and a terrible buzzing threatened to overwhelm her senses. She tasted blood in her mouth and blinked back stars as the woman cocked her arm and hit Mae again. Mae felt her teeth rattle, and tears of pain and fear welled up in her eyes.

"Goddamned bitch!" Ilona had produced another knife, this one short-bladed and double-edged.

Mae spit a mouthful of blood up into the woman's eyes. She knew she was going to die, but she would be damned if she would die whimpering. She steeled herself for the blow.

Jill, standing on wobbly legs, her dress a disheveled mess, her hair a wild tangle, appeared behind Ilona. The redhead cried a warning. Ilona turned to look over her shoulder as Jill struck downward with the thick end of the baton, screaming like a demented banshee. The heavy piece of metal took Ilona near the temple with a dull thud. Jill lifted the weapon again as her first opponent toppled over like a felled tree.

The redhead cried out and lunged over Mae's prone body toward Jill, hitting her at the knees. Both fell to the floor, struggling for control of the baton.

Mae sat up, dazed and bloodied. She heard a scream—high, mournful, filled with pain. She looked at the source.

Mirallyn stood silhouetted against the opening to Annwn, her arms out flung, her long silver hair whipping around her head, stirred by the force of the cold winds blasting into the room from the Underworld. Her head was thrown back, the terrible scream issuing from her throat.

Around the small faerie sorceress, the mortal mages, now joined by the two elder Arnesons, were pressing in.

"No!" Mae's own voice joined the high-pitched cries as her mother disintegrated, bursting into a vaporous cloud of red and silver in front of the portal. Her heavy robes, bloodied and torn, fell to the floor, empty.

Most of Mirallyn's remains were sucked into Annwn, covering the fresh white snow with a dark crimson smear. What did not fall through the portal to the Underworld landed on Chrysandra and Fay.

Mae climbed to her feet. Bloodied, wobbling and unarmed, she moved toward the mages who had killed her mother.

Hodgins, his face and upper body drenched in sweat and blood, gave Mae a panicked look. He released Marie Arneson's hand and, grabbing the unresisting Fay and a startled Chrysandra, dived through the open portal into Annwn.

Marie Arneson collapsed to the floor and lay on her side, her brown eyes wide and unblinking. Her lips kept moving, muttering something Mae could not hear.

Backstrom dropped to his knees. The sound of the older man retching was nearly drowned out by the heart-wrenching wail of Mae's lover.

Mae turned at the sound of Jill's anguished scream. Ilona and the redhead had overpowered Jill, straddling her body and pinning Jill with their weight. Mae watched as the redhead lifted Jill by the straps of her dress, raising her head and shoulders off the floor, then slammed her back down. Jill made a whimpering noise and the red-head raised her again.

Mae changed directions, charging into the fray. The redhead was too intent on Jill; she never saw Mae come up behind her. Mae lashed out with a booted foot, striking the woman in the side of the head. She tumbled sideways as Mae lost her balance and fell to the floor next to Jill.

The heavy smell of burning wood heralded the arrival of Kravis ap Thimp. He was covered in soot, his coat missing and his clothing scorched in places. He was holding his sword in his left hand. Black smoke filled the doorway behind him. Wordlessly, he reached down and lifted the red-haired woman from the floor. She trembled and stared at him like a frightened animal.

He stabbed her in the stomach with a quick thrust and dropped her again. She curled up, screaming and crying.

Mae gasped. Kravis's eyes were wild and he laughed aloud at Mae. Mae felt a chill. He was standing in front of the only mundane exit from the room, the building burning behind him, smoke pouring in, a bloody sword in his hand.

"Kravis!" she screamed.

"Take your lover into Annwn, Mae Malveaux! There is no other escape!"

Mae grabbed Jill by the front of her battered black dress. She needed Jill on her feet. She needed to rescue Fay from Hodgins. They all needed to escape before the remaining mages could rally and overwhelm them.

"We have to go!" Mae cried, rising to her feet, trying to steady Jill.

Jill wobbled up to a standing position, constantly blinking, as if trying to focus her eyes. Holding tightly to Jill's arm, Mae turned toward where Hodgins had jumped into Annwn with her sister and Chrysandra. Marie Arneson had somehow passed through the portal and was running toward the forest and calling Chrysandra's name. Mae pulled Jill forward and pushed her through. Jill landed in the bloody snow and sat up, looking around. Before crossing, Mae looked over her shoulder at the scene in the room.

Ilona screamed and leaped toward the portal, smashing into Mae and knocking her down. Mae grabbed the woman's left foot and pulled, stopping Ilona halfway into Annwn. Ilona twisted around and lashed out with the curved knife. Mae turned her head in time to keep from taking the brunt of the attack on her face. The sharp blade raked her across the right side of her neck and her ear.

A pair of hands grabbed Mae by her sweatshirt, lifted her off the struggling body of the woman and threw her through the faux mirror frame. Mae felt her body surge forward. She collapsed in the snows of Annwn.

Mae sat up on her knees. Jill was next to her, still looking slightly stunned and bleeding from her head.

Mae looked back into the mansion. Smoke had filled the room and there was the bright glow of fire flickering in through the door.

James Arneson was dead, cut down by Kravis. The Arneson matriarch knelt at her husband's side. The red-haired woman, whose green dress was drenched in blood, crawled steadily toward the portal, hoping for escape from the burning mansion. Backstrom and Ilona were struggling with Kravis for control of the sword.

Mae looked through the portal at the mansion. There was a heartbeat of calm, a heartbeat of cold, frozen silence.

They came with the sound of razor wings: a rustling, shrieking, tortured cacophony on the air. The occupants of the burning mansion looked toward the smoke- and flame-filled doorway. The sound grew and burst into the room, heralding the arrival of a flight of silverware. The polished metal slashed through the room. The animated silver swirled around Backstrom and Maureen Arneson, ripping and tearing at them as they wailed. Mae turned her eyes away from the massacre.

The injured redhead made a desperate run for the perceived safety of Annwn. She dove through the opening and fell to the ground with a graceless thud. Ilona stood over Kravis's body, dark blood dripping from her curved knife. The woman looked up toward the ceiling an instant before it collapsed in flames around her.

The portal before them shimmered and wavered for an instant, and the scene of slaughter vanished as if someone had turned off a television, leaving only the cries of the wind and a vast expanse of white landscape before them.

Wednesday, 1st of November

MAE LOOKED TO JILL, who was sitting in the snow, blood running from a nasty-looking wound on her head. Near Jill lay the red-haired woman, whose breaths were coming raspy and shallow. Around them was a dark smear on the snow that Mae wanted to ignore but could not. She turned her eyes away from the grim sight. She would grieve for her mother later. For now, she needed to focus on the living.

Mae leaned in to her lover. "Jill? Jill, are you okay?"

Jill gazed at her in confusion. "I—I think maybe." Jill leaned into Mae's arms, the cold making her body shake. "I hurt everywhere. Especially my head."

Mae looked down at the shivering woman. She needed medical attention. It was obvious Jill was suffering from a concussion.

As for the red-haired woman, Mae doubted there was much anyone could do to save her. The woman was covered in her own blood, pale and gasping, her lips opening and closing as she tried to suck more air into her lungs.

Mae glanced around at the empty desolation of Annwn. There were footprints, four sets of tracks heading toward the frozen forest.

She stood, helping Jill to her feet, and turned in a slow circle, looking at the horizon.

"Please..." a weak voice whispered behind her.

Mae looked at the dying woman. She lay on her back in the snow, her red hair fanned out around her head, her skin so pale it was blue, the front of her dress covered in dark, drying blood. Mae moved to kneel by her side.

"I'm sorry, there's nothing I can do for you." Mae wished there was some way to end the woman's suffering. She frowned and took the woman's hand. She heard footsteps behind her, crunching in the snow. "Death is your only escape now."

Mae looked up into the star-filled eyes. Death stood over the two women holding his briefcase. "And here he is," Mae whispered.

"Hello, Maeve Kathleen Malveaux."

"Death," Mae replied, nodding to the woman in the snow. "Here on business, I see."

"Yes, though my business is not with this unfortunate." He took off his suit jacket and placed it around Jill's shoulders.

Mae frowned at him. She glanced down at the woman and back to Death. "You can't just leave her to suffer. That's—it's inhumane."

Death nodded. "Agreed, Maeve. But I have no power over this one's fate. Only the rightful lord of this place may give her surcease from her suffering."

Mae gave him a fierce glare. "The 'rightful lord' of this place is frozen on his throne, bound by a man who wants me several kinds of dead. The 'rightful lord' of this place caused this mess."

"Mae," Jill said softly, touching her arm.

Mae's hands clenched. "The 'rightful lord' is why Hodgins has so much power. I don't think Gwynn ap Nudd is going to be riding in with the Wild Hunt to end this woman's pain anytime soon," Mae said through gritted teeth.

Death stared at her, watched her for so long that Mae started to shift from one foot to the other, though she held his gaze in her own. At her feet, the red-haired woman made small whimpering noises.

"What did you tell your lover when you feared she would die in this place?" Death asked, nodding toward Jill.

"I told her she couldn't die here. That if she did, she would be trapped forever."

"Why would she be trapped here? Is not Annwn a place for spirits to rest before rebirth?"

Mae frowned and looked from Death, to Jill, to the dying woman lying at her feet. "Yes. But since Jill doesn't believe in this afterlife, her spirit would have been trapped here."

"You know this how?"

Mae looked up at him. She opened her mouth to speak and closed it again. "I just knew. I—"

"When you challenged the alpha of the Cŵn Annwn, what happened?"

"He submitted to me," Mae whispered.

"And did the pack leave as you ordered?"

Mae nodded.

"And your streetcar, it brought you and your lover safely out of Annwn at your command?"

"Yes."

"Are you cold? You are, after all, standing in a frozen wasteland."

"No." Mae said, shaking her head. She had not even considered the fact that Jill was shivering while she seemed unaffected by the cold and wind.

Death smiled at her. "You did not believe I hung you from the Great Oak of Annwn for my own amusement, did you, Maeve Kathleen Malveaux?"

"I died," Mae said, her brow furled in thought.

Death nodded. "Yes."

Mae gave him a worried look. "I'm not *still* dead, am I?"

Death chuckled. "I believe Jillian Lorraine Hall would attest to your corporeal existence."

"Definitely *not* dead," Jill confirmed, pulling the jacket tighter around her shoulders.

"I don't get it. I'm not a—" Mae stopped. She was, in fact, connected to this place by her mother's blood. She might lack the magic of the fae, she might not resemble them except for her small stature, but she was still one of them.

She was a half-blood member of the Tylwyth Teg. Annwn was inside of her, a part of her being.

Mae remembered what Death had told her during their last conversation in Annwn, when she had asked if Arawn had a daughter, he had replied, "Not Arawn, but the later lord of this place, Gwynn ap Nudd."

Gwynn ap Nudd was not the first lord of this place. And he had fallen, the Champion of the Tylwyth Teg. Mae knew the myths. *A fallen Champion had to be replaced.* She understood now.

Mae frowned and looked back down to the red-haired woman. The woman's eyes were closed, her chest rising and falling in an irregular rhythm. Tears stained her face. Mae knelt next to her and touched her blood-covered arm. There were things she wanted to know. Mae needed to understand why. The woman opened her eyes.

"What's your name?"

The woman swallowed and grimaced as she took a breath. "Lara, Lara Campbell. Please help me."

Mae reached out and brushed Lara's hair from her face. "I will. I *will* help you, Lara Campbell, but first I need to know something. I want you to answer some questions for me."

Lara nodded.

"What was Hodgins planning to do to my sister?"

Lara's eyes became confused. "The faerie child? She is your sister?"

"Yes. I want you to tell me what Hodgins planned for my sister."

The woman lay quietly for several seconds as Mae gently stroked her head and waited. Mae knew the woman was trying to decide how loyal she felt to Hodgins, or perhaps how afraid of him she was.

"William Hodgins and the others will not be able to hurt you. You're dead, Lara Campbell. All that matters now is what you do with the rest of eternity."

The woman swallowed again and took a ragged breath. "He planned to place his daughter's spirit in the faerie child's body."

Mae nodded solemnly. "Go on."

"William and Marie were trying to attune their daughter to the magic. She had reached puberty, and it was time to discover if she had any power or aptitude. There was an accident. Something went wrong with the casting. None of us were told the whole story, but most of us thought it was because Marie could not handle the power properly. Everyone knew she had a drug problem, and everyone knew she could barely control the magic she wielded." The woman frowned and tried to shake her head. "And Chrysandra seemed to attract ill luck when it came to magic. She was always getting injured by stray bits of rituals and workings, no matter how well we shielded the space."

Mae nodded. It made sense and it dovetailed nicely with the reports of injuries to Chrysandra that had been filed with Child Protective Services over the years. Lara coughed, dry and raspy. Mae gathered some clean snow and pressed it to the woman's mouth. Lara stopped speaking. She took two hard and ragged breaths. "Then the hounds caught the faerie child and brought her to Hodgins. That's when he started working on a way to save his daughter. It presented him with the perfect opportunity to keep Marie sane long enough to save his child and convince the rest of us to expend the power needed to keep Chrysandra in one piece for an extended period."

"What was the plan? I mean, besides saving his daughter's life?"

Lara gasped. "Once Chrysandra was firmly inside her new body, he planned to use his daughter to destroy the rest of the faerie folk.

Any magic we burned up would be gained five-fold once we gained access to their stronghold."

Mae kept her voice calm as she asked, "And what would have happened to my sister?"

Lara hesitated before she answered. "She would have been trapped in Chrysandra's dead body. I suspect Hodgins planned to withdraw the magic keeping his daughter's body running after that."

Mae nodded, showing no emotion. "One more thing, Lara Campbell. Why were you going to sacrifice Jill?"

Again, the red-haired woman was silent for several moments before answering. Her eyes flicked to Jill and back to Mae. "She was the blood sacrifice needed to power the ritual. As she bled to death, her fear and the power of her soul leaving her body would make it easier for the rest of us to work the transfer." The woman smiled grimly. "The fact that she was Robert's sister would make the magic stronger and solidify his position in the circle. He considered his sister a disgrace to his family. Killing her and destroying her soul would have put him nearly in the same league as Hodgins in magical power."

Mae felt her insides chill. She had come perilously close to losing her sister and her lover.

Lara reached up and touched Mae's arm with a bloody hand. "Please, you promised me."

"That I did."

Mae looked over her shoulder at Death. He stood watching with an impassive expression. Mae realized he would be no help. She would need to figure out what to do on her own. Mae looked into the frightened and pain-filled eyes of Lara Campbell. "You understand that by dying here, your spirit will be trapped in Annwn forever?"

"Yes."

Mae leaned forward and placed a hand over the woman's heart. "Then come with me, Lara Campbell, and leave this ruined shell behind." As Mae stood, the spirit of Lara Campbell stood with her.

The spirit looked around. "Is this hell, then?" she asked sadly.

Mae frowned. "Perhaps for you it is. Do you think you deserve any less?"

Lara knelt next to her own dead body. She touched the place on herself where the sword had stabbed her. "No. I suppose this is my punishment." She stood and glanced at Mae. "What now?"

Mae turned to ask Death. He was gone. Mae sighed. His business in this place was apparently finished.

"Mae..." Jill whispered.

Mae turned to her, grabbing Jill by the arm to steady her. It was obvious Jill was barely staying upright. There was no way Jill would be able to keep up, and Mae refused to leave either Jill or Fay behind and alone in Annwn as long as Hodgins was alive. She lifted her chin and spoke into the empty air.

"Now would be a good time for some transport, Mr. Lowry. A nice streetcar ride would be perfect."

The yellow streetcar came at her call, rolling down metal tracks as they materialized in front of it. Mae read the sign over the top of the motorman's window. Annwn Limited. The big machine stopped next to Mae. The red door opened.

"That's a beautiful sight," Jill muttered.

Mae stepped into the car, leading Jill to a seat and paying Jill's fare. "I need you to stay on the car when I confront Hodgins."

"Mae, your eyes, they're—they're full of stars."

Mae nodded. "I know. I'll explain later. Promise me you'll stay on the streetcar."

"Mae—"

Mae grabbed Jill by the arms. "I need you to do this. You're in no shape to fight, and I need to know you're safe while I deal with Hodgins."

Jill frowned. "I want to go with you."

"I know." Mae released Jill's arms and stepped away from her companion. "I'll get Fay back from Hodgins and we'll go home."

"Promise?"

Mae smiled gently. "I promise." Mae took a quick step toward Jill and kissed her, soft and gentle. "I love you."

"And I love you. Now go do whatever it is you need to do to the bad guy and get your ass back to me in one piece."

Mae kissed Jill again and backed away. She looked at the conductor and the motorman. "Follow me," she said, stepping out of the streetcar.

The shade of Lara Campbell stood waiting for her. She locked her eyes on the spirit of the woman. "Now, Lara Campbell, you run with the Wild Hunt."

Before the newly dead spirit could answer, Mae turned, adjusted the messenger bag on her shoulder and started toward the forest. She knew Hodgins would be there. Mae knew the forest was where she *needed* to be.

She began to run, first in a slow jog, but she gathered speed as she went, her short legs pumping hard. Around her, mist and spray rose up from the windswept snow. Shapes began to loom, low to the ground, four-legged.

The Cŵn Annwn, red-tipped ears flattened against sleek white bodies, gathered around Mae, running with her, surrounding her. Mae laughed aloud and pushed herself harder. She looked over her shoulder to find the spirit of Lara Campbell running among the hounds and the big yellow streetcar carrying Jill following along on tracks that appeared before its wheels in the white snow.

Mae's gaze returned to her goal. She increased her pace again, running effortlessly across the snow and ice of Annwn. She felt a wild joy well up in her chest and gave it leave to lead her where it may. Around her, the pack bayed and howled as they crashed into the forest in search of their prey.

Mae found Hodgins in the only logical place for him to run to. She slowed her pace to a brisk walk as she entered the clearing. The white hounds spread out in a circle, surrounding the Great Oak of Annwn. Lara Campbell and the yellow streetcar were nowhere in sight.

The mage stood behind the wooden throne of Gwynn ap Nudd, his bloody right hand on the shoulder of the fallen Lord of Annwn and Champion of the Tylwyth Teg. In his left hand he held a curved knife, similar to the weapon Ilona had used to wound Mae. Its blade was covered in bright blood.

Gwynn ap Nudd, pale and thin, sat on his throne blinking in confusion. The antlered man gave Mae a bewildered look, his eyes asking a question Mae could not answer. His long gray hair was struck through with brown and lay lank and flat on his head. Bloody symbols adorned his face.

At the Son of Nudd's feet lay Marie Arneson. Her chest was cut open, her internal organs strewn about in the snow. She turned her head to look at Mae with horror-filled eyes.

Mae scanned the area for some sign of Fay or even Chrysandra and found neither. "Where is my sister?" she demanded.

Hodgins stood with sweat pouring off his body and steaming in the cold air. "Fled into the snows with the aid of my rebellious child. But no matter, you're too late, Mae. I've sacrificed Marie to bind the lord of this place to my will, and he shall do my bidding. Once you are dead it will be a simple matter for the hounds to find them. Then I shall sacrifice the master of the Hunt himself to save Chrysandra." Hodgins looked at the Lord of the Tylwyth Teg and pointed at Mae. "Kill her," he commanded in a raspy, labored voice.

Gwynn ap Nudd stood and lifted his long spear, holding it in thin, bony hands. His hunting leathers sagged on his frail frame like an overlarge sack. He took a shaky step toward Mae.

"Your daughter is dead," Mae said, though whether to Hodgins or the master of the Wild Hunt she was unsure. It was a truth for both of them.

Marie Arneson screamed the name of her child to the uncaring sky above, screamed her pain and sorrow as her ruined body writhed helplessly in the crimson-stained snow.

The Lord of Annwn lowered his spear and lunged. The spear pierced Mae between her breasts and exited out her back. The antlered man's ragged face filled with rage as he pulled the spear back through her body. He paused with the broad tip of the spear in Mae's chest, and then twisted the shaft before withdrawing the rest of the tip. Mae swayed on her feet from the force of the blow and withdrawal of the brutal weapon.

Hodgins's pale, sweaty face twisted up in malicious glee. "I told you to stay out of the affairs of your betters, Mae. I warned you, you silly little girl."

Mae frowned, looking down at the place the spear had pierced her body. Gwynn ap Nudd had struck true, straight into her heart, exactly where she had been impaled on the Great Oak. She pulled the collar forward to look down her sweatshirt, checking herself for injury. There was a wound, but no blood. As she watched, the wound closed itself, leaving a thick new scar over the previously healed injury. Mae looked up at the tired and worn face of Gwynn ap Nudd.

Mae stepped forward and touched the Lord of Annwn on the cheek. "I'm sorry," she said. Mae ran a gentle hand along his face.

For a moment his star-filled eyes cleared of their confusion. "Bebhinn?"

"No."

Gwynn ap Nudd looked down at Mae. "Who are you?"

"My name is Maeve."

He sighed. "Then at least I am undone by a warrior of my people, not by some mortal serpent."

"Kill her!" Hodgins rasped out.

Mae looked up to find the man holding a small round crystal, his eyes wide in panic. He was gasping for breath, his free hand holding his chest. She turned her eyes back to Gwynn ap Nudd. He seemed disoriented again. For a moment he swayed on his feet, and then he drew his knife from his belt.

Mae reached out and gripped his wrist, holding the knife down at his side. She leaned up on her toes and kissed him on the brow. As her lips touched his forehead, Gwynn ap Nudd's aspect changed, becoming that of an elderly stag. The creature's once-brown fur had turned gray and silver, its antlers twisted and growing back on themselves.

Mae stepped away from the former Champion of the Tylwyth Teg. "Run, Son of Nudd. Die a free creature."

For an instant the stag stared at her with soulful brown eyes, eyes that showed the stewardship of Annwn had truly passed from him to Mae. The stag dipped its massive antlers in a small bow. It turned to face the pack of hounds, which had gathered and were fairly vibrating in anticipation of the chase to come.

The stag snorted once, rose onto its hind legs for a moment, then crashed through the line of hounds and into the snow-covered forest, bounding away with surprising speed. The hounds looked to Mae for a moment. She gave them a nod of permission. The pack turned as a group and charged into the forest, seeking their prey.

Mae watched them disappear into the trees. She turned back to Hodgins and Marie. The woman had stopped struggling and screaming. Now she simply lay on her back and cried. Hodgins had fallen to his knees, clutching his chest. The crystal sphere lay on the ground.

Mae lifted the spear and approached them.

She stepped past Marie Arneson. The woman was already dead. There was nothing more for Mae to do to her except release her from her ravaged body. As cold as it seemed, Marie Arneson's turn would have to wait. There was more dangerous prey to contend with.

William Hodgins's breaths were labored, thin and reedy. His face was the cold pale color of the dead and covered in sweat. He looked up at her with bloodshot eyes. The last bit of color drained from his face as his gray eyes met Mae's star-filled ones.

"What will you do now, Malveaux? Are you going to strike me down in cold blood?"

Mae felt the feral thing rise up in her chest. She wanted to kill him. She wanted to lift the spear and end his life. He deserved death—worse than death for all the pain and misery he had caused over the decades. Mae hefted the spear and struck down hard, putting all her strength and pent-up anger into the blow.

The spear point shattered the crystal sphere. It hissed and smoked in the snow. In the forest, the howling voices of the Cŵn Annwn rose up in a victory cry. Mae glared at her helpless opponent.

"No, Bill. I'm not going to kill you. I don't want your spirit roaming around in Annwn. This place is going to be a paradise again. You don't deserve to dwell here."

"Truer words were never spoken."

Mae turned to face Death. She gave him a friendly nod. She heard Hodgins make a strangled cry of fear behind her.

"Any suggestions?" Mae asked.

Her answer came with a ringing bell and the click-clack of wheels on rails. Mae looked up as the streetcar rolled into the clearing. She quietly chuckled at the streetcar's placard of Annwn to Minneapolis via Llysllyn.

She turned to Death. "You know, I was just wondering if I would need a steed."

The red door opened. Jill stepped out into the clearing, still wearing Death's jacket over her shoulders. She was followed by an angry, shivering Fay and a confused Chrysandra, both girls still covered in gore and blood.

"Look what I found wandering around in the forest," Jill said cheerfully.

Fay turned and looked up at her. Mae could see the resemblance to both her mother and herself in the young woman's face.

"You *did* come for me," Fay said.

Mae nodded. "Yes. We came for you." Mae swallowed. There was no way to soften the blow. "Fay. Fay, I'm sorry—"

"I know," Fay whispered. She narrowed her eyes and glared at Hodgins with an evil smile. She held out a hand. The man stood on shaky legs. "You made a mistake using my blood to heal yourself, Mr. Hodgins. Or should I call you William Jefferson Hodgins?"

Mae stepped up to her sister. "Don't kill him."

"Why? Why shouldn't I? He killed my—our—mother!"

"Look around you. Look at what's happening."

Mae watched as Fay took in the sight of Annwn. The snow and ice were melting and vanishing into the soil. The Great Oak was beginning to bud, new leaves bursting into life after the long winter.

"We don't want him here. We don't want him in our world," Mae said.

Fay looked into her eyes. Mae knew she was trying to come to a decision of some kind.

"Are you really my sister?" Fay asked in a whisper.

"Yes, I'm really your sister. I promise to explain everything once we're done here."

"He killed Mother," Fay said. Her eyes were filling with tears. "She's gone."

Mae nodded, her own eyes blurry with moisture. "I know. I know." Mae gathered her sister into a hug. "I know I can't replace her. I know we've never been together. But I'm here now and I promise you're not alone." Mae squeezed Fay tightly. "I'll take care of you, sister, and I need you to take care of me too."

Fay pushed herself out of the hug and took a deep breath. She nodded at Mae. "Of course, I'll take care of you."

Mae smiled at her. "Good."

Fay turned to Hodgins and pointed at the streetcar. "Get on," she commanded.

Mae stood and watched Hodgins climb aboard, the terror in his eyes plain. She understood Hodgins had no choice. He had their blood in his veins and he was Fay's to command in this place.

The possible future implications of that fact worried Mae. She was not sure what would happen once he was back in the mortal world. She wondered if it was wrong to hope his heart would stop once he was out of her realm.

As she watched Hodgins vanish through the red doors of the streetcar, the full implication of her thought struck her.

Her realm.

She felt someone touch her shoulder. She looked up at Death. He was smiling.

"Yes, Maeve Kathleen Malveaux. *Your* realm. Keep it wisely. Guard it well." He nodded to the rest of the party in the clearing and walked toward the waiting streetcar.

Mae turned to the conductor and motorman, who had exited the car and picked up Marie Arneson between them.

"Easy now," Lowry said to the woman. "We've come to take you home."

"Does she need a fare?" Mae asked in a soft voice.

Lowry gave her a gentle smile. "No, ma'am. Her passage is paid." He nodded toward Death's back as He climbed aboard the streetcar. "She'll reach the other side safely."

"And you?" Mae asked Chrysandra, who was walking next to her mother's ruined body, holding Marie's hand. Fay stood next to Chrysandra, her face worried, her eyes filling with tears.

The undead girl released her mother's hand and looked up. "I don't know. I—I… Once we cross back over, I'll finally… I've been dead for a long time, I guess."

"I don't want you to go," Fay whispered, the threatened tears spilling down her cheeks.

"You could stay here," Mae said. "I could release your soul in Annwn. You could wait here until…" Mae paused, unwilling to finish the sentence. She didn't want to think about her or Fay's deaths so soon after losing her mother.

Chrysandra shook her head. "Thank you, but I have to go with them. They—they're my parents. Maybe we can be a real family in the next world."

Mae nodded her understanding and moved away, allowing her sister to say her goodbyes to the dead girl in private. She watched as they spoke quietly and hugged. Jill came up and placed her arm around Mae, silently lending her support. Another hug between the two girls, and Chrysandra climbed aboard the streetcar. Mae heard Hodgins's scream, high and frightened, and Marie's manic laughter as the car rang its bell twice and rolled away. Fay sat on the ground and watched the car take her friend and her captives away, sniffling loudly in the cold, still air.

Mae turned back to Annwn. The landscape was thawing. Under Mae's feet the last of the snow vanished, and the long-dormant grass began to turn green.

"What happened here?" Jill asked, poking at the torn front of Mae's sweatshirt.

"Oh, I got run through with a spear."

Jill gave an exaggerated sigh. "I let you out of my sight for five minutes and you ruin your clothes *again*."

Mae laughed and grabbed Jill in a fierce hug.

Sunday, 17th of December

Dear Diary,

I'm starving.

Of course, I'm just being dramatic when I say that, but Mae promised to take me out to breakfast this morning, and if she and Jill don't hurry up, it's going to be lunch.

They're just…incorrigible. And loud. It's kind of sickening.

The one time I complained, Jill snorted and said they'd try to keep it down next time.

And then my sister said that someday I'd meet some nice girl, and then we'd see how I really felt about it, and Jill pointed out that I might meet a boy, or someone who was something else entirely, you never knew.

I told them that my sex life, when I have one someday, was my business. Of course, then Jill wanted to have The

Talk. Mae cringed and said I wasn't allowed to have a sex life until I'm thirty.

I had to point out to her that, technically, I'm thirty-six.

Mae spit her coffee and Jill laughed hysterically.

I love them both.

I've adjusted to living a semi-human life relatively well. Mae says I'm pretty much like any other teen girl. Except for the whole magic and fae-blood thing.

I have my own room in the townhouse. Mae moved into the master bedroom with Jill. Closets were rearranged and bathrooms fought over, but it's all temporary. Once the remodeling and redecorating is finished, we will be moving to the lake house permanently.

One of our biggest problems has been arranging for me to receive a mortal education. There was a birth certificate for me. Mae had found it during one of our frequent weekends staying in our mother's home in Llysllyn. Unfortunately, it showed me to be the same age as Mae. Jill solved the problem by volunteering to teach me everything I need to function in the mortal world. Home schooling, they call it. Mae and Lady Elliefandi arranged tutors to help me learn the ways of the reality underneath the human one. Someday I'm going to have to go back to Llysllyn and take over Mother's position, so we live in the human realms that I might grow and mature faster. Lady Elliefandi needs me to return to her Court and be her swynwraig, her wizard.

It was a tense night when we went to the Seelie Court to retrieve Elliefandi from Lady Rhyania.

Jill simply forced her way into Rhyania's hall and demanded Lady Elliefandi's release. When the warriors and nobles of the Court moved to apprehend her, Mae strode through the doors, the Cŵn Annwn at her heals and infinity in her eyes. I've become quite adept at commanding silver, so the warriors and guards found themselves unable to draw their weapons. Mae informed the nobles of the Llysllyn Court that, as their new Champion, she demanded they restore Lady Elliefandi to her rightful place as Lord of the Court and call off their hunt for her consort, Jill Hall.

Lady Rhyania had barely contained her laughter at the stunned look on her cousins' faces.

Lady Elliefandi ferch Myfleria thanked Mae and Jill for saving her people, then gathered her cloak around her tired body and returned to Llysllyn. There was a short, vicious battle for control of the Llysllyn Court between Elliefandi and the council of nobles who had taken over when they banished her. Sweet, kind Elliefandi exacted a gruesome revenge against those who had cast her out of her home, a revenge that involved hot silver swords and heads on poles. The Court bent to her will after that night. Most do not know that Lady Elliefandi has been negotiating to merge Llysllyn with Lady Rhyania's Seelie Court. Rhyania's mother was of the Tylwyth Teg, so it is a natural match.

The rest of the Tylwyth Teg think Mae's a hero, and as the new Lord of Annwn, the nobles of the Llysllyn Court keep trying to ally themselves with her. The lords believe if they can become Mae's consort, distasteful as it would be to join with a half-human, they'll be able to take over the running of Annwn. After all, she's not only half-human, but a woman too. It's very political and funny, since they have the hardest time dealing with the fact that Mae likes girls. They don't understand that Mae and Annwn are one and the same. This has caused some—well—problems.

One of the minor nobles, an idiot named Baron Kandin ap Runelanor, got the bright idea to force Mae into taking him as a consort by getting her pregnant. However, since Mae would have nothing to do with him or any of those other over-stuffed idiots, he decided to try to use a sleep charm on Mae and impregnate her while she was unconscious. He caught her alone and by surprise on her way home from an audience with the Lady Elliefandi. Fortunately, the hounds warned me about his plot. I summoned Lady Elliefandi and Jill to her aid. When we got there, Mae was on the ground asleep. The moron was standing over her smiling at his own cleverness.

He was damned lucky Jill didn't kill him.

In the end, after he suffered his beating at Jill's hands, Ellie bound his magic and cast him out of Llysllyn. Mae's would-be suitors cooled their ardor after that.

Now that Annwn is working as it should, the spirits of the Tylwyth Teg who had died in Annwn spend their days and nights engaged in eating, drinking, playing music, dancing and loving while waiting for their spirits to be reborn.

Sadly, other creatures did not fare as well during the thaw, especially the spirits of humans who were unfortunate enough to be banished to Annwn by the circle of Mages over the years. Mae managed to set aside a place for them to dwell, away from the Tylwyth Teg and other faerie creatures, and is still working with Death and others of his kind to find a solution to their problem.

Taking over Annwn, though easy in the doing for Mae, was difficult in the beginning.

One of the very first things we had to do was go back to the ruins of the Arneson mansion so that I could make sure the portal there to Annwn was permanently closed. The place stirred terrible memories for all three of us, but Mae had to collect the spirits of our mother and Kravis ap Thimp and guide them to Annwn. I think, for me at least, knowing Mother's spirit is whole and happy in Annwn helps to—not erase—but ease the memories of her final moments. It was good to grieve. It is good to know she's there waiting for us.

We also had to sneak around that night to avoid notice of the local law enforcement. The police had doubted Mae's story. She told them about the personal investigation she had been doing concerning the welfare of Chrysandra Arneson. She told them about the county attorney's involvement with what should have been a routine case.

She talked about being forced to take a vacation from her job and being threatened with unspecified repercussions if she continued to stick her nose into this business. She told them after her apartment was broken into, she became afraid for her life and did not know who she could trust, including the police or any authorities.

The police might have laughed her story aside and locked her in jail, except for the evidence and aftermath of the fire in the Arneson mansion.

When they identified the skeleton found on the grounds as Chrysandra Arneson, the investigation took on a whole new track. The fact that Marie Arneson had been found ritually disemboweled with William Hodgins, dead from heart failure, lying next to her holding a bloody knife made the evidence for a black magic mass murder more solid. After the police identified all the dead bodies in the basement, it lent even more credence to Mae's bizarre story.

The local newspapers had gone mad with sensational headlines about a group of rich and powerful Twin Citians' seamy occult conspiracy and the violent slaughter that destroyed them all. Jill says it's the stuff of cheap novels.

The police are still investigating, but so far, no charges have been filed. A small revolver was traced back to Jill's father, and Robert Hall III had died from what appeared to be a self-inflicted gunshot wound to the head

Mae will probably need to keep a low profile for the rest of her life. I think eventually we will move someplace the human police can't find us—maybe faerie or a spirit realm—but Mae says she's not ready to give up on her human life yet. She's even learned to make her eyes appear their normal brown when she walks in the human world. I'm sure it has more to do with being with Jill. But someday I will have to go home to Llysllyn. And someday Mae will need to move into Annwn for good, and take her place under the Great Oak. And someday Jill Hall's mortal span will end.

But that is all in the future.

I can hear Mae and Jill coming down the stairs, laughing like little girls. Today there will be breakfast in a wondrous restaurant where the servers wear night clothes and the decorations include a buzzard and tiny devils. Tomorrow, well, tomorrow will take care of itself, and that is good enough.

THE END

About the Author

Michael Merriam is a writer, performer, poet, and playwright. He is the author of the steampunk series *Sixguns & Sorcery*, and his essays have appeared in *Uncanny Magazine*, *Cast of Wonders*, and *Andromeda Spaceways Inflight Magazine*. His scripts have been produced for stage and radio, and he has appeared in the Minnesota Fringe Festival and StoryFest Minnesota. Like most artists, he has worked a variety of odd jobs over the years, including short order cook, late night radio disc jockey, international freight specialist, and manager of a puppet troupe. He lives in Hopkins, MN with his wife and two exuberant cats. Visit his website at www.michaelmerriam.com.

About Queen of Swords Press

QUEEN OF SWORDS IS an independent small press, specializing in swashbuckling tales of derring-do, bold new adventures in time and space, mysterious stories of the occult and arcane and fantastical tales of people and lands far and near. Visit us online at www.queenofswordspress.com and sign up for our mailing list to get notified about upcoming releases and offers. Or follow us on Facebook at the Queen of Swords Press page so you don't miss any press news.

If you have a moment, the author would appreciate you taking the time to leave a review for this book at Goodreads, your blog or on the site you purchased it from.

Thank you for your assistance and your support of our authors.